Headlong Into Chaos!

The Diaries of a

Primary School Headteacher

Dedicated to my wife, Alison and my daughters, Erin and Rachel, who kept up the pretence that I was normal.

Published by Panda Publications

Instructions for Safe Usage

This book should be taken twice daily with a glass of diluted water. If any side effects are felt the reader should stop reading immediately and go for a long walk in the rain. If no rain is available, marmalade can be used as an entirely ineffective substitute. It is strongly recommended that the book should be read in the morning; if a reader chooses to ignore this advice and reads the book later in the day, the author cannot be held responsible for any parts of the story that the reader may have missed due to his late arrival on the page.

It is not recommended that you read this book to children as a bedtime story, since it may lead to significant psychological irregularities later in life. The book should also not be regarded as a collection of recipes, nor should it be used as a flotation device, except in surreal circumstances where the preservation of life becomes incidental.

If at any time the reading experience becomes too stressful, there are emergency exits on pages 35, 97 and 176. These should only be used under the supervision of a qualified proof reader.

In the event that the book suffers a technical glitch during the reading process, it can be reset using the following procedure;

- close the book, ensuring no pages are creased;
- place the book on a small, flat surface for two whole minutes;
- re-open the book at page 42 and navigate slowly to your desired starting point.

Please note that whilst every effort has been made to offer maximum accessibility to the work contained herein, this book is not compatible with all versions of Windows, particularly those of the frosted variety, since it can become very difficult to read through the knobbly glass.

Please keep the book upright at all times to avoid loss of words through accidental spillages.

Finally, dear reader, do not attempt to replicate any of the events from this book in your own home; doing so will make you look very, very stupid.

Introduction

It is the late 1990s in a North Midlands former mining town, a place populated by wholesome, genuine characters. If they warm to you, they will treat you as they would treat a member of their own family. Alternatively, if they take a dislike to you, they will treat you as they would treat a member of their own family. On balance, it is best to hope they like you.

I had always wanted to be a head teacher, from first starting out as a student until approximately the end of my first day in the job, when I realised it had probably been a badly thought out ambition. Put simply, what goes on behind the scenes in a primary school is almost beyond comprehension and certainly beyond belief.

As the new head of the local school, aged in my mid-thirties, there was a lot to learn and very little time to do it. Every one of the three hundred children had a distinct personality that needed to be understood quickly. And every one of the three hundred children had parents, who, it seemed, ranged from the delightful to the terrifyingly unstable. Of course, the delightful ones lived their own lives and rarely ventured into the school. The lunatics visited me every day, sometimes more than once every day.

Fortunately I was surrounded by a team who knew the place well. Of course, they knew it far better that I did, and that's quite a challenge when you turn up as 'the boss'. I inherited a techno-phobic secretary who 'didn't use spreadsheets on her computer but she did put a cloth over it at night'. The caretaker spoke in words that educated the primary school children in ways that their parents might not have wished for and he made no secret of his two main loves in life; cleaning his urinals and categorising his nuts.

My deputy head, Gillian, terrified me, as she did everyone, but nobody dared mention it. Deep down inside her was a well-meaning individual but it had never found the courage to rise to the surface and may well have regretted it if it had done so. Alan Barnett, the Year 6 teacher, whilst supremely intelligent, had not the faintest clue regarding social relationships, tact or empathy. To hear him commenting on the microphone at sports day with such phrases as

'Boy with big nose in the lead, fat one's fallen over…' was a unique experience indeed.

The behind-the-scenes picture of the school would not be complete without the myriad visitors; the health and safety officer who broke a shelf and injured three children; the vicar who hated Christmas but found funerals a reliable source of income, because 'nobody books a themed funeral in Palm Springs' like they do with weddings; the mayor who insisted on coming to make speeches that made no sense whatsoever to eight year olds; and the Chair of Governors who was a pompous, self-important prat. Apart from that, I liked him.

With three hundred children, thirty seven staff and a building that struggled to remain standing in anything more than a stiff breeze, life was never going to be simple. Read on and find out just how much it wasn't!

Autumn Term: Week 1

Does anyone know the name of those meteors that fly through space?

They're called haemorrhoids, Sir…

She was short and plump and dressed in a tracksuit that had once been vivid pink. She had both an angry look and a large spot on her face. And she marched across the playground like she was leading an army of imaginary troops into battle. I, it appeared, constituted the enemy. And yet beneath the bristling and indeed, prickling, exterior I sensed a somewhat nervous individual trying to get out, but not having the courage.

"Are yoo t'new headmasster?" she demanded. I confirmed to her that this was an accurate assumption and began to smile politely. Her reaction to my unexpected smile was to arrest it in its infancy and my faint grin was interrupted before it was allowed to take hold and become something more substantial.

"I thought you'd've been older!" she snapped. I explained that in fact I hadn't been older, but if it was any help, I had been younger for the majority of my existence. She simultaneously grimaced and winced, and led her troops away, back to where her child was waiting.

She was the first parent I had met and I had not made a good impression on this lady. Within seconds of our first meeting I had become too young, smiled too much and I answered questions using strange words that she understood individually, but not when they were joined together in a sentence.

It was five to nine, time to signal the start of the first day of the new term. I had stood on the school yard, being stared at like an exhibit at a freak show by my new pupils and their elders, but now it was time to return to the sanctuary of the building. Soon the playground would be empty and quiet and the buzz of activity would transfer inside with me. The building itself was thrown together in the late-1960s. It was a concrete-sided, flat-roofed colander, a caravan without wheels. It had been cheap to build and with every subsequent year, its entire original building cost was spent on keeping it standing. Yet through the considerable efforts of the staff, the place was bright and cheerful. I had yet to marvel at the feature waterfall that followed heavy rain on the hall roof, but in anticipation of such an event, I had been instructed by Walt the Caretaker to not leave electrical or valuable items anywhere but within the confines of a waterproof container.

The woman was there again when I reached my office. Clearly, she knew her way around better than I did and I felt it might be beneficial to learn some of the short cuts that she undoubtedly knew. I may need them for a rapid departure one day.

This time the woman was without her child but had gained an accomplice called Kelly. Kelly was a young mother who had apparently supplied the school with so many children that she perhaps should have qualified for some form of discount. Or failing that, some kind of operation.

“This is ‘im.” The Mad Woman announced with unfailing accuracy. “I telled yer, I thought ‘eed a bin older, burree int. I telled ‘im miself, I said I thought you’d’ve been older. He answered me but I couldn’t follow what ‘e said.”

“Hello again. What can I do for you?” I asked, aiming to maintain a bright and cheerful approach, to complement the inside of the building, which had begun to suddenly feel a little oppressive.

“Well *I’ve* come to complain,” said the woman, “but you can see Kelly first. She just wants to get her youngest put down.”

At this point Kelly's youngest appeared from around the corner where it had been installing a sticky lolly into the photocopier. My first reaction was to suggest that she had left things a little late and that the child should have been put down shortly after birth, but I knew what was really required. Kelly wanted the child's name put down for school and this should be a relatively quick and simple task.

I was to learn, however, that nothing was – or would ever be – simple. Kelly was unsure of the child's exact date of birth and was noticeably put out when I insisted that 'Early Spring' would not suffice on the official admission forms. She reluctantly promised to find, and then check the birth certificate and return with a little more detail. She could, fortunately, remember the child's name. It was Sandringham! Sandringham was the seventh child to emerge from Kelly's loins, each child apparently a little less cerebrally endowed than the previous. By the time Sandringham started school I would have to consider the possibility of removing a desk and replacing it with a large plant pot for him.

With Sandringham successfully in the process of being put down, it was time to turn to the matter of the Mad Woman's complaint. She came into the office on my invitation and sat down. She spoke without pausing for breath, thus building up further evidence that she was not wholly human.

“It’s our Michael,” she informed me. “I want him to be on that there special needs list and nobody’ll put him on it. I came in more times than I can remember to see your predistresser and he did nowt. He just telled me as our Michael’s not doing bad enough to get special help. Well I don’t think it’s right and I’m going to t’education if you don’t put him on t’list. That’s all I’ve got to say.”

I had a feeling that it most definitely wouldn’t be all she had to say.

“It’s an unusual complaint,” I said, “because it seems your son is too bright to be put on the Special Needs list. To get him on there, we’d have to try and make him less bright and that goes against what schools are supposed to do.”

“Nobody knows what they’re talking about. I’ve had him to doctors, psychologists, dyspraxia clinics, incontinence clinics, hyperactive experts and they all say there’s nothing wrong. I’ve got him booked in wi’ one of them cycle analysts next week but I know what they’ll say.”

I struggled with a dilemma, unable to decide whether to picture a cycle analyst or a hyperactive expert bouncing around his office. But no matter. I also knew what they'd say. I knew what was wrong with this child and I hadn't even met him. He was what I could only describe as 'parentally challenged'. The poor lad had been born to a parent who desperately wanted something to be wrong with him. And because he was normal the boy had turned out to be something of a letdown. I found myself staring incredulously at this woman, imagining how disappointed she must have felt on the day she gave birth to him.

"Congratulations, Mrs. Mad Woman," the midwife would have said, "you've got a healthy baby boy."

She would have sat bolt upright at this point. "Healthy? Are you sure? I'm not at all happy about this. How can I get special treatment and extra benefits if he's healthy and normal? Check again, you must be able to find something wrong with him! I'm complaining to the Health Authority, I am!" she would have replied.

I was jolted back into the present moment by her sharp voice.

"So what yer going to do about it? Does he go on that list, or what?" she enquired politely.

I copped out. “Leave it with me. I’ll get to know him a bit better and we’ll see if there are any problems we need to address.”

“Nineteen Sorby Avenue, do you want the post code?” She replied, efficiently.

“No, that’s fine. Thanks for coming.”

With the Mad Woman now leaving the premises, I hoped that life could perhaps get back to normal. And that was the point when I realised I had no idea yet what ‘normal’ actually was. This was a strange building full of people I didn’t really know. It had a history that I knew little about, it had successes and failures that I had yet to discover and somehow, I had to convince its entire population that I was able to take charge and run the place. First, it might be necessary to convince myself and that might take some time.

But sitting and pondering was not going to be an option in this office. The room was magnetic, I decided. As soon as one person left it, another was drawn towards it. The knock on the door this time was from a small child, aged about six.

Upon entering the room he uttered the word “Mig.” This was not meant to be the start of a discussion, merely a display of nervousness and a lack of ability to say anything comprehensible to the ferocious new headmaster.

He thrust his workbook in my face. On the first page was something he had done with a pencil, one day it would become writing. Clearly his teacher had sent him to show me this work. There could be two reasons for this: either the work was so astoundingly good that the child deserved commendation and a sparkly sticker from the lofty heights of my office. Or else the work was so poor that I should reduce the child to tears with a sudden display of anger. But which was it to be? How, when a six-year-old makes curious marks on a page, is it possible for the uninitiated to tell which is good and which is bad?

"Who sent you to show me this?" I asked in a friendly voice.

"Mig." Was his reply.

"Was it Mrs. Crosby?"

The word 'mig' was this time accompanied by a nod of the head; so I assumed I had judged his age correctly and chosen the most likely teacher.

"Was she pleased with you?"

"Mig." This time expressionless, offering me no help at all.

"Have you worked really hard this morning?"

"Mig."

I seemed to me that such a quiet and nervous child was unlikely to have been the perpetrator of evil deeds so early in the term, so I made my first executive decision. The work was good.

"Would you like me to put one of these stickers on it? Look, it says 'excellent work'."

"Mig."

I affixed the sticker and offered to accompany the child back to his class, this act would help both Mig and me find our way around a little better.

I opened the classroom door and smiled inanely at Mrs. Crosby, the Deputy Head. She was a large ebullient lady in her late forties who presented a fearsome figure to young children.

"I've brought this young man back." I announced.

She smiled at me and then looked at the boy. Her eyebrows began to dip towards the bridge of her nose.

"I hope you'll treat that as a lesson, young man. I won't put up with rubbish like that now you're in my class. Twenty-five minutes to produce that! You're lucky you're not missing your play time."

“Mig.” The child answered and went to sit down.

“Thank you for dealing with him, head master. I hope it’ll show him we mean business.” Mrs. Crosby said to me.

“Mig.” I said, and left the room quickly.

I figured that I might attempt to avoid Mrs. Crosby for approximately four days.

Walt the caretaker was marching along the corridor as I sheepishly left the classroom. Walt was a huge man in every direction and he emitted a strong odour which allowed him to be tracked down easily when he was needed.

“Morning, Walt. Everything OK?” I asked.

“Well I’m not one to moan,” Walt remarked, “but I’ve got a dodgy ball valve.”

“Oh dear! Do you think you’ll need time off?” I laughed.

“No, it’s a toilet thing. I’ll need to get it fixed, I’m proud of my toilets, I am. I don’t like toilet problems, I don’t.”

“None of us do, Walt. The consequences can be tragic!”

“I’ll tell you this and I’ll tell you now and when it’s said it’s said. It’s nice to hear that you think toilets are important. He didn’t, t’last gaffer. He were a right pancake, he were. I’m not one to moan but he never once commented on my urinals. And they're spotless, my urinals are, you could eat your dinner out of 'em. Have you got time, I'll show you."

"No thanks, Walt, I'm not hungry. In fact my appetite seems to have mysteriously disappeared. Do you need to go and buy a new ball valve?"

"I do. I'll go now and I'll be back later."

I chose to not mention that going now and coming back later would be a better option than going later and coming back now. I didn't think either of us could cope with the ensuing discussion. Besides I was becoming slightly asphyxiated.

I sat at my desk and watched Walt set off in his yellow Jeep, wondering if he was really the target market for such a vehicle.

Maybe now I could begin to do some work. A pile of official looking letters had landed on my desk whilst I had been out. They really should be read and dealt with. Unfolding the first envelope produced a knock at the door, however. It was Ann, my secretary. Peering over her shoulder was a man aged about forty.

"I know you're busy, but Mr. Bailey has made a special trip to see you. He says it's important." Said Ann.

I invited Mr. Bailey in.

"Gary Bailey," he barked.

Already I was staring at his head. I had only seen this in pictures before but Gary Bailey had three strands of hair dragged across his gleaming scalp. His words were drifting around the room and not registering with my brain because I found myself too busy concentrating on remembering that he was *not* called Gary Baldy.

I jogged alongside his words until I felt that I had caught up with the conversation. He was in full flow when I got there and it appeared that he had visited me in order to slag off his wife.

"And she won't let me see our Julie now. If she knew I were 'ere she'd go mental. If she knew I were talking to you she'd kill us both. She's turned our Julie against me and now she won't even talk to me on t'phone."

"It's an awful situation," I agreed, trying to sound like I had listened to the whole story, "I don't really know how I can help directly, but I could do some assemblies about families and so on, you know. That might make Julie think about not losing contact with you."

"Well, this is it, headmasster! I've come here because there *is* something you can do. We're going to court in three weeks and some welfare bloke'll be contacting school. I need you to give me a good character reference. I need you to make her sound like she's a rotten mother. I need you to say things like she ran off with another bloke and that she's poisoning our Julie against me. Will you do that?"

"I can't really get involved in a marriage break up. And even if I did, someone in court would want to know how I had so much information about your family. I haven't been Julie's headteacher long enough to get all this background."

"Look, I'm desperate to see mi daughter, pal. Surely you can figure out how to get round a few little questions to help a mate!"

"I can't promise anything. I really do have to try to be impartial, otherwise I'd have to get involved in every marriage problem in the school."

"Oh, I get it! Don't worry, I'll make it worth your while!"

"No, no, it's not that….."

"I've got business contacts. They'll do whatever I ask, they owe me. If I tell 'em to give you a helping hand, they'll do it. Of course, you wouldn't want to get on t'wrong side of 'em."

"Could your business contacts not give you a character reference?"

“I’m not sure they have the right background. I mean, they’re used to being in court and all that, but for – shall we say – different reasons. Look I know you’ll make t’right decision, you just need to think how to word it. I’ll leave it with you and I’ll call back next week. Sorry to have taken up your time.”

“Look Mr. Bald…..Bailey, I really can’t……”

“See you pal!”

And he left. And my choice was perjury or broken kneecaps.

I sat and stared out of the window. I didn’t expect this on my first day. I thought there was supposed to be a honeymoon period in the early days of the job. Then I had the fearsome thought – perhaps this *was* the honeymoon period! Maybe things would get heavier.

I picked up the letter that had previously produced Gary Baldy’s presence, and I began to read it. It told me something about some new initiative that was going to cost money we didn’t have, but it was compulsory. And before I reached the third paragraph, I was aware of someone behind me. Perhaps it was one of Gary’s mates! I looked round to see a rather creepy looking man, thin, pinched and greasy and aged about thirty five, wearing a sweatshirt emblazoned with the Local Authority’s logo. I greeted him with a startled grin.

"I've come to service your PE equipment." He said in a slow, nasal voice. "I come every year. I check your attachments and grease your nuts, that kind of thing. You're new here aren't you."
"Er, yes. Nice to meet you. Do you know where everything is?"
"Well not everything, but I know where your PE equipment is. I come every year, you see. I've got a mate in t'van. He comes every year with me, except one year when he had angular fever and they kept him off work. He's good with rope ladders and sprockets. We've got a new van this year, it's a Transit."
"Excellent! Well, give me a shout if you need anything, won't you!"
"I'll probably come and knock on your door, rather than shout, if you don't mind."
"Whatever!"
Maybe he could give Gary a character reference, I wondered, as I watched him collect his mate from their shiny new van. They came in with a tool bag each and began banging things in the hall, just a short distance from the office. I shuddered a little. The thought of this curious little man fiddling with equipment that children were then going to climb on filled me with dread. Maybe the man from the van had a little more about him. I hadn't heard of any nut-

greasing related deaths over recent years so one of them must be reasonably competent.

The man appeared again at my door.

"Would you like to see some photos of my wife?" he asked.

A million thoughts went through my mind and they all condensed into a single reply, "Er!"

And before I had time to elaborate, he whipped out a small photo album and began to show me pictures of his wife. My fear that she would be indulging in peculiar practices was unfounded. She was a young, happy, Oriental lady, who clearly had mistaken the words 'Will you marry me?' for the similar sounding, 'Would you like me to bugger off and leave you alone?'

"She's lovely." I commented, really wishing I could get on with at least one job today.

"I bought her." Came his nasal reply. "My brother had bought one last year so I went over and did it as well. It cost eight thousand pounds but that included flights."

My mind had evaporated. I could think of nothing to say to this man. The wedding photos he thrust into my face showed the bride's family eating an Oriental banquet whilst the proud husband munched a chicken leg. Perhaps this was a test. If I could react well to this, maybe things would begin to resemble normality.

“They’ve gone up, though!” he continued. “Last year my brother only paid seven grand. Another thousand makes a bit of difference, but it might be aviation fuel that’s done it.”

“Well, I’m sure you’ll be very happy together.” I remarked.

“You have to be at that price, don’t you. Mind you, she were t’nicest one in t’catalogue, so I’ve done well. And when she can understand what I’m saying it’ll be even better.”

I had doubts about his last comment, but I decided to let fate take its course. Particularly as his mate had appeared to have done all the work and was ready to go.

“Well, it’s been nice meeting you.” the nasal one said. “Your nuts shouldn’t need any attention for the next year but you know where to come if anything unexpected comes up.”

I walked to the door with him, to ensure he was really leaving.

“That’s our new van,” he said, pointing to what was obviously their new van, “it’s a Transit, and it’s new. Do you like it?”

“It’s lovely.” I replied. “Goodbye!”

A woman was dashing up the path as I waved the men off. She was slightly out of breath when she reached the door.

"Hello," she said, "I couldn't beg a minute of your time, could I?"

The phrase, 'No, sod off, I'm busy!' remained inside my head and instead I replied, "Yes, of course."

We walked to my office and sat down.

"It's ever so good of you to see me like this," she began, "I wouldn't come without an appointment normally but I need to put you in the picture as soon as possible."

She seemed, at the moment, to be the most ordinary person I'd met all morning.

"My name's Diane," she informed me, "Diane Bailey."

Bailey, Baldy, she was his wife! I now could predict everything she was going to say to me. And yet I hadn't a clue what I was going to say to her!

"Look, it's like this. I'm in the middle of a messy break up with my husband. I kicked him out a while ago because it were going nowhere and now he's wanting to get in touch with our Julie. She's nine and she's in this school. She's not interested in seeing him and I don't want him hanging around. If he comes to school, I need you to kick him off t'premises or get t'police."

"Well, it's not quite that easy, Mrs. Bailey. I can't stop a parent from seeing their child unless there's a court order involved. Without that, he has as much right as you do to visit school, pick her up, or whatever. There really is nothing I can do to stop him, I'd be breaking the law if I did."

"Oh I see. It's like that, is it? Look, my father is a very influential fishmonger and he'd take it very badly if Gary started giving us a hard time. There must be something you can do."

"I can let you know if he picks Julie up, but I can't stop him. Not without a court order."

"I'm hoping to get one of them. We've got to go to court soon and they'll decide what's right. My father's going to help see to that. Listen, if they ring you from that welfare office, I want you to tell them about Gary. I want you say how he treats us badly and he's a danger to our Julie. You can do that, can't you? Me dad'll back you up."

“It might look a little fishy…. er, strange if I claim to know your family history in such a short time. I’m not really in a position to get involved.”

“Oh come on. They’ll believe you, you do a respectable job.”

“But people will stop believing me if I stop telling the truth. I have to be honest and the simple fact is that I don’t know your situation well enough to comment on it. I’ve been here for less than three hours and I haven’t even seen Julie yet. I can’t make life-changing statements.”

“Look, I’ll let you think about it. I’ll get my dad to ring you and work out a story.”

She got up and left and for a brief moment I wondered how I would react if the fishmonger extraordinary accused Gary of battering his wife!

The yellow Jeep streaked up the driveway like a bolt of lightning. Walt slammed the door and stormed into school.

“Bloody pancakes, the lot of ‘em!” was his opening remark. “I’m not one to moan but I’ve been in that shop for nearly an hour while their bloody computers went down. I’ll tell you this and I’ll tell you now and when it’s said it’s said and I’ll say no more, these computers aren't worth t'paper they're written on. You don't fix a ball valve standing in a queue while a bunch of pancakes poke about on a keyboard. I've got dinner tables to put out in t'hall and I've only got a few minutes to get it done. Well I'm sorry but I can't stand around talking, I've got things to do even if nobody else has. Bloody pancakes, I tell you!"

Nearly lunch time! I reflected on the huge amount of work that I had done this morning. That's right, I'd unfolded a letter and read a few lines of it. That must be why I felt so exhausted. I decided that this afternoon would be different. I would tell Ann the secretary to turn away any visitors and I would take a trip round the school and get to see some staff and pupils. It wouldn't reduce the pile of jobs on my desk but it might focus my mind on the school a little more.

First thing in the afternoon I walked into Ann's office, next door to my own, to tell her of my plans. I found her looking exasperated as she tried to fire up the computer. To be fair, Ann was a little old to be learning about new technology and she was finding it hard. But things change rapidly and she was finding herself with little choice but to get to grips with her hi-tech assistant.

“Having problems, Ann?” I asked, watching her wave the mouse around near the screen.

“It’s this damn rodent thing that I’m supposed to use!” she snorted. “I bought a book in summer and it made it look so easy. I’m supposed to click this in the bottom corner of the screen and it isn’t working.”

“Ann, you don’t put the mouse on the screen, you have a pointer on the screen. The mouse stays on the pad.”

“That’s not what it said in my book.”

“Trust me. Think of it as a kind of short cut.”

“But where do I get one of these pointers from?”

I explained my plan of action to Ann and left her alone to overcome her fear of mice.

I swiftly marched past Mrs Crosby’s room and continued to the other end of the school where the older juniors were located.

The children in Alan Barnett’s class were in their final year of primary school. This afternoon they were about to begin a study of the Solar System and Alan, a very serious, tall, thin man with a bushy beard, was drawing a plan of the planets on the whiteboard at the front of the class.

“Don’t mind me,” I said, “I’m just having a look round.”

Alan clearly did mind, but carried on with his lesson.

“So that’s, as it were, the planets,” Alan said, “but does anyone know the name of those meteors that fly around close to Mars. Interesting things, meteors. Like them a lot. I’m a lover of space issues generally. So, meteors, we need to put them on the plan. It’s the ‘Something’ Belt.”

Most of the children were desperate to impress their new teacher and headteacher so all hands went up to answer the question.

A rather goofy looking boy called Mark was chosen to provide the answer.

“They’re called haemorrhoids, Sir.” Mark said proudly.

“Ah, distinctly untrue. They’re called Asteroids, Mark!” Alan yelled. “Haemorrhoids are rather nasty things that you get on your, er, backside, as it were! You don’t, on the whole, find haemorrhoids flying around in space. And if you do, then those astronauts are braver than we give ‘em credit for! Ha, not terribly good at joking, it’s not a thing I do well, but quite proud of that one. Jot it down later, I think.”

I smiled and left Alan to get on with his lesson. I had a quiet snigger as I walked down the corridor. Perhaps asteroids were to be found near Mars, I mused, but maybe haemorrhoids were in the vicinity of Uranus! I decided to take a long walk before going into another classroom.

I walked all the way to the infant department and decided to pay a visit to the youngest children, who were, like me, enduring their very first day. Alma Robertson was their teacher and in true infant teacher style she........spoke.........very.........very.........slowly.

"Ooh!" she said as I entered the room. "This is Mr. Jeffcock, children. He is our new headmaster. Let's tell him what we've been learning to do today."

A minuscule being raised her hand and said, "We've been learning to thit up thtraight, Mith Wobbot-thon."

"That's right Cleopatra. We've been learning to sit up straight. And we're all very good at it. They're very good children Mr. Jeffcock."

"I'm not!" yelled a scruffy little lad from the back of the room. "My mum says I'm a little bugger."

"Yes Nathan, but no-one asked you to tell us that." Said Alma, calmly.

“She says I’m a right little bugger, my mum does.”

“What’s a little bugger?” asked a sweet little girl at the front of the room.

“It’s another name for a boy.” Said the child next to her, quite knowledgeably.

“Ooh, we’ve got a lot of little buggers in our class. I’m going to tell my mum.” Said the sweet little girl.

“I think it might be best if I left.” I told Alma. “You might want to have a good long chat about something that’ll take their minds off that conversation.”

“Bugger, bugger, bugger.” A little boy sitting on his own began to chant as I left.

Funnily enough, that was exactly what I was thinking!

I had now visited two classes out of a possible ten. Perhaps there would be time to disrupt a third before checking that all was well in the office. I chose to drop in on a class of eight-year-olds and their teacher, Jenny Bryant. Jenny, apparently, was the school squirrel. Her cupboards were full of pens, pencils, rulers, rubbers, old wartime soldiers, and various other indiscriminate articles. Anyone who needed to get their hands on equipment that we had ‘run out of’ was advised to visit Jenny's European Stationery Mountain and instant satisfaction would follow. At least to those who were easily pleased!

Outside Jenny's room was a boy. He shifted awkwardly from one foot to the other as I approached.

"What are you doing out here?" I asked him.

"I didn't mean to do it!" was his reply.

"You didn't mean to do what?"

"I didn't!"

"Tell me what you didn't mean to do."

"Kick Laura!" he said sheepishly.

"So, let me get this right. You've kicked Laura, but you didn't mean to kick her."

"I didn't. And she's got a big bruise."

"Where did you kick her?"

"Next to the fire exit."

"No, I mean where on her body? Where is the bruise?"

"Top of her leg."

"How can you kick someone on the top of their leg by accident? What was your foot doing near the top of her leg?"

“I didn’t mean to.”

“I don’t see how this can be accidental. Explain to me how you came to kick her, but didn’t mean to. Go on, I’m fascinated.”

“I was aiming for Danny’s balls but she got in the way.”

“So you’re trying to tell me that it’s OK because you were really aiming to kick somebody else!”

“Mmm.”

“Stay there till you’re eighteen!”

Well, at least we now had an outstanding pupil. The trouble was, he was out standing in the corridor!

Jenny was about to begin a number game with her class as I entered. She had her back to the door and didn’t see me come in.

“Before we can play the game, I need to check that you all know what I mean by the word ‘remainder’ when I’m talking about a solution to a sum. Who can tell me what a remainder is?’ she announced.

Her eyes fell on a girl who was clearly daydreaming and gazing out of the window.

“Jessica, you tell me. What is a remainder?”

“Erm, it pulls Santa’s sleigh, Mrs Bryant.”

The entire class descended into a fit of hilarity and at that exact moment, Jenny caught sight of me standing near the door. Her face flushed with embarrassment for a brief moment until she saw that I was also laughing at this unfortunate child. She waited to see what my comment would be.

"Rudolph the Red Nosed Remainder!" I said. "I'll think of you every time I hear that song!"

I turned to Jenny and said quietly, "Who's this Laura that got kicked in the fire exit? Is she OK?"

Jenny pointed to a girl whose head had bucked teeth sprouting out of the front and pigtails sprouting from each side.

"That's her over there. Her dad's the Chair of Governors, and she's, shall we say, a little precious!"

"So we can expect to see him some time?"

"Oh God, yes! He'll be after reviewing discipline policies, introducing the death penalty, you name it! You'll have to hose him down once he gets started."

"Thanks for the warning!"

Well, at least when *he* came in, I'd know what it was about. That would be a big advantage over the visits I'd had so far. I left Jenny to get on with the game she was about to play and walked back to the office. Ann was sitting at her computer, staring intensely at the screen.

“Everything OK?” I asked.

“No, it’s all gone wrong. I used the rodent and got the thing on the screen. Then I went to make a drink because I was a bit worked up. When I came back, the thing had gone from the screen and it’s been going mad ever since. It’s got lines flying about all over it. I never told it to do this – I wanted it to wait till I’d got my drink. So I’ve rung the technical people and said it’s just gone haywire and it won’t do what I want it to do. They’re coming out quickly. It costs thirty pounds but if they don’t come, we can’t use it.”

I looked at the computer.

“Ann, that’s called a screen saver! You left the computer on when you made a drink so the screen saver came on. It’s quite normal. Hit a key and it’ll go back to how it was. When did you ring the repair man?”

“Oh, forty minutes ago, he said it sounded like I was really worried so he’d come straight out. Look, this might be him now.” She indicated a man walking to the front door.

“Thirty quid for him to press the space bar!” I said.

“Assuming we don’t need any parts.” Ann replied, confidently.

“I’ll let you deal with him, Ann. I’m going to make a cup of coffee.”

Before the kettle had boiled, Ann returned with a huge smile on her face.

“Ooh, he *was* good. He fixed it in no time. I’ll use them again with no worries. I’ve given him a cheque. Oh, and he’s shown me a quick way to fix it if it happens again.”

“Oh, I am glad! Ann, did you use the computer much, you know, when the last Head was here?”

“Not since we got this new one. He did all the computer stuff.”

“So he typed all the letters, downloaded all the invoices, all that sort of stuff?”

“That’s right. You’ll have to see if *you* can get any training on it!”

“So, I’m just a little puzzled. What did *you* do in the office?”

“Ooh everything. I counted the dinner money, put plasters on children’s cuts, mended reading books. Oh, and if any mums came in to help out, I looked after their babies and toddlers. I enjoy that.”

The telephone rang and Ann looked at me with an expression of revelation in her eyes.

“That’s another thing I did, answer the phone. And then it sometimes needs putting through to another extension, or they need putting on hold. It’s quite complicated, but I’m fairly good with technological things.”

“Except computers.”

“Oh, they’re not technology, they’re just a mystery.”

The phone continued to ring.

“So, Ann, are you still planning to answer the phone now that the new term has started?”

“Yes, I’ll do it now. I almost shut it out, you know. You get used to hearing it ring, don’t you!”

“Not if you pick it up!” I answered, getting more agitated with every passing nanosecond.

She finally picked up the receiver and began to speak. She struck up an immediate conversation with the caller and chatted casually for an interminable period of time.

“Ooh, I know, dear!” she said. “You’re right, it happened when my sister had hers done. You just never know when, do you! Really? I

wouldn't have guessed, but then I don't go there very often. No, not at all." She looked across and caught sight of me, her new boss, wondering how important the call was. "Well, it's been lovely chatting but I'll have to go, got a lot of work to do. Bye love."
She replaced the receiver and smiled at me.
"Wrong number!" she said. "But I don't like to be rude."
The school day was about to end, at least for the children. As it did so, one of the teachers, Mick Adams rushed into my office.
"I'm just letting you know that Michael's mum is coming to see you. I don't know what it's about but I heard her say 'We're going to see that new headmasster' to him as he came out of school. Do you want me to say you're out?"
I immediately recognised the person he was describing as the Mad Woman.
"No, I'll see her. What's her name, by the way?"
"Mrs. Klimp. We get some bother nearly every night. It sometimes helps to not be around!"
"I've met her already. Is there a Mr. Klimp?"

“Yes, poor man. He’s disabled, permanently in a wheelchair. Legend has it that’s why she married him. He was the only one who couldn’t get away quick enough!”

Her dulcet tones could be heard down the corridor and I steeled myself for battle.

“I’ve got a complaint!” She barked at Ann, “Where’s t’headmasster? I need to see him, it’s urgent.”

“Come in, Mrs. Klimp!” I shouted from my office. And she did.

“Our Michael’s been bullied today and nobody’s done a thing about it! What yer gunner do?”

I turned to Michael and said, “Tell me what happened Michael, and tell me who you told about it.”

“What happened? What happened?” the woman yelled, “they beat him black and blue and nobody stopped ‘em. That’s what happened.”

“I can’t see any marks on him, Mrs. Klimp.”

“They’ve gone now. But they’ll affect him cycle logic like. He won’t be able to sleep tonight. He’ll have nightmares.”

I so much wanted to ask how he could have nightmares if he wasn’t asleep, but it would have only made the episode last much longer.

“When he told his teacher he was told to sit down. It’s disgusting. It’s a big cover up, this place.”

“When did you tell your teacher, Michael?” I asked.

“Straight after lunch break.”

“And what did you say to him?”

“I said ‘Can I go to the toilet?’”

“Why did you say that? How does that tell him you’ve been hurt?”

“I panicked and said the wrong thing.”

“So, let’s see. You went to your teacher straight after the lunch break and asked to go to the toilet. He refused and told you to sit down, as you’d only just come back in from an hour’s break. But by saying ‘I want to go to the toilet’ you actually meant to give the message that you’d been bullied.”

“That’s right.” Said Michael.

“And nobody did a thing about it!” yelled the Mad Woman. “Not a thing. It’s appalling!”

“And who had really bullied you, Michael?” I asked.

“One of the infants bumped into me on the yard because they weren’t looking where they were going.”

“But that isn’t bullying, Michael.”

"No, Sir."

"Oh that's right, defend the little infant. He'll grow up to be a thug, you just watch!" she barked. "And anyway, our Michael lost his new pen and nobody bothered about it. What have you got to say about that?"

"A pen? What did it look like? Can you describe it, Michael? The cleaner might find it."

"I'll show you." Michael said, and he held up a pen.

"It was like that, was it?" I asked.

"No, it *is* this one. I found it again. It had rolled off my desk."

"So you didn't ask anyone to help you find it?"

"No."

"Then why are we talking about it?"

"My mum didn't listen to the whole story. She just got mad and said we had to see you."

I stared at Mrs. Klimp. "Well, I think we're about done, aren't we. Now if you'll excuse me, I have things to do!"

She left, a little quieter than she came in and passed Ann in the corridor. Ann was coming to ask if I could take a phone call. The caller had told her who they were but she had forgotten! After what seemed like an eternity, she transferred the call to my phone.

“You’re through now.” She said on her telephone.

“Thanks, Ann.” I replied on mine. “Hello.”

“I’ll put mine down now.” Said Ann.

“Thank you Ann. Hello.”

“That’s what makes yours connect, you see, when I put mine down.”

“Ann, please put your phone down now!” I waited a few seconds and then said, “Hello.”

“I’ve just remembered who it was,” said Ann, still on the line, “it’s the Chair of Governors.”

“Well then put it down. He’s probably ringing to moan about what happened to his precious daughter this afternoon….”

“That’s right, I am!” came a rather pompous voice from the other end of the line. Ann clearly had put her phone down. “And I’ll be in first thing tomorrow to find out what action you’ll be taking!”

Autumn Term: Week 2

Walt! Are you OK? Have you broken anything?

Just me watch strap…

I was sure the start of the second week would bring with it a sense of peace and normality. The first week of term in the new job had taken its toll in many ways. I had spent far less time at home than I should have. Yet I still felt I knew very little about the school and its community. This was largely because I had spent my time reacting to unexpected circumstances, rather than being in control of events. However, I had only endured four visits from the Mad Woman over Thursday and Friday and this was a positive sign, I kept telling myself.

As for the Chair of Governors and his damaged daughter, I feared that this would be an episode bound to drag on for many centuries. He had, as promised, visited me the day after our unfortunate telephone conversation. He was as I remembered him from my interview, pompous, bombastic and rather lacking in grey matter. He had hoped to put me firmly in my place by staring at me over the top of his glasses when he spoke. It hadn't worked on a number of counts. Firstly, his demands that we rewrite the discipline policy were met with my response that the entire Governing Body would have to agree to that. Secondly, his wish to introduce expulsion, or failing that, the death penalty, for all bodily contact was somewhat illegal. And thirdly, staring over his glasses and pontificating made him look a prat.

He had left on a sour note after reluctantly agreeing to discuss school discipline at next week's governors meeting. Given the right opportunity, I might be able to publicly teach the man that getting over-involved in his own child's problems could make him look foolish in front of the rest of the governors.

But the week had begun smoothly and by Monday evening I was able to relax at home with my wife and children. True, I had started dreaming about a curious beast that was an amalgamation of the Mad Woman and the Chair of Governors and this made me somewhat reluctant to go to sleep, but resting in front of a good film and drinking a glass of wine helped numb my brain before bedtime.

I was woken from a reasonably pleasant sleep at two-fifteen in the morning by the telephone. I had only ever had two phone calls at such an hour in my life. The first was when my grandmother died and the second was a wrong number from San Diego. Not knowing what or whom to expect, I picked up the receiver. I was informed by a man with a fiercely strong Glaswegian accent that the school alarm was ringing and, not being able to contact Walt the Caretaker, the company had turned to me, being the next name on the list. The police would be waiting when I arrived.

Throwing on an old T-shirt and a pair of jeans I left the house and drove the nine and a half miles to the school. A police car was already waiting and as I approached the main entrance I was greeted by PC Blunt.

“Are you the caretaker?” he asked.

“No, I’m only the Headteacher.” I replied.

“Oh, sorry. Can you open up and switch the alarms off? I’ll follow you in. If there’s anybody in there I’ll call for back up.”

“So there’s no chance of you going first, then?” I asked, hopefully.

“No! I don’t know my way around the building.”

“I’m not sure I do either. Especially in the dark.”

Struggling to remember the code, I turned off the alarm and we set off into the building. It was silent, very dark and extremely unpleasant. To know that round the next corner could be an axe-wielding murderer, or even worse, the Chair of Governors, was a fearsome thought indeed. PC Blunt followed at a safe distance whilst I opened each classroom door and tried to peer under desks in the hope of *not* uncovering an intruder.

"There's no damage to speak of, is there?" the policeman whispered.

"Don't think so."

"Do you reckon you've lost anything?"

"Only a decent night's sleep!" I grumbled. "I feel a bit cheated in way. You'd think if you had to get up in the middle of the night, the least you could expect would be a good trashing!"

PC Blunt looked at me with a curious expression and smiled pitifully.

"I think we can lock up," he said, "there's nothing here. Sometimes spiders set alarms off when they walk across the sensor."

"I blame the Japanese!" I commented. "They've miniaturised everything. You used to get cat burglars and they were big enough to see. But spider burglars…"

"No, no I mean real spi… you were joking, I'm sorry."

As I reset the alarm, PC Blunt's jacket began talking to him. He pulled out a radio receiver and spoke into it.

“Can I leave you to lock up?” he asked with a renewed sense of urgency. “There’s a robbery going on down on the estate and I’m needed at the scene.” And he rushed off to his car before I had the opportunity to make some comment about being left alone in the dark with the school keys, no torch and surprisingly little courage. Keys, of course, always know when you’re alone and nervous. They refuse to fit the lock and then they insist on not turning until you begin to sweat and swear. The fifth expletive did the trick. The door locked and I walked towards my car, only to be met by PC Blunt once again.

“Look, this is a bit embarrassing.” He said. “You know I have to get down to this robbery, well I have a problem. My Panda Car won’t start. It’s stone dead. You couldn’t give me a lift, could you?”

With the prospect of sleep diminishing by the second, I opened my car door and smiled.

“Of course!” I said. “Jump in.”

Now that I was part of the team, PC Blunt saw fit to inform me that his name was Nathaniel and then proceeded to direct me to the scene of the crime, which was a small house on a quiet street. I parked my car and Nathaniel dashed into the house to apprehend the miscreant.

It was an unusually warm September night and I was still feeling rather hot as a result of my tussle with the school keys in the dark, so I sat and rested with the engine running, being suitably cooled by the air conditioning.

Lights appeared in my rear-view mirror. Nathaniel's colleagues were here to help and I was pleased that he would not have to tackle the criminal alone. I expected to see them dash, Sweeney-like, towards the house but it was not to be. Instead, they reversed their car in front of mine, climbed out and flung open my door.

"Out of the car!" one of them demanded.

"Ah, but you don't underst...."

"Get out of the car! Do it now! And no funny business!"

The officer clearly meant it. I did as he asked and planned to tell him that this was actually not the getaway car at a more suitable time.

"Would you mind telling me what you're doing sitting in the car alone with the engine running at this time of night?" said one of the officers.

"I was waiting for one of your colleagues." I stupidly replied.

“Oh, a comedian! Mick, we’ve got a comedian. He was sitting here waiting for a policeman. Looks like he’s found one, eh? Where did you get the car from?”

“It’s my car. I’ve given a lift to…..”

“Get a number plate check on this car, Mick.”

Mick began to do as he had been instructed whilst the other officer, with whose name I had not yet become acquainted, continued to try to arrest me.

“Let’s see your license, then.”

“I don’t have it with me. I got up in a bit of a rush and didn’t bring anything.”

“What a surprise! And why were you rushing, go on, entertain me!”

“Well, it was because of the break in.”

“Last minute job, then, eh?”

“No, no, you really don’t understand. Look, let me start from the beginning.”

Mick returned and whispered something to the nameless officer.

“What’s your name, address and postcode?” the officer asked.

I told him my name, address and postcode and Mick nodded.

“Seems like this *is* your car, then.”

I breathed a sigh of relief.

"But just because it's your car, it doesn't mean you're not on a job."

He informed me.

At that moment, Nathaniel came out of the house with a scrawny looking youth.

"Hiya, Mick, Dave. I've got him. Caught in the act."

"And we've got his driver!" said the newly Christened Dave.

Nathaniel burst out laughing. I, alternatively, hadn't reached that stage of emotional development yet. Nathaniel explained the whole situation to his colleagues and they began to roar with laughter. Nathaniel, Dave and Mick staggered around in fits of laughter, pointing at me with tears rolling down their faces. I allowed myself to break into a relieved smile, quickly halted by the piercing voice of an old lady who had flung open her bedroom window and shouted,

"Shut that noise up or I'm ringing t'bloody police!"

I began to feel sorry for the scrawny youth who had waited patiently in the working Panda Car as the officers discussed my plight.

Nathaniel told them a little more about the evening's proceedings and then Dave looked up and said,

“You’re t’new Headmaster at t’school up on t’hill, are you? Hilltop Primary?”

“Yes, that’s right.” I replied with a smile.

“My little lad goes there. Matthew, you’ll know him, won’t you. Oh, this’ll be a good tale to tell t’other parents on t’playground. Oh, it’ll be a cracker.”

I stopped smiling.

Tuesday began in a sleepy haze. I really needed this to be a quiet day, which meant it wouldn’t be. You just know these things!

“Morning Walt.” I said as I stepped into the building.

“Morning. I’ll tell you this and I’ll tell you now and when it’s said, it’s said, and it’s this. You look tired.”

“There’s no fooling you, is there! I had a call out last night. The alarms were ringing.”

“Some bloody pancake messing around, were it? I’m not one to moan but I’ll tell you this and I’ll tell you now, there’s some right bloody pancakes round here. I’ve lost count of how many pancakes we’ve had on t’roof of this place. Local adventure playground, this is. Me and our lass stayed at her sister’s last night, looking after her, like.”

"Is she poorly?"

"No, she's married to a nutter. Complete cheesecake, he is. Left home three months ago, keeps giving her grief. That's why we stayed there. Tried to sort out her plumbing while we were there but he'd got no suitable equipment. You wouldn't believe what state his nuts were in. So you got called out, then? Did they do any damage?"

"Nobody here at all. It was a false alarm."

Walt explained in immense detail about the way spiders and other small creatures can crawl across the sensors and trigger the alarms. He relived his many call outs, explaining how each and every misdeed was committed by a pancake. By the end of his story I felt mentally drained but now realised that the school alarms were only triggered by small insects or mixtures of flour, eggs and milk. So there was really nothing to worry about.

Ann approached with news of a phone call. I offered to take it in her office, as this would save at least fifteen minutes of 'putting the call through'. It was, as Ann explained a call from the medical centre and was something to do with child welfare.

It was nothing to do with the medical centre at all. It was the Court Welfare Officer dealing with the case of Diane and Gary Baldy. This was the man who would help determine the future of the members of this malfunctioning family. I had never spoken to an individual who was so nervous and subservient. I felt uncomfortable simply listening to the man.

"I'm so sorry to take up your time," He wittered. "I'm sure you're a very busy man, and I don't mean to intrude on the many jobs you're probably doing. But I wonder, if you could, if at all possible, sometime soon, well, to suit you really, but preferably sooner rather than later, allow me to make a appointment to see you, not for long, of course, but it is rather important and I would appreciate it."

"Yes!" I replied. "Have you got a day in mind?"

"Oh that's very good of you. I know you'll be busy but the earlier the better for me. That is if that's alright with you. Please say if that's no good."

"No, really, the sooner the better. How about this afternoon, say one thirty? Get it sorted quickly, you know?" I suggested.

"Oh that would be excellent. I'm very grateful. More than you could ever imagine. You must have such a lot to do and seeing me so soon is a real bonus. Thank you so much. I'll look forward to meeting you. Goodbye. Oh, and thank you again." Assertiveness training courses had been designed specifically because that man was born, I decided. He really should attend one, but was probably too scared to ask his boss.

Someone who categorically did not need assertiveness training was my Deputy Head, Mrs. Crosby, or Gillian, as I now knew her. She oozed assertiveness from even the merest follicle. She was a born leader and she terrified me. She had warned me that this morning she was meeting a parent who wished to complain about the way children were treated in her class. Apparently, some parents felt that Gillian was too loud and frightening to be an infant teacher. Some of the children were scared of her, too! She was big, loud and exuberant but in fact she was an excellent teacher. Once the children really got to know her they tended to really like her. Unfortunately, many children were forty-three before they really got to know her.

However, today's parent was not scared. She was coming in to sort things out once and for all. And as she marched along the corridor to Gillian's room, I realised that I knew her. It was Melanie Barratt. She had been one of my pupils. I was her teacher when she was ten. She was one of those people whose physical age had overtaken her mental age from a very early point in her life. She had caused me endless trouble when she was a child and was now back for a second go, this time as a parent.

Within two minutes of her walking into Gillian's room, I could hear shouting. It was time to intervene, or referee. Or perhaps, sell tickets! I burst into the room to see Melanie in full flow, treating Gillian to a display of every expletive known to mankind and simultaneously demonstrating just how contorted the human face can become when one is angry. Gillian's mouth was firmly closed and consequently it took me a moment to fully recognise her, but then I decided I should do something.

"Melanie!" I shouted over her screams, "I think you'd better calm down!"

Melanie turned and looked at me and the most amazing transformation took place, right before my eyes. She became a little ten-year-old again. And I was her teacher, telling her off. Only this time round, she actually took notice! And as we took our respective roles in re-enacting a classroom scene of twelve years previous, she looked at the floor and shuffled her feet.

"I'm very sorry." She said behind her breath, "I shouldn't come in here shouting, it was very irresponsible of me."

I was very impressed that she knew such a big word. I assumed that she must have been practising it. Either that or she'd been so irresponsible for the last few years that the word was imprinted on her brain.

"I think Mrs. Crosby's got the message, Melanie, along with half the school and residents at selected postcodes. Now, leave it and give her a chance to think about what you said. There's no point just shouting for the sake of it, is there!"

"No, I'm very sorry. I shouldn't have done that and I'm very sorry. Sorry Mrs. Crosby."

Gillian looked quite stunned. She wasn't exactly sure what I'd just done there. But I knew exactly what I'd done – I'd improved my credibility no end! I'd rescued the vicious and vociferous Deputy Head from an angry parent with the minimum of fuss. And she didn't know how I'd done it. And I wasn't going to tell her!

I took Melanie back to my office for a chat. I was interested to know how one of my ex-pupils was getting along, although hopefully, she wouldn't be a representative selection.

"Oh, I'm alright," she informed me, "things have got a lot better, recently. I've just about cleared my drug habit so they're not taking the kids off me. And my partner, he was a bit violent, but he could be lovely, he's in prison for a bit so I'm safe there. My new boyfriend's got a court order stopping him from seeing me so that's OK, and my suspended sentence finished last month. So I'm doing well."

I quietly presumed that the only 'well' she could possibly be talking about was a deep hole in the ground.

"I've got a new social worker and I'm trying to visit the rehab clinic when I'm supposed to. And I've started making sure my kids have got food because I was a bit lax with that at one time. But you don't know till somebody tells you, do you? My social worker's ever so pleased with how I'm looking after my house. It's not a palace, but I don't have dog mess on t'floor like I used to. Because they said it weren't healthy for my kids, that."

This was almost surreal. Melanie was a child last time I knew her and now she was a major employer. She travelled with an entourage of social workers, therapists and probation officers. She relied on these people in the way a president relies on his advisers, to guide her through the tough decisions that were required in the course of a day. Maybe there were bodyguards waiting outside the door and a bullet-proof limousine to whisk her off to the drying out clinic.

But I also felt strangely humbled listening to her. She had probably had more unpleasant experiences in her twenty-three years than most of us would ever have in our entire lives. She had gained the ability to choose boyfriends who treated her as a punch bag, she had inhaled and injected hundreds of curious substances and she had already begun producing and no doubt training her successors to this grand lifestyle. And in spite of all this, she was happy that things were going well.

“Do you see much of your parents and your brothers?” I asked, remembering her foul-mouthed father from her childhood. And then remembering her mother, whose favourite phrase had been ‘No, our Melanie didn’t do it. She’s a good lass and nobody can tell me different.’

“I don’t see ‘em a lot.” She said thoughtfully. “My mum and dad disowned me when I started mi drugs. Or when I had mi first abortion. I can’t remember, it’s all a blur. Anyway, they kicked me out and I’ve only seen ‘em in court since then.”

“In court?” I asked, hardly daring to hear the reply.

"Yeah. They had me bound over when I started chucking bricks at their house after they'd kicked me out. I were stupid doing that, I know now. I should have chucked bricks at their car cos I could have got away quicker and they wouldn't have caught me."

I smiled. There were no words to fit the situation.

"Do you remember our James? Well he's dead now." She told me with a knowing nod of the head.

"Oh that's awful. What happened?"

"Joyriding. He nicked this car and it had faulty brakes. Smashed into a wall. We've got a lawyer trying to get compensation from t'owner. It weren't roadworthy, that car."

I frowned. There were no words to fit this situation either.

"And you've got a couple of children of your own, now." I said, trying to change the subject.

"Yeah. They were both accidents but you can't keep aborting, can you! My oldest one, Summer Breeze, she's six. She's a little twat, er, devil sometimes, but her dad were a nasty bastard. He's inside for child abuse but he only messed with other kids, never her. My younger one, Ophelia, she's only three. Her dad were in t'paper a few weeks ago. He'd done an old woman's house over. It were a good picture of him. I've cut it out for when she's older. She'll be able to say she's got a famous dad. Look, I've got to go. I've heard that my social worker's doing a surprise visit this morning so I need to go and hide mi needles."

"I thought you said you were off the drugs."

"Yeah, I did. I am, mostly. I've cut right back."

The distant look in her eyes suddenly made a lot more sense. As she left the building I picked up a small exercise book, titled it 'Summer Breeze Barratt' and forced myself to not place an exclamation mark after the name. I then logged as much as I could remember on the first few pages. Soon, there would be a case meeting about Melanie and I would get to meet her entourage and selected members of her fan club. I would have to begin my whistle blowing activities for the sake of the kids. Summer Breeze, it seemed to me, was destined for a dark and wintry life.

As I filed the book in the drawer of a filing cabinet, I overheard two nine-year-old boys walking past my office. I was on the verge of starting a second exercise book as I listened to what they said.

"Did you have sex last week?" said one of the boys.

"Yeah, did you?" said the other.

"Yeah, I love sex."

"I hate it when you've had your turn and you have to wait four weeks till next time."

"I know. It should be every week."

"It should. Some days I'm desperate."

I had to know who, what and when they were talking about. I ran out of my office and followed them down the corridor, apprehending them just before they reached their classroom. I asked them to elaborate and they were happy to do so.

"We were saying that we wish we could have sex more often, Sir."

"Sex more often? What do you mean?"

"At lunch time, Sir. Extra food when they've finished serving, you know, seconds. We only get secs every few weeks and we'd like them all the time."

I walked away, bemused by the fact that in one building and in the space of a few minutes, I could witness both the innocence of youth and the degradation of a once-innocent individual.

I didn't need my second exercise book after all. In the exercise book department, I would go without secs today!

It was time to begin attacking my list of things to do. Although I added many items to the list each day and it now numbered sixty-seven, I was pleased to be able to report to myself that I had ticked off the first two items. The list of jobs stood a real chance of being completed before my three hundred and forty-ninth birthday. My sense of achievement yielded to my sense of smell as a pungent odour drifted down the corridor, and then I heard the dulcet tones of Walt.

"Bloody pancakes!" he was muttering to himself.

"Got a problem, Walt?" I asked, hoping that my eyes were not hinting towards the subject of personal hygiene.

"We've 'ad a bloody pancake on top of that lamp post on the drive." He informed me.

"Wow! Somebody must be a heck of a tosser!" I joked.

"That they are!" he replied, not grasping even the slightest hint of the joke. "I'll tell you this and I'll tell you now and I'll tell you reight and straight and when it's said it's said and I'll say no more. We've got more pancakes round here than, than….."

"Denny's at breakfast time?" I suggested, trying to help him out of his conversational hole by the use of a transatlantic interjection.

“What? More pancakes than, than, anything!” he stated, looking very pleased with himself for concluding so eloquently.

“What have these pancakes done, Walt?” I asked.

“What have they done? I’ll tell you what they’ve done. I’ll tell you, and since you ask I’ll tell you now. They’ve been up that lamp post and pulled its cover loose. Now it’s an elf and safety. One gust of wind and that could be down on somebody’s head. Then it’ll be thee and me in t’dock, won’t it!”

“It will indeed, Walt. We’d better call someone in to fix it.” I suggested.

“No, I’ll get mi ladder. I’ll do it.” he bravely offered.

“Well I’ll stay with you. You’re not supposed to climb above eleven feet are you?”

But he’d gone to get his ladder. I think he quite enjoyed little tasks like this, although he would never admit that he enjoyed, well, anything really!

He leaned the ladder against the lamp post, requested that I place my foot on the bottom rung, and then began to climb the ladder. Despite the fact that he was fixing a lamp, Walt was not a light man. His weight appeared, at least to me, to be causing the lamp post to rock rather more than I felt it should.

"Walt, are these things set in the ground OK?" I shouted.

"I should think so. Why, what's up?" he yelled, by return of 'post'.

"It's just that it seems to be rocking a bit. This plate thing at the bottom looks like it once had bolts in it, but there aren't any now. It all looks a bit loose."

"It'll be fine. It's been up for years and never needed any work doing."

It continued to rock as he climbed. And then, when he was more than half way up the ladder, the rock became a sway. I looked hard at the base of the post and could see that it not only was devoid of bolts, but was also badly corroded.

"Walt, I want you to get down!" I shouted up to him.

Ever obedient, Walt stepped one rung higher. The post gave a final creak and lurched forward taking Walt and his ladder with it as it plummeted to the ground. This, in the car park was a terrifying sight to behold. Insurance and injury claims were playing leap-frog inside my brain as I stood and helplessly watched the events unfold in slow motion.

As it became clear that the trajectory of the lamp post was leading it into a space between two parked cars I momentarily relaxed until I caught sight of Walt leaping clear of the pole and coming to earth like an airborne hippopotamus. As the pole crashed safely in a space between two vehicles, Walt broke his fall by landing on the roof of the nearest car, which happened to be rather new and not inexpensive, and belonged to Gillian, the Deputy Head. As he landed, he created for himself a Walt-shaped nest in the roof of the car as it buckled under his considerable weight.

"Well bugger me!" Walt exclaimed from the roof of the car. "I've never had that happen before and I'll tell you this and I'll tell you now, I shan't be wanting it to happen again in a hurry!"

"Are you OK? Have you broken anything?" I asked.

"Just mi watch strap, I reckon. Mind you, this'll be a bugger of an insurance claim for somebody to put in, won't it! Cause of damage – caretaker landed on roof. They'll think she's a right bloody pancake! Nah then."

Walt scrambled down from the roof, knocking off a door mirror in the process and I quietly rehearsed how I might let Gillian know the fate of her unfortunate vehicle. I suggested that Walt took the rest of the day off but, to give him his due, he was not one to let a little matter of falling from twenty feet interfere with the lavishing of love upon his urinals. He insisted that after a cup of tea, he'd be fine and besides, his wife was at home today so he'd rather be at work.

By one-thirty I had eaten half a sandwich and was fully nourished and ready for my meeting with the Court Welfare Officer. He arrived, wearing a dark suit and incredibly thick spectacles that only just escaped being mistaken for binoculars. He came into my office and placed his black briefcase on the floor.

"Hello." He said. "Thank you so much for seeing me, I do appreciate it."

I needed to prepare for the fawning that was about to follow and so to buy a little time, I offered him a drink.

"Oh, could I? That's so kind. I'd love a coffee with a little milk and about five eighths of a teaspoon of sugar, but don't go to any trouble. It's very nice of you to offer, I don't want to impinge."

How does one 'impinge', I wondered. Are there impinging courses that you can attend? Might there be grades of impingement that you must achieve before becoming a fully qualified impinger? Or does this man 'not want to impinge' because he really doesn't know how

to? My mind had begun to wander and we hadn't even begun our discussion. I picked up the phone and buzzed through to Ann, requesting that she made two cups of coffee and that she brought the sugar bowl with her. Ann, despite her technophobia, could do kettles and I knew this had the makings of a successful mission for her.
The Court Welfare Officer, it appeared, had decided to visit me in order to find out which parent 'Our Julie' should place the majority of her trust in. It therefore came as something of a blow when he discovered that I had only met the parents once in my entire life. The only conclusion I could make with any conviction was that 'Our Julie' would probably be better off being raised by a pack of wolves.
"I was visited by the father," I informed him, "who wanted me to fabricate a story about the mother. He wanted me to paint a picture of an unfit mother who was poisoning the child against him." I explained.
"So, if I may suggest, if you don't mind, it is possible that the father has, shall we say, something to be afraid of, should the case be discussed, as it were, in court." He nervously suggested.

"But later the same day I was visited by the mother, with the aim that I fabricate a story about the father to prove that *he* is the unfit parent." I added.

"So, we could, perhaps, suggest that, maybe, it is the mother who, shall we say, is concerned…….ah, I'm beginning to see a problem here."

"Absolutely! Now I don't know these people very well but I don't like the way they think they can put pressure on others to get what they want. They clearly have manipulated people in the past and I suspect that both are guilty of trying to manipulate their young daughter into declaring which one she loves or wants to be with the most. In the process, they're involving anyone they can, to influence both the decisions of the courts and of their little girl. My concern has to be for the child and I have think she is being pressurised from both sides to make a decision that no child should have to make. The simple fact is that the girl is too young to be subjected to this sort of manipulation and, equally, the parents should be old enough to put their child's feelings ahead of their own. The kid is spending sleepless nights worrying about pacifying her parents when all should really be doing is getting on with growing up. As should the parents!"

"Excellent! May I quote you in court?"

With my mind drifting from broken kneecaps to angry fishmongers, I knew that I had given an honest opinion and that neither parent would be popping in to thank me for my help.

"I'd rather you say that I can't make a judgement in such a short time. But yes, you can tell the court my concerns. How do you expect the decision to go?"

"Usually, in this, as it were, type of case, there would be no order against either parent. Access will be shared but, if you don't mind, I would suggest that, if I may, your concerns are heard and that the manipulation situation, as it were, is monitored by either a reliable family member or a professional intermediary."

"So the wolf pack is out of the question?"

"For the, er, as it were, moment, ha, ha."

I envied the nervous little man as I watched him fumble with his briefcase and drop his pen three times on the floor before finally making notes of the discussion. He could give his opinions, well actually he could give *my* opinions and then probably never see the family again. As for me, they knew exactly where I could be found.

Autumn Term: Week 3

I'm a councillor. I can get an erection in a matter of days.

I had been dreading the third week of term ever since receiving some events for my diary, back in early June. This week, the third week of term, contained my first meeting with the Governing Body. I had already been in the building eleven hours by the time the meeting began and did not therefore relish the idea of a further three to four hours of being put on the spot. But no matter, it was a legal requirement.

As the Governors arrived they reminded me of their names and then sat down to look at their agendas. There were fifteen Governors, made up of parents, staff, councillors and other local personalities who had been appointed by the Local Authority. By and large, I mused, there are two kinds of people who choose to give up their free time to become school governors. Firstly, there are those worthy characters who genuinely want to serve their community in some way, to put something back in. But there are also those who are there to while away their spare time, and get to know the confidential stuff, which they can then drip out to selected acquaintances when the time is right. I needed to quickly find out which camp each member of the Board worked in. As the Chair of Governors arrived, I remembered that there was an additional category of person who takes on the role – the pompous pillock who likes to feel important. And that is probably the most dangerous kind of them all.

When it seemed we had our full complement, the Chair sat at the table, so to speak.

"Good evening ladies and gentlemen of the Governing Body and welcome to our first meeting of the new school year." He barked. "I should like to officially welcome our new Headteacher and hope that he quickly settles into our way of doing things."

I wasn't sure about that comment. Was it possible that it hadn't occurred to him that I intended to settle into the *correct* way doing things? If this happened to match their way, then that would be fine.

"I should also like to welcome our new teacher governor, Louise Johnson." Said the Chair.

"I should point out," I said, "that when I informed the staff that we needed a new teacher governor, the response was quite amazing."

"Excellent!" said the Chair. "There was quite a rush, was there?"

“Indeed there was. But Louise was last out of the room so she had to do it!”

“Hmph!” is the nearest approximation to the Chair’s remarks.

He shuffled some papers importantly.

“Right! On with the meeting. First point, apologies. Does anyone have any apologies?”

“Yes!” I chortled, “I’m sorry!”

No-one laughed. All the governors looked sheepishly either at the Chair or at the floor.

“I am asking for apologies for absence, Headmaster. That is how we begin the meeting.” He grunted.

“I know, I’m just… well, never mind. Sorry. Oops, there’s another apology!”

The Chair peered over his glasses and sneered. “If there are no genuine apologies we shall proceed with the next item. Please read the minutes of the last meeting for accuracy.”

Minutes of the last meeting! They went on for pages and pages. They should have been called the *hours* of the last meeting, or maybe the epochs of the last meeting. And of course, not having been to the last meeting, I had no idea if they were accurate or not.

So I sat and looked round the room trying to remember names. Polly Stone was a social worker, Barbara Griffiths was the lollipop lady, Islwyn (Izzy) Thomas was a councillor, Paul Parry was a parent of a child at school, a member of an obscure Environmental Party, and an active anti-car protester who travelled everywhere by bike, he told me. I imagined him attempting to go on holiday to Spain with a wife, three children and five suitcases on his bike. In fact this drift of the imagination stopped me from continuing round the room and suddenly I was startled by the Chair talking.

"I'm going to go straight into correspondence." He announced. And as he did so he produced an immense pile of mail that had been addressed to the Governing Body. He then, to my horror, proceeded to open, read and discuss each letter in turn. This may have made sense for the three important letters, but the majority of the pile was junk mail. The man seemed unable to distinguish between what was important and what was not. And time – and my life – was ticking by furiously.

He opened the ninth letter and described its contents.

"This is from a company that helps teachers with their professional development. It says here, 'Do your staff feel that they are working in a stable and supportive environment?' What would be your comment on that, Headmaster?"

"Er, both!" I said. "The staff here feel that they are working in a supportive environment and because of the state of the building, they often think they're working in a stable!"

"Please be serious, Headmaster." The Chair replied. "There may be useful products contained in this letter."

"OK, I'll be serious." I said, now heartily sick of this man's know-it-all pomposity. "Before you continue with that letter, let me tell you that the Local Authority provides courses at a fraction of the cost of the ones you're reading about. You are reading a mailshot from a couple of teachers or headteachers who got out of the job because they couldn't do it and now think they're qualified to train other people. I don't respond to junk mail. The school will decide what our training needs are and then we will look for the best provider. I'm not going to be told what someone at the other end of the country thinks we need just because they can provide a course on it."

"So are you saying you won't give each item fair consideration?"

"I'm saying that as a Board of Governors you should be able justify what the school spends its budget on. There is very little spare cash floating around in schools and every penny you spend on an overpriced course that you could have got cheaper elsewhere is a penny you can't spend on educating the children."

"I'm sorry, Headmaster, but it's your job to see how the money's spent. Our job is to receive reports from you and monitor what you're doing. I have to justify nothing."

"Are you aware that if a school knowingly mismanages its budget, all of its governors are personally liable and can be held financially responsible?"

Clearly he wasn't, and neither was the rest of the Board, for there was a stunned silence. I detected a slight dent in his credibility. He was on the road to becoming a wobbly Chair.

The junk mail was binned and the meeting progressed. The first real item on the agenda was discipline.

The Chair wished to recommend a thorough overhaul of the policy as information had come to light that acts of badness were not severely dealt with.

He cleared his throat, pulled his spectacles to the end of his nose, peered over them and began his speech. "As Governors you may not be aware that a brutal attack on an innocent child took place in school last week. You will probably be disgusted when I inform you that the perpetrator is still at large. It is my view that he should have been suspended by the Head. Would you care to comment, Headmaster?"

"Yes, I'll comment. First of all, being suspended by the head is otherwise known as hanging and I think that is a little barbaric in a primary school. The criminal who is still at large is an eight-year-old boy who kicked another child. The boy was reprimanded and given detention for a couple of days. I have threatened that, should another incident occur, I will bring in his parents and we will discuss serious measures to teach him how to behave appropriately, in accordance with our already comprehensive discipline policy. Accidents do happen in schools. There are a lot of people in a relatively small space. Bumps and bangs happen. Children lash out and sometimes hit an innocent victim and we deal with it on every occasion. But suspension is reserved for more serious offences."

"So you're saying that my daughter being kicked is not serious!" the Chair barked. As soon as he had finished his sentence he realised that he had just informed the entire Governing Body that the child in question was his own daughter. It was now clear to them that he was trying to use his position to gain special privileges. The Governors eyed him with cynicism and he visibly squirmed.

"Your daughter is a member of the school and is treated like everyone else. The child who kicked her has been punished. If your daughter had kicked someone else, would you expect me to have suspended her?

He was now on the defensive, attempting to salvage his credibility.

"Somebody's been getting at you, haven't they! There's been allegations before about me wanting to have special treatment. I don't like allegations like that and I intend to find out who the allegators are."

"The alligators are slimy reptiles…."

"You're damn right, they are!"

"…That live in the Everglades!"

The other governors had not seen the Chair quite so rattled before and the room was now filling with whispers and sniggers.

"I suggest that we don't rewrite an entire policy on the basis of your daughter's single misfortune, but that we continually monitor the way the school puts its policy into operation." I snapped. "Before deciding upon divisive and draconian measures that will cause an outcry amongst the vast majority of parents, I suggest the Chair becomes familiar with both protocol and legal issues surrounding school discipline. It is only by following the correct guidelines that we can expect support from the Local Authority's legal and insurance services, should a serious problem or complaint about our handling of a situation arise. I also recommend that any governor with a child in school remains impartial. Bear in mind that if we punish one child severely for a misdemeanour that might have been an accident, we have to follow the same pattern every time. And next time it could be your child who gets the punishment."

A resounding vote of support rippled around the room and the Chair, red-faced, made a pompous noise and picked up his agenda.

"Next item." He said.

By ten thirty we had discussed not only discipline and the inevitable falling lamp post, but also the choice of vegetables for school meals, the carpets in the library, the pothole in the playground, the leaky roof, the speed of traffic on the main road a quarter of a mile away, (which, we were informed by Paul Parry would be solved if the road was closed to everything but bikes) and the possibility that one of the dinner ladies wore a wig. Finally, we reached Any Other Business. It was nearly time to go home, fourteen and a half hours after arriving.

"So, is there any other business?" asked the Chair.

"I feel I'll have to bring up dog mess." Said Izzy the councillor.

I was unsure whether to call a doctor or try to find a large bucket. In the event I did neither.

"Dog mess?" I repeated.

"It's something I think about a lot is dog mess. It's very close to my heart and I wonder if the school understands the implications." He stated, importantly.

"Are we talking about the implications of having dog mess close to your heart? Or are we supposed to be worrying that you spend a lot of your time thinking about dog mess?" I asked.

"I'm concerned that a lot of parents are responsible for dog mess around the school gates."

"Sorry to be picky, but I actually think you'll find it's the *dogs* that are responsible for at least the vast majority of it!"

"You know what I mean. So, back to my point, I have composed a letter to distribute to all parents. I've brought a copy with me for approval and if it is approved I suggest that we send this to parents tomorrow."

Izzy unfolded the letter and began to read it in his serious councillor's voice.

Dear Parents,

I am sure that, like myself, for many of you, dog mess is a prominent feature in your mind. I have looked very closely into dog mess and the results are frankly, not pretty. A young child, mistaking the dog mess for a toy, could pick it up and put it close to his or her face. This could result in eventual blindness. I would like to pass a motion at this point. My motion is that the school will provide a bin to be used specifically by dogs at the gate. I shall ask the school to elect mess monitors to stand at the gate and ensure that if a parent is responsible for producing dog mess, they will be brought in to the headteacher. I would also suggest that where possible, parents leave their dogs tied to the railings of the toddlers' playground down the road, thus keeping the school free from such mess. I am sure that if we all work together we can eradicate dog mess from our school, thus making the school a happier place to be.

Yours sincerely, Izzy Thomas.

“I commend my letter to the Governing Body. Any comments?”
Where do you start? Of course, all the Governors had a look of horror on their faces, but all looked at me for an official response.
“Well, Izzy, I think we have to be a little careful how we word things.” I began.
“You mean tread carefully. I’m sorry but you won’t catch me treading carefully where dog mess is concerned!”
“No, Izzy! But wading into dog mess is never advisable, is it? We need to ask for general co-operation before we start promising bins and crap monitors. Bins have got to be provided by the council on the premise that we will expect the council to empty them, so that’s a long job because councils work on a different time zone to the rest of us. If we promise it now, parents will complain when it hasn’t been done in a couple of weeks.”
“I can get an erection in a matter of days. You’re forgetting I’m a councillor.” He proudly stated.
“Well, that’s useful to know, but there are other problems. If we appoint children to the post of crap monitor, it’ll really hit the fan when their parents find out and I’ll have a queue of angry mums outside my door. And if a child brought in a parent to be told off by

me for fouling the footpath, well… I don't have to explain that one do I?

"So you think I'm going in too deep?"

"In a manner of speaking! And I have to say, the lack of dog mess doesn't automatically make the school a happier place. No-one gets depressed on catching sight of a small pile."

"I do! So my letter isn't appropriate? Do all Governors feel the same way?"

There was a general nod that made the room appear to have just driven over a bump.

"The world isn't ready for your letter yet, Izzy."

I could sense the discussion was nearly over and I was proud to have not used the words 'full of crap' in reference to his letter.

The phrase 'is there any other business?' had a faintly surreal ring to it when it was repeated and the resounding silence that followed the question meant that it was time to go home. I said goodnight to the members of the Board and all but the Chair said a cheery goodnight to me. Then I wandered around to check the doors and windows were locked. The locking up process involved securing two inner doors with a key that was then placed in a locked cupboard, then setting the alarm and finally locking a very badly aligned final exit door. The knack to securing this in place centred around twisting the key whilst simultaneously bouncing the door with the left hip.

My task complete I set off to my car, only to hear the phone ringing in the office. My first thoughts were to ignore it, heeding Walt's wise words of 'There's only more work or trouble on the end of them bloody things!' but my conscience got the better of me. A limited number of people knew where I was and so the call must be from my wife or perhaps one of the governors who had just left. I bounced the main door and unlocked it, disabled the alarm, retrieved the key to the cupboard from where I could obtain the two keys for the inner doors and then raced along the corridor. The phone was still ringing as I dashed into my office and picked it up.

"A large pepperoni with extra cheese!" said a voice at the end of the line.

I explained that schools are not regular providers of late night pizza and suggested that the caller must have the wrong number. The caller, however, did not agree with my assessment of the situation.

"Well I rang this number last week and got a pizza delivered!" he said.

"No-one was here at this time last week!" I replied. "Honestly, this is a school, you must have dialled the wrong number."

"Are you sure? I mean, what's a school doing open so late at night?"

I could have begun to tell the caller that we were here so late because we had been discussing dog crap but I felt it might have a detrimental effect on his appetite and ruin his eventual pizza.

Instead, I put the phone down and began the long process of locking up. This time I was going home. But I might call and pick up a pizza on the way.

Back in school at eight o'clock the next morning, I hoped the day might be quiet. That hope was shattered by the first phone call, at ten past eight. Sarah Brown, a Year Four class teacher would be unable to get in to work until lunchtime. Her child was sick. And now I was also sick, as I would have to spend the morning teaching Sarah's class. Supply teachers were both too expensive and in very short supply, suggesting that their title was rather inappropriate.

I spent the next half-hour in Sarah's room, reading her plans and getting the lesson materials prepared. Armed with a pile of papers, I marched efficiently to the photocopier and began producing the day's work. Like all photocopiers, it seemed to be fitted with an invisible sensor to detect when the operator was standing close by. If you stood and watched the machine, it worked faultlessly. However, should you walk away and leave it to get on with its job, it would jam the very second you were out of sight. Upon your return, you would thus find that you were no further ahead than when you left! Making that very mistake, I went to inform Ann of my revised plans for the morning and on my return, the copier had jammed. Opening the machine, I found no evidence of jammed paper, but the copier knew better, and refused to operate until the jam was cleared. I switched it off and reset it and upon warming up it proudly informed me of a paper jam. The queue of staff now waiting to use the machine was growing longer by the minute and as each teacher tried in vain to find even the merest scrap of jammed paper, it became clear that the machine was about to have a day off. Ann rang the repair company and I had a pain killer.

Being in the classroom with the children brought back memories. Twenty-six of the thirty-one children started the day with me. Two arrived late with the usual well-thought-out excuses. The first claimed that his mother had overlaid, a phrase that conjures up an image of an over-enthusiastic chicken every time I hear it. The second simply explained that her mum had got pissed last night and after going to bed at three in the morning, nobody had woken up in time for school. I preferred the second excuse because it didn't involve chickens.

Sarah's plans for the first lesson involved the children learning new vocabulary. It was a novel idea, as most children pick up their new vocabulary on the playground. The children had to look up words in a dictionary and then compose a sentence using each word. As I walked round the room I became aware that not every child was using a dictionary. Some were just guessing.

"Tom, have you checked the meaning of 'aspect'?" I asked a boy sitting near the window.

"Yes, sir." Replied that same boy.

"Then why does your sentence read 'When I walked through a field of geese I got my aspect'?"

The boy took on a crimson glow and admitted he may have not checked carefully enough. We both agreed that a second attempt may result in an improvement.

Walking around and reading the words of wisdom written by the children, I learned many new and exciting things that I had never before been aware of. I learned that your fortune is told when you read a horror scope, that at the beginning of a new page in the science text books they give you an egg sample, and that Jesus was raped in a blanket shortly after birth. Looking further back in one child's book I discovered that during the war, Morisson shelters were obtained from a major supermarket and that two local villages are four miles apart, as the *cow* flies. I intend to keep clear of the flightpath.

The morning break arrived and I learned that Sarah, the absent teacher was scheduled to supervise the playground this morning. Consequently I, being Sarah for the morning, was scheduled to supervise the playground this morning. And as the architect was visiting me to discuss the design of a pair of new classrooms, our meeting would take place in the refined environment of the schoolyard with three hundred children shouting, screaming, racing and falling over.

The architect, who insisted I call him Rob, was talking to me in as business-like a fashion as he could manage, but kept glancing downwards and to the left, and twitching. The focus of his attention was a seven-year-old girl staring intently at him.

“The site is built on reclaimed land.” He told me. “Old mine workings and so on, you know. We’ll have to fence an area off and drill some test holes so that the structural guys can look at the….”

His eyes wandered to the girl once again. He wasn’t accustomed to working in schools and had no idea that every move would be watched with interest.

“So that they can work out the foundation……” he stopped. He was losing his train of thought. Given time he would learn that it is unwise to even *have* a train of thought in the vicinity of children. And then he made the crucial mistake. He smiled at the child. He had initiated a relationship.

“My mum and Rebecca’s mum are second cousins.” The girl informed him.

Clearly glad to have to been awarded this knowledge, Rob replied, “Mmph.”

“So we’re relatives, me and Rebecca. We’re, we’re…”

“You’re distant cousins I think!” Rob suggested.

“No we’re not, she only lives on the next road!” the girl remarked.

I attempted to rein Rob back into the world of the only slightly surreal by ignoring the child and resuming the discussion.

“Can you ensure that the contractors contact me to discuss access times to the site. I need to avoid delivery lorries driving over the yard at times when the children are outside. And we’ll need to close off certain doors so I could do with knowing in advance in case we have to move an extra eighty kids through a different exit route.” In the midst of this I became aware that Rob was once again distracted and was not listening to anything I was saying. The object of his attention this time was a ten-year old boy waiting to speak to me.

“Sir, we’re trying to play football and Zak keeps moving the goalposts.”

“Then he’ll have a rewarding career in Government, won’t he! I’ll speak to him when he’s Education Secretary.”

The boy walked away and Rob smiled.

“So that’s how you do it!” he said.

“Confusion, it’s the key to being a successful teacher. No-one can put up a good argument if they haven’t got a bloody clue what you’re talking about!”

In order to maintain our discussion it was necessary for Rob to follow me back into Sarah’s classroom and become involved in a mathematics lesson. With the children hard at work, we could thrash out a few of the finer details of the extension. It was a successful chat and by its conclusion we had decided the following: eight test holes would be drilled; the main digging would commence in a half term holiday; no you can't take nine from four; the scaffolding would need to be inaccessible to vandals; no, this man isn't an inspector, he's an architect; no an architect isn't a type of vegetable; safety stays would need to be fitted to the windows; seven threes are and always have been twenty-one so you must have made a mistake somewhere; there's an 'h' in 'chart', you've just claimed to have drawn a pie cart; and no, I don't believe you got the same answers as Mark because you borrowed his pencil.

Rob left shortly before the lesson ended. I suspected he might never return.

The photocopier was being repaired when I broke free from the classroom. Walt was offering advice to the engineer who was not only trying to clear the jam but was also attempting to find out why the copier had such a curious smell.

"I'll tell you this and I'll tell you now and when it's said, it's said. They're complicated things, these machines. I said they're complicated." Walt informed the hapless engineer. "They're alright when they're working but when they're not working, they don't work."

"Well, you need to know what you're doing," said the engineer, trying to be polite. "And some places I go, it's hard to tell what people have done to get in such a mess."

"I bet you find some pancakes on these sometimes, eh?"

It was clear that the engineer was picturing some depraved individual photocopying pancakes. He smiled at Walt and then disappeared once again into the bowels of the machine.

Walt looked at me and nodded towards the machine.

"It's buggered, pal." He informed me.

"Is that the technical term for it then, Walt?"

"No. Technical term is knackered. Same thing though. Some bloody pancake's jammed it up. It'll be Celia, she's useless with these things."

"Actually it was me, Walt. But it just jammed itself. It thinks there's something stuck inside it and it won't work until we get it out. Trouble is, no-one can find anything inside it, so it's a bit tricky removing it."

"You want to turn it off and turn it back on."

"Done that! It's got a memory!"

"Well then, you want to open all its bits up and pretend to fiddle about. That'll fool it."

"Done that as well!"

"Well you'll need a repair man, then. Bloody awkward things, these are. I'd rather have a urinal or a cistern any day. They don't have memories and switch themselves off, do they!"

"They don't, Walt. But your copies would come out all soggy, wouldn't they!"

I received a curious look from Walt.

Ann came around the corner with a small child who was feeling ill.

"Sit here, dear, and I'll ring your mum. Will you be OK?"

"What's that man doing?" the child asked.

"He's mending the copier, it's broken down. I bet you've never seen inside it before, have you?"

At that point, the engineer, tugging on a part of the machine, caused a snapping sound.

"Bollocks!" he said.

"What's bollocks?" said the boy to Ann.

“Er, er, it’s a part of the machine.” She replied.

“Which part?”

“Er, the bit that the paper wraps round. I think the man must have decided to take that bit out. That must be the part that’s broken.”

The engineer stood up and looked at the bit of machine that had snapped.

“Have you broken its bollocks?” the boy asked the man.

Curiously, the engineer said nothing. He went outside and switched on his mobile phone.

Moments later he returned to inform us that he would have to come back in a few days with a replacement part. This was a disaster for a school that relied on around eight hundred copies a day. I began to worry about how the staff would react to the news. And then I began to worry a little more when I heard the little boy exclaim to Ann,

“I’m going to tell my mum that I watched the man get inside the machine and rip its bollocks out.”

Autumn Term: Week 4

Her overall, caught in a gust, lifted to reveal things that instantly promoted Walt to being the more attractive of the duo.

Monday morning of week four arrived and the copier still was not working. The news of this was almost bad enough to force me to close the school. It was a disaster only one step short of total kettle failure.

But the week was going well. I had been in the building for fifteen minutes and there were no signs of impending doom, no absent staff and no angry parents. And then, at five-past-nine, I was visited by Diane, the cook. Diane was small and fat and had perpetual pimples growing on her face. As one disappeared, so another took its place, as though a rota system had been devised and it was an interesting diversion on a Friday afternoon to try and guess the location of next week's pimple.

Diane had never visited me before. Instead she paid weekly calls to Ann in order to match up the number of meals actually taken with the amount of money actually paid. The two frequently did not match and time was spent each week making the figures appear consistent. I had once called it 'cooking the books' but this had not gone down well.

Today, however, Diane had a problem far deeper than even her rate of pimple production. Today she had wasps. To be precise she had dead wasps, hundreds of them littering the floor of her kitchen. In what must have been a terrible day on the wasp stock market, these creatures had thrown themselves to their inevitable death upon the tiled floor, the metal worktops and even in the deep fat fryer. They crunched under my feet when I stepped into the kitchen to investigate and I was already hoping that chocolate chip cookies were not on the menu this lunchtime.

"Can you see them?" Diane asked.

"Funnily enough, I can." I replied.

"I can't cook a thing. It could poison somebody." She informed me.

Not being sure whether she was talking specifically about the current situation, or being more general, I nodded and smiled.

I decided to make two phone calls. The first would be to the catering service to find out if they could ship in some meals from another local school, the institutional equivalent of sending out for a pizza. The second phone call would be to the council to see if they could send in the tanks, fighter planes and grenade-equipped personnel to rid us of the infestation. I had already decided that, if the wasps would be with us for some time, I would give each one a name and include it on the school roll. Every pupil generates money for the school budget and I could make use of a sudden and unexpected increase of six thousand pupils. This had more potential than my previous idea of including children's imaginary friends.

The council would send someone out today, I was informed. Given that councils work on something of a geological timescale, I decided that I would expect the team of 'waspbusters' any time in the next four weeks. The news from the catering service was less encouraging. Other schools, as I had suspected, had no spare capacity to produce such a large number of additional meals. They had two suggestions for me. The first was that I send all the children home and close the school. The second was that Diane should make sandwiches in a relatively wasp-free area of the kitchen.

A secondary school can send its pupils home in the middle of the day quite legally as they are old enough to fend for themselves. Not so a primary school! The children, being often quite young, have to be handed over to a responsible adult, or failing that, their parents. It would be impossible to contact every parent and even more impossible to guarantee that they could all drop what they were doing and collect their children and therefore, option two was the only reasonable course of action.

I went to inform Diane of her task and as I entered the kitchen I picked up the aroma of Walt. He had decided to give his opinion of the situation, and very accurate it seemed as I joined them.

“These are your wasps, you see.” He explained, hitting the nail right on the head.

“I know, and they were all over my floor when I came in.” Diane told him, once again indisputably correct.

“Buggers, wasps, that’s what I think. Better dead than alive, but not on your kitchen floor. It’s not hygienic having dead wasps on your kitchen floor, especially this many.”

“I know. And they’re in my fryer, come and look.”

Almost flirtatiously, Diane led Walt to her fryer so that he could observe the dead wasps floating in the fat. She smiled with a certain degree of pride as Walt peered into the fryer and saw for himself that her story was indeed true.

“I mean, what does a bloody wasp want with a deep fat fryer?” Walt postulated. “You’ll end up having to change your fat now, nah then! And that’s a mucky job, I’ll tell you that and I’ll say no more. Mind you, it’s not as mucky as cleaning dead wasps up from your kitchen. They look like rabbit crap at first glance, don’t they!”

“Ooh, they do. Eee, it’d have been a poorly rabbit though, wouldn’t it! Mind you, if it were rabbit crap there’d be some weight here if you bagged it up.”

I contemplated the fact that you can never tell what will be a good stimulus for a conversation. This was clearly an excellent stimulus and quite a relationship was developing. But despite being knee deep in wasps, it was destined to be a shallow relationship. When the wasps were gone, there would be little substance.

And then Ann came through to the kitchen to tell me that the council people had arrived.

“Have you asked to see their ID?” I asked. “A council workman arriving less than two hours after you’ve called them is highly suspicious.”

The men came into the kitchen and looked at the floor.

“Wasps.” One of them proclaimed.

“There’s no fooling you, is there!” I commented.

“You’ll have got a nest. I’m guessing it’ll be in your roof space. Have you got rotten timbers?”

Walt, sensing a maintenance conversation was in the offing, responded with lightning verbal dexterity.

“Rotten timbers?” he chirped, “Rotten timbers? I’m not one to moan but I’ll tell you this and I’ll tell you now and I’ll tell you reight and straight and when it’s said it’s said and I’ll say no more. These timbers are so rotten that you could put an ‘ole in ‘em just by peeing up one. There’s only paint holding ‘em together. See them rooflights? Can you see ‘em? It’s a bloody miracle how they stay up. They’re as good as floating, they are. All you’d need is one bloody pancake on that roof and the lot could end up in t’sink. Nah then.”

“Have you got dry rot then?” the man asked.

“I’ll tell you this, we’ve got dry rot, wet rot, concrete cancer….”

“And there’s a funny smell as well.” Said the waspbuster.

“Can’t say as I’ve come across that!” Walt replied, “But nothing’d surprise me.”

The men went away with Walt who would provide them with ladders on condition that they take a tour of his boiler room, inspect the tidiness of his storage facility and marvel at his gleaming urinals. I began to wonder if dry or indeed wet rot could be at the root of Walt's personal problem. I decided to not dwell on this matter for very long and besides, a photocopier engineer with replacement bollocks had arrived. I took him to the office and pointed out where the copier was. This was a futile gesture owing to the fact that firstly, as a photocopier engineer, one might assume that he would recognise such a machine and secondly, it was difficult for even a novice to confuse a photocopier with a desk, telephone or personal computer. This held particularly true when one considered the fact that the machine was as large as a small house and, filling a huge proportion of the office, was rather difficult to overlook.

The man worked efficiently for some time. Not only did he replace the broken part and ensure that the machine worked, he also kindly installed a squeak that had never before existed. This, I concluded, must be a free gift along the same level of usefulness as a ten pound holiday voucher. In fact it was more useful than a holiday voucher as it meant that I could hear when the machine was being used and thus never had to come out of my office and wait in a queue.

The sound of footsteps on the roof convinced me that there must be great activity taking place on the wasp eradication front. Diane, in her kitchen was creating sandwiches with almost inhuman rapidity but my attention was drawn to the fact that this week, not one but two pimples existed on her face. This must have been a proud moment for her and I felt sad that the wasp episode had earlier detracted from her glory. But no matter, she was in her element now. She had a sandwich production line working with a fluency that had to be seen to be believed. And completed sandwiches were being laid along a freshly cleaned worktop, ready for the fast-approaching lunch break.

And then, to add to the success of the situation, I heard a shout from the roof.

"Found it! There's a bloody big nest here, look."

Walt, still in active service on the extermination trail offered to hit something with his hammer. And as he did so, a shower of plaster, dust, rotten wood and any number of indeterminate objects fell from the ceiling. They were prevented from falling all the way to the floor by a neat row of sandwiches. The worktop that had been chosen to support the sandwiches was directly under the point at which Walt was banging.

Diane watched helplessly as her morning's work was covered with debris. I wanted to suggest that she tried to pass it off as whole grain bread with all the goodness left in, along with a considerable portion of the ceiling. But, quite frankly, I daren't say it. I didn't actually say anything at all.

Diane took a long, hard look at her ruined rolls and assessed the situation carefully. Finally, having decided the best course of action to take, she looked up at the ceiling.

"Stop 'ammering on that bloody roof!" she yelled.

Sadly she yelled this at the precise moment that Walt began hammering again and consequently, he neither heard her, nor stopped hammering. As the next bang brought down another layer of toppings upon the day's delicacies, Diane raced out of the kitchen to investigate the reasons for Walt's continued disobedience.

Outside the kitchen she looked up at the roof and shouted at a rate of decibels only equalled by the occasional airliner.

"You soft bloody pillocks! You've brought t'bleeding roof down on me baps. What the 'ell are you doing?"

Walt approached the edge of the roof cautiously.
"We've found where they are. We've got to get this wood loose so we can pull this big nest out. You might need to cover your stuff up in t'kitchen."
"Cover it up? You could have said that before you started bloody banging. You've wrecked mi bleeding sandwiches. They're all covered in crap, every one of 'em. I might as well have just served a portion of bloody wasps and have done with it, it'd have been more healthy! At least they're not riddled with asbestos like my baps!
Bread rolls riddled with asbestos. My mind drifted momentarily to the question of whether it would be possible to make toast from asbestos-riddled bread. And then I was brought back to earth by the sight of Diane leaving it! She had decided in her exasperation, to climb the ladder and deal personally with the matter in hand.
The ladder rattled against the side of the building as she raced skywards.
"Get down, you bloody pancake! You're not insured to be up here." Walt advised.
"Insured? Insured? Come and look at my baps and you'll be needing insurance! What am I going to give all these kids for their dinner?

They've got two choices, dead wasps or asbestos sandwiches. Either one'll kill the little buggers."

It was clear that Diane was not going to be able produce a meal today for a variety of reasons. First, it was too close to lunch time to be able to prepare anything of an appropriate magnitude. Second, she was far too happy screaming at Walt to spoil it by attempting to make lunch and third, should they ever come down from the roof, she would be taking Walt aside to display her baps for him! I decided, therefore, that a phone call to a local fast food restaurant might do the trick.

Difficult situations, particularly those with a good story, often bring out the best in local businesses. After a brief chat to the manager of a rather well known burger bar, I secured an order of two hundred and forty six assorted kids' meals, complete with toy. These would be provided free of charge on condition that much excellent publicity was afforded the company, both in newsletters to parents and by way of a story in the local press. The meals would be ready in twenty minutes but we would have to collect them.

At lunch time an army of teachers agreed to collect the meals and I agreed to remain on the premises for supervision of the children. I dashed outside to inform Diane of the situation and upon looking up to the kitchen roof, I found her standing rigid and, more unusually, silent. It appeared that in her frenzy she had forgotten her morbid fear of ladders and heights. And now that her frenzy had subsided, her fear had returned. She would not move. She dare not even turn her head or move her arms, let alone walk.

"Diane!" I shouted. "Are you OK?"

"She's not bloody OK!" Walt replied. "She's scared of heights. I told her not to come up, I said 'don't come up' but did she listen? I'll tell you this and I'll tell you now, she didn't! And now she's bloody stuck! I can't get her to move and God knows how we're going to get her down. We look like having a bloody helicopter on t'job!"

A small, but growing, group of children had gathered round to watch. The Dinner Ladies had first tried to encourage the children to go and play elsewhere but this was much more fun. And besides, the Dinner Ladies were rather enjoying it too.

"Diane, listen to me! You can't stay up there for ever, can you! The ladder is perfectly safe. Why don't you let Walt guide you down? You know it's safe because you climbed up it!" I called out.

“I’m staying here. I can’t move. I’m not getting on no ladder, it’ll tip up.” Diane said through gritted teeth.

“Diane, there’s no other way down, you have to use the ladder. Besides, this is a low roof, it’s perfectly safe. You’re only one floor up.” I shouted.

“I’ll tell you this and I’ll tell you now and when it’s said it’s said. Since I’ve been up here I’ve been having a good look at this roof and I didn’t know it had got to this state.” Walt remarked for the benefit of both Diane and me. “I’ll put it this way, she won’t be up here for all that long looking at these timbers. It’s just a matter of whether she comes down t’ladder or falls through t’roof. I’ll leave it with her!”

“Oh that’d be all I’d need! I’d end up landing on my baps!”

“Not if you bend your legs as you land!” Walt helpfully advised.

The waspbusters had finally retrieved the nest, an immense circular community that had lodged itself into the roof space. Entry for the wasps had been through rotting timbers as the men had so brilliantly predicted. They held up their prize and stated that this was one of the ‘biggest buggers they’d ever seen’ and that it must have been there since the dawn of time. They leapt onto the ladder and brought the nest down.

“You can keep it!” said one of the men. “You could put it on display. There’s no wasps in it so it’ll be safe. Mind you, looking at some of these little buggers on your playground you’d be better off if it were swarming!”

The men drove away, passing the return of the teachers with their quarry of burgers and chicken nuggets. As the children cheered their arrival, my thoughts turned once again to Diane and her rooftop vigil. And Walt, the rooftop vigilante! He was still talking to her up there, trying to convince her that life on the roof would get dull and tedious after a time and that a ladder was a perfectly safe way to descend.

“I don’t know what else I can do.” Walt said, “I can’t rig a winch up and lower you down on it. Tell you what, I’ll go down and have a think.”

“You’re not going down and leaving me up here on mi own. I’ll be more scared than ever if I’m on mi own up here!”

“Well I’m not planning on living up here with you for t’rest of my life, you bloody pancake. I’ve got things to do down there. There’s my toilets for one thing. You have to keep on top of toilets. If you don't keep on top of your toilets all hell breaks loose. Have you ever seen my toilets? They're spotless are my toilets and my urinals are better than any I've seen and I've seen a fair few, I'll tell you that. You could eat your dinner out of my urinals."

"I'm not interested in your sodding toilets. And I don't care how clean your urinals are, nobody's in t'mood for thinking about folk eating out of 'em!"

"I'll tell you this and I'll tell you now, if I had a choice of eating in my toilets or your bloody kitchen as it looks now, there'd be no contest. I'll leave it with you!"

"Will you stop talking about toilets!" Diane said, adopting a rather contorted position.

"Oh, you want to go, don't you! Well don't do it up here! I've said it before and I'll say it again, them timbers won't stand it. You'll have t'lot down before you know it, and then you'd have a story to tell your grandkids!"

As if to add to Diane's woes, the dark clouds that had been gathering for the past twenty minutes were now beginning to do exactly what dark clouds do. Big, heavy drops of rain were falling onto the roof and, more significantly, onto Diane and Walt. This was not good news for Diane's bladder. It also began to affect her ears rather adversely, as Walt became somewhat more agitated.

"Well I'm sorry, love, but if you think I'm standing up here getting wazzed on, you're wrong. I'm getting down and if you want me to help you, you'd better tell me now. If I get down I'm going inside to dry off. And I'll tell you this, them Dinner Ladies'll have let all them kids in and there'll be wet foot marks everywhere. That means I'll be too busy to come out and see to you."

And Walt began to walk towards the edge of the roof. Diane, realising that she would have to do something, shouted after him.

"Walt, are you sure them ladders are safe?"

"I'll tell you this, I've been up more ladders than you've had hot dinners. Well, perhaps not in your case 'cos you're a cook, but you know what I mean. And I've hardly ever fell off..... I've never fell off one in my life. So, are you coming or what!" Walt asked, conveniently forgetting the lamp post debacle for the purposes of this argument.

Diane paused for a moment and then said, "Alright, I'll let you carry me down."

Walt's face did things it had never done before. It twisted, bulged and displayed emotions that had been lost since his first forays into maintenance. I briefly turned away to laugh and when I looked back, he still had the same startled expression. If the roof had been a few storeys higher, he would probably have leapt to his death.

"Well come on then, before I change my mind!" Diane barked.

Walt picked up the curiously shaped lady and put her over his shoulder in the pose of a Fireman's Lift. The wind and rain now lashed at Diane's nether regions and her overall, caught in a gust, lifted to reveal things that instantly promoted Walt to being the more attractive of the duo. For someone who is afraid of ladders, descending face down over another person's shoulder is hardly a good way to overcome those fears and, of course, once on the ladder, Diane began to scream and squirm.

"Stop wriggling about, you bloody pancake! You'll have us both in hospital." Walt instructed.

"I thought you said these ladders were safe!" Diane yelled.

"Aye, well I don't normally come down 'em in pouring rain with some bugger over my shoulder doing a bloody war dance. Keep still!"

“I’m not enjoying this, Walt.”

“Well if you think I am, I’ll leave it with you!”

Walt’s foot touched the ground and he gave a huge sigh of relief.

“Here, you’re back on terracotta. You can get down.”

“Ooh, you’re an ‘ero, Walt.”

“Aye, and you’re a bloody pancake. I can’t believe it, coming up there when you’re scared of heights! I see where they got that book from now, Wittering Heights. That’ll be a similar tale, I’ll bet.”

Diane smiled once more at her hero and Walt smelled once more at his damsel in an overall. She walked back into the kitchen and was seen to get out a sweeping brush and a huge number of rubbish bags. Walt came across to where I was standing and we both went back inside to the dry.

“So Walt, what’s it feel like to be a hero?”

“It makes your back ache, that’s what it feels like. I’ll tell you this and I’ll tell you now, she’s got some bloody weight on her, that lass has! Mind you, she’s sturdy. It’d take more than a gentle breeze to blow that one over. In fact I’d be surprised if a bloody tornado could do t’job.”

I couldn't decide whether it had been a successful morning or not. In the sense that every disaster had been resolved, it was highly successful. But if it was successful, why did I feel a burning desire to hibernate for a very long time?

Standing outside my office when I arrived there was a man. He was tall, stocky and had the most incredibly greasy black hair it was possible to imagine. And there was lots of it, flowing in every direction, as if trying to escape from his head. His name was Ian, he informed me. When I continued to look blank he explained that he was the Educational Psychologist. That was the point when I remembered that an Educational Psychologist was due to visit, about now, actually. And curiously, his hair turned out to be far less greasy than his personality. He was a smarmy git.

Since the delegation of Local Authority services, schools were allocated a small number of hours of various experts' time. The hours were based on the number of pupils at the school and if any extra time was required it had to be paid for, through the nose. This, I reminded myself was another good reason to include all those wasps on the school roll. It no doubt seemed a sensible way to operate the system if one was sitting in an office at least thirty miles from a school, but in reality it was a major cock-up. The hours were allocated to the school in April but ran from September to September. The actual timetable of visits had to be fixed by June and were then set in concrete. Of course, this was fine until a wild child moved into the area and joined the school after the visits had been arranged, or worse still after they had taken place. Then the school had to pay a fortune for advice, for the pleasure of gaining the child and all its troubles.

Ian had come to see me to discuss children who were having significant difficulty, and also to sneer. With my mind still loitering around visions of a cook on a flat thin roof, I was probably having more of a significant difficulty than ever to focus on any type of discussion. We began with the youngest referrals and worked our way up the school, looking at what needed to be put in place for each child. He spoke in a condescending manner about every child and its family, suggesting that simply by speaking to the child, and perhaps donning a 'Superpsych' cape, he could put them to rights. But it was the last child who caught my attention. Ian was intimating that Lizzie, the autistic girl in her final year was going to have her help reduced as she was maturing and would learn to cope with her condition.

"She'll be at secondary school next year," Ian said, "and it's likely to be a case of sink or swim. She's a bright kid and with a bit of maturity she'll handle it. I don't see there's much more our programmes can do at this age."

"I think she needs help more than ever." I said.

Ian twitched and then stared at me intently.

"How can you justify the cost? I mean, you'll cop the bill and the secondary school gets the benefits!" he said.

"No Ian, Lizzie gets the benefits. Isn't that what's important?"

"Whatever. But you're still spending cash on a kid who's leaving. It's cash you can't spend on the ones who are staying. Why bother?"

"I've seen this girl a few times, Ian. Part of her condition is that she takes everything literally, without question. Last week she walked through the hall whilst a teacher was talking to a class of infants. When she walked between the teacher and her class, the teacher stopped her and said 'Lizzie, walk round me,' meaning go behind. Lizzie, to the infants' delight did just what she thought the teacher wanted. She walked round her. Round and round and round, encircling the teacher until the instruction was changed."

"Priceless!" Ian laughed.

"But she does things like this all the time."

"She'll grow out of it. It's a maturity thing. I don't know why you're worried. Have a laugh about it."

"Well, think about this. She's going to secondary school next year, right?"

"Right."

"And at secondary school she'll meet loads of new kids who haven't grown up with her."

"She'll learn fast, don't worry. She'll have to!"

"Now, go and look at her. She's a nice-looking girl. She's very nice-looking actually. Just think for a minute about some dodgy lad who realises that she'll do as she's told, without question. Do I have to spell it out?"

Ian's condescending grin melted away and was replaced by a look of anxious concern.

"I see what you're getting at. Any suggestions?"

“We have to get her to think for herself, make her own decisions, say no! I never thought I’d say this, but we need to teach her to be a bit rebellious. We have to encourage her to answer back. I don’t know how many teachers are qualified to do that – most spend their time doing the exact opposite – but your department needs to help this kid.”

“We’ll find somebody. We’ll work out a programme. I see your point, honestly I do. I’ll get back to you soon. We’ll have her sorted.” Ian reassured me, scribbling frantically in his note book.

He left, a little less smarmy than when he had arrived and I felt a little more confident that we would get a result.

As I stood at the door and waved him off, I became aware of two things. One, you can occasionally get a result from a bureaucratic pillock and two, there was somebody standing behind me. I turned round to face both Diane and her pimples.

“I’ve got a bloody great bag of dead wasps here. What shall I do with ‘em?”

I had a wonderful suggestion in mind, but the operation to get them removed would be too painful to contemplate. Instead I told her to offer them to Walt as a ‘thank you’ gift. He would dispose of them in the right place. It wouldn't be advisable to interfere with his dustbin organisation. I felt sure that he would have an aversion to just any old rubbish being put in his bins.

Diane requested that I take a look at her kitchen now that it had been cleaned up. It was spotless. It was almost, but not quite, up to the standard of Walt's urinals. Tomorrow, the children would be disappointed to not receive a take-away for lunch but life can be cruel like that. Diane offered me the last remaining unclaimed fast food lunch and I gratefully accepted it, having not eaten since six thirty in the morning. She agreed to warm up the food in the microwave for me. The bag contained a burger, chips, ketchup and a curious toy called Betty Spaghetti. I ate the food but didn't play with my Betty Spaghetti toy.

I would save that until I was at home.

Autumn Term: Week 5

"Well you'd start wriggling if you 'ad an hymn book shoved up yer bum when yer trying to say t'Lord's Prayer."

I was visited at eight-forty by Paul Richards, one of the teachers in the lower junior department. Paul was a very laid-back character. He was about forty and always dressed in a smart but casual way. The children loved him but part of the reason for this was that they could, and possibly did, get away with murder at times. My first view of him had been in the first week of term when I entered his classroom and found him sitting at his desk. Behind him was a display board covered in children's work and entitled 'The Alien'. He appeared to not realise that, when he sat at his desk, the title was directly above his head and looked as if it were referring to Paul himself.

I had not seen him when I visited the school in the previous term as he had been on a teacher exchange and had been working in Australia. In return, my school had been the recipient of an Australian teacher who I met once during my early visits. He was full of praise for the school, describing it as 'bonza', but had already decided that the British education system suffered from too much government interference and too many ‘bloody stupid targets’.

“Why do they think that testing the little buggers every five minutes’ll make ‘em smart?” he had once remarked. “You don’t make a sheep fatter by weighing it all the bloody time!”

His remarks had struck a chord with me and, in true boomerang style, kept coming back into my head when I read documents about the latest set of hoops for us all to jump through.

Paul had seen the sense of the Australian system, he informed me. You could get on with teaching the kids. You could even do things you thought were relevant. And you could surf, though not actually during the process of teaching. All things considered, Paul had decided that he wanted to emigrate and this was the reason for his visit this morning.

“I rang up and spoke to the people about it and they sent me these forms.” He explained. “Basically, you need to sign one of them to verify that I am actually a qualified teacher and all that. They’re very tough on who they let in.”

I signed the appropriate part of the form.

“Are you well on your way with it then, Paul?”

"Pretty much, although I'm not planning to go over until summer. It'll probably take till then to process everything. You wouldn't believe what they ask you! There's all the usual stuff about work and things, to make sure you can fend for yourself when you get there. They want to know if you've got any kind of criminal record."

"Really? I didn't realise it was still compulsory!"

I quite envied Paul. Nothing ever worried him and even this, a major move to the other side of the world, wouldn't be a big deal. The children would miss him, but it meant we'd be able to interview for a new teacher in summer. Then, I'd have one member of staff that I'd actually chosen, rather than inherited.

The rest of our conversation was cut short by the arrival of Ann. Opening my office door, she looked furtively and said, "You've got a visitor."

"Who is it?" I asked.

"It's an entire family!" Ann replied. "A man, a woman and a girl about seven. I think they're looking for a school place."

Paul left and Ann showed the family in.

"Would you be the head?" the woman asked in a very affected tone.

“Not if they asked me again!” I replied. “But yes, I am. What can I do for you?”

“We’ve moved into the area.” She informed me. “At the top of the hill, you understand. Well away from the rented properties of course. We need to choose a school for our daughter and we’ve shortlisted three. We intend to interview the headteachers of each and take a tour of the school before making a final decision. You were recommended to us by our neighbour although I have to trust that her taste in garden furniture is no indicator of her taste in schools.”

“Oh darling!” her husband giggled.

I was not at all convinced that I wanted this family in my school. They had turned up out of the blue, expecting me to drop everything and see them, they were derogatory and condescending and they would probably be much more trouble than they were worth. Nothing would ever be right for their offspring and they would let me know that on a regular basis.

Offering to get them a school brochure, I went to Ann’s room and instructed her to let all the teachers know that I would be bringing this monstrous woman and her family around school. And then I returned brochure in hand, to my office.

“So, what’s your little girl’s name?” I asked.

“Precious.” Replied the mother.

“Precious!” I repeated. I turned to the girl and said, “So, you’re Precious, are you?”

“Yeth.” She lisped.

“OK, so you’ve just moved into the area. Where did you live before? Was it reasonably local?”

“We lived in the Home Counties.” The mother informed me. “We moved because of Simon’s job. He’s something of a high-flyer and it can mean relocating from time to time.”

“Daddy’th a banker!” Precious stated.

“Yes, I had a feeling!” I said, and wished I hadn’t.

“Normally get little Precious fixed up with a private school,” said the Banker, “but quite frankly, not enough of them around this neck of the woods. Nearest one, twelve miles. Long journey for a little girl twice a day.”

“You’re right.” I said. “And she wouldn’t have any school friends to play with in the evenings if it’s such a long way away.”

"Well I suppose. Although we don't encourage other children. Nasty little habits some of them have. Don't really want her mixing that way." The ever-caring mother told me.

I suggested that we might take a look round the school and that this would prompt a discussion about its various aspects. The mother needed no prompting.

"Tell me about the children who come here." She said. "What sort of child will my daughter be mixing with?"

"Oh we have every variety, something to suit everyone. The catchment area covers the district where you live, the new development and the council estate. It's a wide area and we have just about every background you could imagine. It's a good mix, just like the real world."

"So you have children from the council estate?" she confirmed.

"Yes we do."

"What level of segregation do you offer? I wouldn't want my Precious to be in the same class as those children."

"We offer absolutely no segregation. Children are children. They all get an equal chance and they all get equal treatment. If they're good they get equal praise and if they're bad they get equal punishment."

"But aren't they dirty?"

"Some of the brightest and most sensible children in the school live on the council estate. I'm sure when you look round you'll not be able to pick out where specific children live."

She didn't look convinced but she agreed to walk around and see if the school came up to expectations, despite finding a bit if dust on top of a radiator.

Leaving my office the first port of call was the main hall. Here, the morning assembly had just finished and the last class was walking out. The teacher in charge had apprehended two nine-year-olds, a boy and a girl. They had clearly committed some form of badness during the assembly time.

"It wor 'im, Miss!" the girl protested. "He were poking me in mi bum wi 'is hymn book."

"I weren't! She were wriggling about and she sat on mi hymn book. I were just trying to gerrit back." The boy explained eloquently.

"Crap!" the girl suggested. "I wor sitting still. It were only when 'is book went up mi bum that I started wriggling. But you would if you 'ad an hymn book shoved up yer bum when yer trying to say t'Lord's Prayer."

"But there was no need to shout so loudly and there was certainly no need to say what you said, Jade!" the teacher insisted. "It's not good for the infants to hear 'Forgive us our trespassers as we....gerrof mi arse you prat!'. They learn from you older ones and we don't want an infant going away and thinking that's part of the prayer, do we!"

"No Miss." They both replied.

As the two miscreants went back to their classroom, the teacher, seeing me with Precious and her family, came over and said, "Boy, we've got some right ones here!"

The mother laughed a rather pathetic laugh and said "Quite, dear."

Turning to me, the mother snapped, "Do they all use that sort of language?"

Assuming she meant the children rather than the teachers I replied, "We discourage bad language at any time. But the fact is that some children hear so much of it at home that they often don't know that what they're saying *is* wrong. So we deal with it as it crops up."

"Well that's one mark down for you, I'm afraid. I said I don't want my Precious mixing with those children from the estate and I think you'd agree that we've seen a good example of my fears. Now, tell me again that I can't pick out a council house child!"

"I don't know whether you can or not." I replied. "But the girl you just met doesn't live on the council estate. She lives in the huge place right at the top of the hill. That's probably just round the corner from you!"

Fortunately for the mother, Precious demanded her attention at that point. Unfortunately, when she had her mother's attention, Precious asked, "What egthactly ith an arth, mummy?"

Feeling a need to change the subject I started talking again.

"The hall will be empty for a while now. Most classes have their Literacy and Maths lessons in the mornings, while they're all fresh and wide-awake. We try to timetable the hall for late morning and afternoon for PE and Games activities. So we'll have a wander down to the classrooms. What year group is Precious in?"

"Year two." Mother stated. "But that's at a private school. I don't know if these places have the same system."

"Looks about right. Will she be seven during this school year?" I asked.

"Next week. We've got a big bash planned. Marquee in the garden, entertainers, everything."

"Oh, excellent. I'm surprised you know enough children for all that, having only just moved here."
"Oh no, there won't be children. Simon will use the event to impress some of the board of directors and I'll take the opportunity to show the coffee morning group what sort of a spread I can organise."
"Well, if she's seven next week, she's a Year Two. Let's go and see the class she'd be in."
What a poor deprived child! On the surface, she had everything but in reality the kid had nothing. She was a fashion accessory. She probably came with a Gucci label attached to her backside. And her own birthday party was a vehicle for her father to try and become even more of a banker than he was already.
The classroom was at the end of the corridor in the infant department. The teacher, Amanda Chaplin, was only two years into her career but was proving to be quite exceptional. Amanda looked up as we entered the room. She had all the children sitting on the carpet looking at an oversize copy of a book which was attached to an easel.
"Hello." I said. "I'm just showing these people around the school. If this young lady comes to our school, she'll be in this class."

All the children listened to what I said and stared intensely at Precious.

“This is Miss Chaplin.” I explained. “No relation to Charlie, as far as we know!”

“Hello there.” said Amanda. “What’s your name?”

“Prethiouth.” Precious attempted to say.

Amanda looked at me incredulously and I nodded to confirm that this was accurate. Five children laughed.

“Why are there so many children in here?” the banker asked.

“This is a standard size class. There are thirty children. It’s quite normal.” I replied.

“Why is she called Precious?” a boy in the front row asked in a loud voice.

Amanda, sensing that this was likely to degenerate rapidly, calmly explained, “Because her mummy and daddy obviously thought she was very precious when she was born.”

The mother almost smiled and then was stopped by the little boy’s reply.

“We should a’ called my little brother Useless. That’s what mi dad says he is!”

"Well, we don't all call our children something to do with what they're like, but it's something we can do if we want to." Amanda tactfully suggested.

"Our Kylie can't read and she's twelve. She should have been called Thick." A rather unkempt girl commented from near the window.

For the second time this morning, I felt the need to change the subject.

"This is a Literacy lesson, isn't it Miss Chaplin?"

"Yes it is. Do you like reading, Precious?"

"Yeth. I'm a thooper reader. I've got lotth and lotth of bookth. I've got a big thelf in my room and itth full of bookth."

"Well that's excellent." Amanda said, happy that there was no likely disaster following that particular conversation.

I turned to the parents and said, "It's a very attractive classroom. Miss Chaplin's wall displays are always quite something."

"Yes, I'm pleasantly surprised how attractive it is, for a state school. But I still find it hard to see how a teacher can give enough attention to so many children." She turned to Amanda and said, "We've always used private schools in the past. You know what you're getting with a private school. But there are no local preps. We're having to alter our standards by the minute since moving here. Are there any smelly children in the class? If so, I'll expect you to keep my daughter away from them, should we choose this school."

"Are you looking at any others?" said Amanda.

"Ya! We're looking at two more. If we choose you, I shall call in to discuss our requirements more fully with you prior to Precious commencing."

She looked once again round the room, desperate to pick out the council house kids, and I whispered to Amanda, "Don't worry, I'll make sure she hears how good the other two schools are!"

And then the girl sitting at the end of the row nearest to Precious suddenly and unexpectedly threw up. All the children jumped out of the way as the girl's breakfast began to first land on and then soak into the carpet. At that moment the mother noticed that a tiny morsel of vomit had found its way onto her daughter's shoe.

"Aaagh! That child has been sick all over my Precious." She screamed.

"It's only a tiny bit and it's not on your daughter, it's on a shoe." I reassured her.

"She could catch things! Do you know how much those shoes cost? My child is wearing designer label footwear. It is not intended that other children vomit on designer footwear."

She cuddled Precious and spoke baby language to her and simultaneously scowled cruelly at the poor unfortunate puker.

"Damn bad form!" The Banker said. "Chucking up on top quality shoes and all that. Should've tried to avoid them. Hope it doesn't stain."

"It won't stain," I said. "At least not if one of you wipes it off pretty quickly."

A look of horror crossed the faces of both parents.

"Wipe it off?" they said. "One of us?"

"She's your daughter!" I remarked.

This was an alien experience to these people. They did not have a child in order to become involved in the messier aspects of living. Children such as Precious existed to look pretty and to prove to one's boss that one was capable of sustaining a family. Children such as Precious were not permitted to crap or puke. It was simply not the done thing.

An impromptu break time was put into action as the class left the room so that it could be cleaned. A child was sent to find Walt so that he could perform the task of restoring the room to its former glory. He also had the effect of magically cancelling out the pungent odour – with a worse one.

I ushered the family out onto the corridor so that we might continue with our tour.

"Well, that's the class." I said. "They don't normally throw up for visitors. You probably should feel quite honoured."

"Mmm." The mother replied. "I still think there are too many children for just one teacher. At our last school, Precious was in a class of ten."

"That's the difference between private and state schools. You'll be lucky to find classes much smaller than thirty. And ten's really out of the question!"

The banker stuck a finger into the air and I looked at the ceiling to see what he had spotted. Nothing was there. He had simply thought of something to say.

"Thought I saw on the news that you couldn't have more than thirty in a class. If Precious joins that class, she'll be number thirty-one. So you'll get a new teacher. Spread the load and all that."

"I'm afraid not." I replied. "The infant class size limit is a headline grabber. There's always a cop out when the government puts out these great statements. You see, the law says I can't *plan* to have a class bigger than thirty at the beginning of September. If circumstances change during the year, such as a new child joining us that we didn't know about back when we were planning, that's tough. We have to go over the limit."

"So it could go even higher if someone else moves in?"

"It certainly could. And if they move into the catchment area and insist on coming here, I can't turn them away."

"But next year, you'd get another teacher, surely?"

"Not necessarily. There's no *junior* class size limit. I could end up having to move a teacher out of the juniors and into the infants to keep to the rules. But then junior classes would be huge. It all depends if the government is prepared to fund an extra teacher. There's no way I can afford one from the school budget – I'm struggling to afford the ones I've got!"

"But the government promised this!"

"They promised plenty of things! When this promise first came along, the government had found the money to pay for extra teachers. But then a lot of schools asked where these teachers were going to work as they didn't have any spare rooms. The government hadn't thought of that. So they had to spend a fortune on an unexpected building programme. That's probably why the promise isn't holding out so well."

"Damn bad show, my opinion." Said the banker.

The appearance of Walt halted further discussion. He marched down the corridor to where I was standing.

"Some bloody pancake's blocked my egress!" he announced. "I've got to go and stock up on that there puke cleaner seeing how I've just finished my last bottle on that carpet in your infants. I've gone outside to my car and some bloody pancake's parked a sodding Mercedes in front of me. I can't get out."

I explained to Walt that the gentleman standing next to me was the bloody pancake in question and it was agreed that the car would be moved. Walt hung back and when it was clear, said to me, "How does he manage to run a motor like that?"

"He's a banker, Walt." I replied.

"He bloody is, parking it there!"

The mother, standing a short distance away, was gazing at Walt in disbelief. She either found him utterly gorgeous or truly repulsive.

Precious began to sniff and as Walt walked away she said, "I can thmell thomething howible! What ith it?"

"I'm not sure, dear." I tactfully replied.

The mother, with just as much tact said, "It's probably the smell of some dirty children. This will be one of the problems of attending a state school, darling. But don't worry – we'll try to move on as quickly as possible."

"But I will be able to make thome friendth, won't I?" Precious asked.

"Yes sweetheart. We'll just have to choose the right ones. I'll get to know a few parents and then I'll tell you which children you can make friends with."

This woman, it appeared, was going to interview potential friends for the child. She would expect them to prepare a presentation beforehand and then complete a series of tests. She would probably then go into a second round where only the most successful could return for a further interview before being granted permission to befriend her daughter. How would she choose, I wondered. Clearly smelly kids were out, as were kids from any form of rented accommodation. Presumably, if a child's parents were noticeably less well off than her, they would be eliminated. But I guessed she wouldn't want to get too close to someone who was noticeably richer, either. All in all, it was something of a foregone conclusion – nobody would be good enough and the poor kid would not be allowed to make friends with anyone. God help the first boyfriend in years to come!

We walked quickly through the junior department and I explained that this was where Precious would be working when she moved up to the next class. A group of children were working in the corridor, around a table. A classroom assistant was leading the group in their literacy activity. The group was made up of a number of children who were struggling with their work.

"So let's try to remember what we've learned before we have our break." Said April Walters, the classroom assistant. "What do we call that punctuation mark? A line with a dot under it. It's an……"

"Excitement mark!" said Jason, who was always desperate to impress, but rarely did.

"Not excitement, but it does begin with 'ex'."

"Excrement mark!" said Sheryl.

"Experiment!" said Trafford.

I watched, cringing, as the children eventually arrived at the answer. The family wanted to stay and watch a little longer.

"So, next question. What do we call the writer of a book? What's the proper title?"

"He's called Arthur!" Jason blurted out.

"Author, well done Jason." Said April.

I convinced the family that we must move on. We walked down the corridor, still able to hear one final question.

"Now, what's a glossary?" said April.

"I know, I know!" Jason shouted. "It's shiny!"

I took the family back to my office because they clearly wanted to discuss test results, inspection reports and the private lives of the staff. Ann brought coffee but they didn't drink it because it was the wrong brand. The discussion went well until the subject of out-of-hours care was broached.

“We don’t offer any.” I explained.

After a stunned silence, the Banker explained that this was essential to their entire existence. Precious must be deposited at around eight o’clock in the morning and could not possibly be collected until six-thirty in the evening. Clearly, I thought, she was not so ‘precious’ that she deserved any of her parents’ time.

“We’re bursting at the seams. We don’t have a spare room.” I told him.

“Then use a classroom. They’re empty when the children go home.” He advised me.

“Teachers don’t go home when the kids do. They have work to do. They mark work, write reports, plan lessons and sometimes have discussions with each other or people from outside. They need their classrooms for their jobs. If we had a kids’ club in a classroom, it would mean hiding confidential papers, locking away teaching materials, not being able to set out stuff for the following day, all sorts of problems. Besides that, a kids’ club needs access to toilets, a dedicated phone line, outside play areas. We have nowhere to create a space like that.”

“So what do other parents do?”

"They look after their own children. Or failing that, they organise a childminder."

"And do you have a list of childminders?" he asked.

"No. But I know of a lady that many parents recommend. She's registered, highly respected and very organised. There's just one problem I can foresee."

"And that would be?" he asked, rather snootily.

"She lives on the council estate!" I said with a smile.

Eventually they left. I led them to the door to ensure they went out of it and the mother tapped her daughter on the shoulder and said, "Say thank you for showing us round the school, darling."

"Thank you for thowing uth round the thcool." Precious said to me.

"A good attempt." I said. "Goodbye."

They took away our brochure and they left with Precious and some excellent reports about the other schools they were due to visit. I really, really hoped that I would never see them again.

I went directly to Ann's office and instructed her to not let anyone else see me this morning. She was to tell them I was in a meeting, writing a report, drunk, visiting a lap-dancing club or anything else which sprung to mind.

“I’ll get rid of people, from now.” She said, contorting her face as if to suggest she was worried.

“How do mean, from now?” I asked. “Is there something I should know?”

“Well, I’ve got someone waiting for you in the staff room. It’s that man who saw you before, Gary Bailey.”

Gary Baldy! The court hearing must have taken place. Gary and Diane will have sat there and listened to my comments. I tried to think back to my meeting with the welfare officer. I couldn’t remember what I’d said, only that it was not remotely complementary about either of them. I searched the archives of my brain and vaguely remembered saying something about the child having to make unreasonable choices and that she’s be better off being brought up by a pack of wolves. This would have all been said in court and now Gary was back to thank me! He possibly had a few of his ‘business connections’ collecting their weapons together right now. And when that was over, I would have Diane and the angry fishmonger to contend with. Perhaps I would be found, in days to come, haked to death by members of the Boning Society.

I steeled myself, stood up straight and marched to the staff room ready for my confrontation. I swung the door open and there in front of me sat not only Gary, but also Diane. I invited them to my office and we walked silently along the corridor. Inside, the door closed with a clunk, we sat down and looked at each other.

"Nice to see you again." I lied. "How's it going? Have you been to court yet?"

"Yes, we've been to court!" Gary barked. "Sat around waiting for God knows how long until somebody got round to seeing us."

"And how did it go? Was there a decision made?" I asked.

"Oh yes!" Diane answered. "There were plenty of decisions made. I sat there with my parents and I had to listen to them talk about my private life. I don't think I told you before but my dad is big in fish and he's not used to having his daughter talked about in public."

"Everybody had their two-penneth." Gary explained. "My mates and family gave me some good reports and her family and this friend she's got gave her a good report."

"So, was that about equal? Did it help the court decide?" I asked, wondering when they were going to give me hell.

“No it didn’t help at all.” Gary said. “But then we got to your statement. That was a bloody eye-opener and no mistake!”

I shifted uncomfortably in my chair and my chair responded by making a noise like a fart. I did not need a farting chair at this moment. I resolved to remain still for the rest of the discussion.

Gary continued. “We’ve talked to the headmaster, the welfare officer said. Well this is where I thought I’d won. A bit of good write-up from somebody respectable, I thought, and I’m home and dry. Turns out that Diane were thinking that as well, on account of she’d been to see you like I had. So we’re both sitting there thinking we were due for copping a winner.”

Diane picked up the conversation. “So this welfare man says he’s seen you and first off you told him that you didn’t know us very well with you only just starting here and all that. So I thought it’s going to be a let-down is this. He’s not going to have telled ‘em anything. But I were wrong, weren’t I!”

I heard my chair fart once more. I must have squirmed involuntarily. It was going to be difficult to listen to how I’d insulted them and simultaneously keep still.

"Well it turns out," Gary said, "that you might have only known us a short time but you'd made a fair few decisions of your own. So this welfare bloke says we're putting pressure on our Julie and making her have to worry about stuff she shouldn't be worrying about. Then it turns out we're being selfish and not considering her point of view. He says t'poor kid can't get on with learning on account of being too wound up with what's going on between her mum and dad. And then it turns out that she'd be better off being brought up by a bloody goat or a chicken or something."

"We didn't know where to put ourselves!" Diane said. "Court started saying as our parents should be looking after our Julie and we should leave her to be a kid. Everybody in t'room were agreeing and we felt like a pair of selfish gits. Bloke in charge, Judge type fellah, he said arrangements should be made to move our Julie in with my mum and dad and that welfare people would sort out when we visited. Then they said my mum and dad had to see as we didn't put pressure on her again."

Gary leaned forward and I suspected that this may be the start of the attack.

"So, after meeting us for that bit of time, you managed to tell that welfare bloke enough about us to get that court say we weren't adult enough to look after a kid."
"Well I have to look at it from Julie's point of view, Gary." I said, in my defence.
"Aye, you do. And let me tell you this, I have never felt so small in all my life. And I'll tell you why. It's because at that moment I realised that you were standing up for a kid you didn't even know, while me and Diane had given birth to her and we *still* weren't standing up for her. We'd got carried away with these stupid bloody arguments and neither of us had noticed that we'd got this poor kid who loved us both and wanted us all to be a family. She could see we were self-destructing and so could you. And we were too bloody wrapped up in crap to notice."
"So we're getting back together and we're going to get it right this time." Diane proudly informed me. "We're going to get sorted out and then she can be back with us and we'll be a real family." She continued.
I allowed my chair a long awaited fart and breathed a sigh of relief. They needed to hear the truth and yet they spent so long putting

pressure on their friends that all they ever heard were lies. And maybe, just maybe, they might see this as a wakeup call for their relationship. And maybe Julie would get what she really wanted – a couple of adults for parents.

"So we're arranging to go back to court and get it resolved." Gary told me. "Only thing is, we need somebody to give us a good reference in court. Now what you said carried a lot of weight last time. So we thought if you could tell these welfare people how everything's all right and how we're transformed characters and all that, it'd do the trick. There's a drink in it for you!"

"But I don't know if you have changed yet. I mean, it's looking good so far, but is it going to last? Like I said last time, I have to tell the truth."

"Well I'm counting on you, and so is Diane. And all my mates and her dad think you'll crack it. You can't let us down. I'll see if I can get that welfare bloke to give you a bell soon."

And Gary and Diane left, hand in hand. The picture of the perfect loving couple disappeared down the driveway. And I had to admit to being surprised at still having all my limbs intact.

But why did I get the feeling that the hole, like Gary's bald patch, was just going to keep getting bigger?

Autumn Term: Week 6

Walt, whilst not quite having a spring in his step, had a spring in his pocket because he was on his way to mend a faulty thermostat.

Since the end of July, the school had been operating with a reduction in cleaning staff. One of the cleaners had unexpectedly resigned and left immediately. This had, apparently been something of a blessing as, although I had never met her I was informed by Walt, her line manager, that not only was she a member of the higher order of pancakes, but she also had quite an irritating body odour problem. On my arrival at the school in September I advertised the job and today was the day of the interviews. Three candidates had been chosen and an interview panel had been decided upon at the governors' meeting. The panel consisted of Walt, as the cleaners' manager, Izzy Thomas, as a governor with a great interest in health and safety, and me, because I had to.

A large notice had been placed on the door of my office, at the height of a child's eyes, stating in large letters DO NOT DISTURB – INTERVIEW IN PROGRESS and a picture version was badly drawn next to it, for the benefit of passing infants. My office had been equipped with jugs of water and each member of the panel had a clipboard containing three identical copies of the questions, one for each candidate. The panel would write their notes on the question sheets, ready for the final decision making process. Everything was above board and oozing equal opportunities from every pore. In final preparation, before the candidates arrived, I opened a window. After all, Walt would be in the room for the whole time.

Two of the candidates had arrived already and were sitting on the comfy chairs in the entrance. As they chatted, the door opened and to my horror, in walked the mother of Precious. She could not see me from where she was standing and I liked it that way. She was not going to interrupt the interviews at any cost. I stood in the corner of the office and beckoned to Ann to get rid of her. Before Ann had left the office, one of the candidates began chatting to the lady.

"Hello, duck. What are you here for?"

"I'm here to see the headmaster." She replied, sensing an opportunity to pour out a gallon of snootiness.

"So are we, duck. Is it for t'cleaning job?"

"I beg your pardon?"

"Are you being interviewed for t'cleaning job? We are, and he said there were three of us. I hate interviews. I've only ever had one and that were to clean in t'club. It were easy, like. He gave me a drink, boss man did, and then he asked me if I wanted t'job. I said I did and that were it. I'm hoping this interview will be like that."

"Madam, I am not here to be interviewed as a cleaner. I am here to see the headmaster regarding my child."

"Oh, say no more! Little bugger is he? They're always in trouble and it's horrible when you get called in to see t'head. You feel like it's your fault, don't you! I've got six, two girls and four gorillas. Every one's been in bother. I've had three suspended and one on a final warning. What's yours done? Mind you, it'll be serious whatever it is if you've been sent for. I hope they don't get suspended for you, it means they're in t'bloody way at home."

Mrs Precious was squirming so frantically that she had almost turned her entire body inside out. And to make matters worse, she couldn't get a word in edgeways to stop this woman talking at her. Finally she spoke over the woman's voice.

"I have come to accept a place for my child. She is not in trouble, nor will she be!"

“Oh, moving here, are you? What’s up with the last school. On the verge of getting kicked out, is she?”

“No, we’ve moved house.”

“Oh, it’s that bad, is it? Well you tell t’council you won’t put up with living in some dump just because your kid’s gone off a bit. They need telling or they’ll fob you off. I’ve been moved twice and I know all about it.”

Exasperated and desperate to prove that she was not the kind of person that was being described, she began explaining herself.

“Madam, we are not being moved by the council. My husband is a banker.”

“They all are, duck! You think you’ve found a good ‘un but it never lasts. I’ve had more than I can remember and I’ve yet to be happy with one. He’ll be part of your problem. Kick him out and replace him with a dog. Then you can get a little place of your own and start again. Your kid will thank you for it. They like dogs, kids do.”

We had laughed long enough. Ann went to speak to the lady and told her that I could not see her as I was interviewing candidates for a job. She gave her the forms to fill in and suggested a starting date for the child. The mother was indignant that she could not inform me of her list of requirements for her daughter's treatment at the school but eventually accepted the situation. She left rapidly before the lady-in-waiting in the entrance started talking again.

Izzy arrived and greeted me. We spent a moment or two looking at the questions that I had prepared and then Walt, fresh, so to speak, from his urinals, came to join us.

"Bloody hell it's parky in here!" he announced. "Some bloody pancake's had this window open. We'll freeze to death." And he promptly closed it.

After deciding who would ask which questions, I set off to bring in the first candidate. It happened to be the lady who had so eloquently engaged Mrs Precious in conversation. I wondered whether she would be prepared for an official interview. She seemed to expect the only question would be 'do you want the job?'

She walked in the room and turned to jelly. Her fears of a proper interview were realised. I explained that she had nothing to worry about and this boosted her confidence not one bit. She poured herself a drink from the jug and then discovered that her hand was still shaking and consequently, most of the water had missed the glass. I pretended to not notice and began introducing the panel.

“This is our caretaker, Walt. He’s directly in charge of the cleaners. And this is one of our governors, Izzy.” I said.

“Is he what?” she replied.

“Izzy Thomas.”

“Well how should I know? I’ve never seen him before.”

Once the interview began, the lady, who was called Joan incidentally, managed to find a way to steady her nerves. She did this by belching at regular intervals as she spoke. Whilst it may have worked for her, it made it a very difficult interview for the rest of us. By question three, it was Walt’s turn to speak. He read the question to himself and put his own slant on it as the words came out.

“Nah then, duck. Let’s say you’ve had to mop summat up from t’floor. You know, like one of t’little buggers has pissed ‘imself. Nah, what would you do to let folks know there were a wet patch on t’floor so as nobody slipped and did ‘emselves a mischief?”

“I’d put one of them (Burp) them there yellow signs up. (Burp) Them signs as what says Wet Floor, I’d put one of them up, I would (Loud Burp). It’s so as nobody goes and slips on it. You need one of them signs up, that’s what you need (Burp).

"Good lass." Walt said encouragingly. "Nah, I've got another question. Mop heads! When you've done your moppin', how do you stand your mops? It's important, is this."

"I've learnt this. You have 'em (Belch to rock the entire local area) with their heads up. It's so as they don't go mouldy (Burp, Burp, Burp) when they're in t'bucket, duck. Aye, that's it. You stick their heads up (Massive Belch)."

The interview went reasonably well. She answered the questions correctly and burped in all the right places. I could see potential here and Walt was clearly attracted to her knowledge of mops and dusters. The fact that she had constant wind possibly might swing it for her in Walt's view. And in years to come we could perhaps harness the power and become the world's first radish-powered school.

The second candidate was male and was called Baz. He had been sent by the employment office and I was not at all convinced that he really wanted to be here. I introduced the panel and began my first question, exactly as I had done with Joan.

"Right, Baz. Can you tell me why it's important to have certain equipment for certain jobs? In other words, why would it not be right to clean a kitchen worktop with the same thing that you'd used in the toilets?"

"What d'you mean? That's a bloody daft question! How am I supposed to know – I don't work here?"

"Well, thinking generally. If you'd cleaned the toilet and then went to clean in the kitchen, why would you not use the same thing to clean with? It's to do with hygiene."

"I don't bloody know. But you're not going to clean a kitchen worktop with a bog brush, are you! I mean, it's all wrong. Wrong shape and everything!"

"Can you think of another reason?"

"No."

"OK."

I asked him a second question.

"If you came across a piece of equipment, like a vacuum cleaner, and found that it was broken, what action would you take?"

"What do mean, if I found summat broken what action would I take? I suppose I'd bin the bugger if it were knackered. Or I might have a go at fixing it – bodge it together a bit."

"But bearing in mind that someone else might try to use it later, is there anything else you should do?"

"I'm buggered if I know! You ask some bloody daft questions, you lot!"

We moved on and he messed up every question. He was either doing it on purpose, or he was extremely stupid. At the end of the interview, Izzy wanted to ask an additional question on a matter that was still, sadly, close to his heart.

"Would you be prepared to take a stand on dog mess?"

"Would I what? I usually walk round it, pal!"

"No this is important. I think a great deal about dog mess."

"Well I think a great deal about Man United and I bet I have a better time than you do!"

"Sir, I am asking you if you take dog mess seriously! Please answer the question!"

"Seriously? Do I take it seriously? I don't know, pal. I've never burst out laughing at a dog turd so I suppose I must be serious about it!"

"Would you take it upon yourself to clear it away?"

"Not if mi gaffer hadn't told me to. Anyway, who is mi gaffer if I get this job?"

Walt sat up proudly as I announced that he was the man in charge of all things sanitary. Baz looked a little disgruntled.

“And what does he know that I don’t?” he grunted.

Walt did not feel happy with this comment and rose to the occasion.

“I’ll tell you this and I’ll tell you now and I’ll tell you reight and straight and when it’s said it’s said and I’ll say no more. I’ve been doing this job nigh on nine years and I know my work inside out. I defy anybody to find fault with what I do. I’ll tell you this, I’d be happy to let royalty inspect my urinals. And I’ll not have some bloody pancake like you coming in here and making out that he’s better than me. Nah then!”

“Bollocks! I could do your job wi’ my eyes shut!” Baz retorted.

“I’ll shut the buggers for you in a minute, pal. With my fist. You wouldn’t last five minutes here! I’ll tell you this, I’ve got a knowledge of boiler systems and lavatory cleaners that people would kill for.”

Izzy and I steered Baz out of the room and calmed Walt down. As I stood up I spotted my excuse to open a window and mused that, whilst travel expenses regularly appeared on interview claims, I had never noticed hospitalisation costs on those same forms.

As I guided Baz to the door, he turned and said, “So when will you let me know?”

“I think you already do.” I replied.

Back in my office Walt was fired up.

“I hope you’re not thinking of having him! I couldn’t work with somebody like that. He’d spend his bloody life moaning about one thing or another. I can’t stand people who moan and complain.”

“Absolutely Walt. Don’t worry, he’s out of the running. I think when an interview nearly ends in a punch up it’s a bad sign for working relations.”

“Aye, I could never work with any of my relations either.”

The third, and last, interview was with a lady called Margaret. She was pitifully quiet seemed to not be in a talkative mood at all today.

“Have you ever heard of a risk assessment?” Izzy asked.

“Yes.” She replied.

“Could you tell me what one is?”

“Yes.”

“So, what is one?”

“It’s assessing risks.”

“OK, and do you know why we do them?”

"Yes."

"And could you tell me?"

"I could."

The lady answered in instalments. She was clearly a temptress, keeping us all hanging on until she finally revealed her answer. The problem was that there was a real chance we may all be dead by the time that happy event came along. At the end of her interview she had told us nothing and yet getting there had taken twenty-five minutes. I led her out of the room and came back to look at our options.

We didn't have any options. Joan and her wind were the only choices. Margaret may well have been a good cleaner but she had given us no clues as to whether this might or might not be the case. Baz, on the other hand, had given us plenty of help in making our decision about him. He was now on Walt's list of all time top pancakes and was destined to stay there for some time. Joan had given us the right answers and in so doing, had 'breezed' past the other candidates, so to speak.

She had chosen to wait in the staff room until a decision had been made. I went along and told her the news that she was our chosen one. On hearing this, she leapt from her chair and flung her arms around me, telling me that this was a wonderful day for her. For me, it was now not wonderful. I was squeezed like a breakfast time orange and was on the point of losing the feeling in my legs when the excitement overcame her and she belched in my face. This had its up side, as she jumped back in embarrassment, thus permitting blood to once again flow freely through my veins. I suggested that she might like to come back to my office and meet Walt, being vaguely aware that her wonderful day would also evaporate rapidly after this moment.

Izzy left, satisfied that he had taken part in a fair round of interviews. He returned a few moments later to inform me that he had found some dog mess on the edge of the driveway. I told him that if nobody claimed it within three months it was his and he pointedly did not laugh.

Walt and Joan to my surprise were hitting it off spectacularly. I came across him giving her a guided tour of the urinals and other less significant parts of the school, such as the classrooms.

“If you’ve got time I’d like to show you my equipment.” Walt said, with an excited look in his eyes. “I’ve got a couple of scrubbers that I keep in this room, come and have a look.”

She was impressed by his scrubbers, which turned out to be machines that did things to wooden floors, as opposed to what I was originally thinking.

“And these are my buffers.” He announced.

“Eee! I’ve never seen buffers as big as that before. Are they hard to handle?”

“Well you need to know what you’re doing. But once you’ve got a bit of experience you’ll handle ‘em like a trooper. Come and look at my nuts.”

Walt had a clever system of categorising nuts, bolts and screws. His storage facilities for such items led Joan to be very impressed and in a very short time Walt had achieved his goal. He had gained the admiration of his new colleague such that she would never doubt his knowledge or integrity regarding all things premises-related.

“I’ve never met anyone with such knowledge when it comes to rawlplugs!” said Joan. “I’m going to love working here.” And she sighed a comfortable sigh, smiled at Walt and belched contentedly.

"Will I have my own vacuum?" she asked her hero.

"Aye, and your own cloths. You'll get a bucket and your own 'wet floor' sign to take round with you."

Overcome with emotion, she put a hand to her chest as if to gasp. Instead she belched, but in an emotional sort of way.

She left, a happy woman with a new job and a potential new flame. With a rekindled fire in her heart and regular gusts of wind from her stomach I was pleased to consider that she was now equal to two thirds of a seventies pop group. Walt, whilst not quite having a spring in his step, had a spring in his pocket because he was on his way to mend a faulty thermostat. He might, I wondered, even take the unprecedented step of using a deodorant, providing this would not make his wife suspicious.

As she walked down the driveway Joan passed a man. She stopped to tell him that she had just been appointed to the post of cleaner and that this was indeed a happy moment. The man wore a dog collar and it was with some relief that I noted Izzy was well off the premises. The man approached the main entrance of the school and on entering introduced himself as Reverend Bob, the new vicar from the local church.

Reverend Bob was not young enough to be trendy, but he was not old enough to be traditional. I decided he must therefore be transitional. He was a cheerful character and made it known to me that he wished to become as involved as possible in the life of the school. He volunteered to take school assemblies and to work with children in their Religious Education lessons. Believing that his enthusiasm was genuine, I informed him that next week held the school's annual Harvest Festival celebration.

"Ah!" he mused. "Would I be right in thinking that you'd like me to take part?"

"Take part, attend it, run it! I'm quite happy to use it as a way for the children and their parents to get to know you." I replied.

"I need to look in my diary. Got a couple of funerals next week and I don't want to clash."

"Of course not. I wouldn't expect you to let anyone down." I told him.

"Oh, it's not that. There's other vicars who could do the funerals. It's just that they're good little earners. Better than weddings and a lot less preparation. I remember an experienced clergyman telling me when I first started. ‘Get a few funerals a week and you’re laughing,’ he said. “And he was right.”

“Mmm. I never thought of it in that way before.” I pondered.

“Oh yes. You see weddings have gone to pot a bit. All these people nipping off to Las Vegas and Hawaii is damaging for business. But funerals, they’re different. Nobody’s going to book a themed funeral in Palm Springs, are they! It’s never going to happen. You can get four or five some weeks and it boosts your earnings no end. A good week of funerals makes life worth living, I always say.”

He consulted his diary and discovered that the date and time of the Harvest Festival were convenient to him. He reacted with some dismay as he realised that he would now have to hold true to his word and become involved with the school.

“So, what have you got planned for this Harvest Festival?” he asked me.

“Well, all the kids are going to bring something in, tins of beans, fruit, that kind of thing. Their parents are invited to stay and watch and each year group has prepared a short item to perform. Now I was going to do a meaningful story about life in countries where tins of beans don’t grow readily in the fields and get the kids to think about the issues surrounding all that. But of course, it would probably sound better coming from you. They see me every day in their assembly. It'd make a nice change to hear a different voice."

"Well, I suppose I could. I could put a story together. Unless I could borrow yours?"

"Not planned it yet. Too many things will happen before next Tuesday. It would probably get planned three minutes before the thing started!"

"Ah. Well, I'm sure I could sort something out." He replied hesitantly.

"You sound a bit concerned." I said.

"I've never done children before. And I've heard so many horror stories. I suppose I'm a bit nervous, but I'll have to do it one day, so I might as well have a go."

He began asking for advice so that he might have a successful session. I explained that it was easy as long as he didn't pitch the story too high, otherwise the kids would be confused and start messing about. Of course, he should also not pitch it too low, otherwise the kids would be bored and start messing about. Bearing in mind that his audience would range from four to eleven years, he should give some serious thought about the level he should pitch the story. He shouldn't ask too many questions because each one required an answer. Three hundred children would put up their hands and some would answer inaudibly, some would get the answer as wrong as it's possible to be and others would tell you they had a dog called Rover. He shouldn't throw anything into the audience, such as sweets. Children will happily throw themselves to their death for a chewy sweet and the resultant scrum on the hall floor will always lead to a lawsuit. He should not bring in any props unless he could guarantee that they would work perfectly, first time. Children make very cruel audiences and any opportunity to laugh at a dodgy prop will be seized upon with gusto. He should not sound too serious because the kids would lose interest and fool around. He should not sound too jovial because the kids would think they were *supposed* to fool around. If he spoke too fast his words would be lost in the acoustics of the hall and he would also lose the interest of the younger children. If he spoke too slowly the older children would start to think he was aiming the story just at the little ones and would consequently stop listening.

"Apart from that, it's simple. Just be yourself and relax!" I said.

Reverend Bob clearly wished he could start all over again. He wished he could visit for the first time and say something along the lines of; "I'm the new vicar but don't expect me to come anywhere near the school when there are children in it. But if you know anyone who wants a really classy funeral, here's my card."

So in the space of one day, Joan the new cleaner had been appointed and Bob the new vicar had been dis-appointed. I ensured that he had the correct date and time in his diary so there was no excuse for not turning up and then he left. I never did get the chance to mention the possibility of a weekly assembly slot for him.

Autumn Term: Week 7

I was going to have to find somewhere for that food to go. I really needed a good old Victorian workhouse or orphanage, but they're just so hard to find. Progress, they call it!

The morning of the Harvest Festival was upon us. As the children arrived at school they were laden with bags of offerings. When I stepped onto the yard in the morning, many rushed to show me what they had brought.

"I've brought this tin of rice pudding because it's out of date and we'll never eat it." said one.

"This can of soup got dented so my mum said I could bring it." said another.

"Dad said I could bring this fruit cos it's going bad." Said a third.

And so it went on. Some children had brought more than one item. Some had even brought items that were edible.

Back inside the building there was a buzz of activity. Gillian, the Deputy Head, was busy organising staff with duties to perform at various points in the celebration. As was often the case, I had no idea what she was up to.

"It's my raffle!" she announced.

"Your raffle? I didn't know you were doing a raffle."

"Yes. I always do a raffle at events like this. Harvest Festival, Christmas, Easter. They're good money raisers."

"Yes, I'm sure. I just didn't realise. I mean, where did you get the prizes from?"

"Oh they're from all sorts of places. There's some things that weren't sold at the Summer Fayre, there's a couple of presents I got from last year's class and I've got a friend who can organise free concert tickets."

"Right. So we'd better tell everyone what the money will be used for. What will it be used for?"

"It goes into my slush fund! It bails us out when we need it."

"But you can't do that Gillian! It's public money. We have to be accountable for it. How do we account for slush funds when the auditors come? You know what it's like, they inspect us down to the last postage stamp and they'll want to know how we get the prizes, what the spending plans are, where the records for funds already spent are, and on and on."

“Oh, it’s alright, we don’t tell them. I take the money home and keep it there, cash. I can’t be bothered with all these financial regulations and things.”

“You take it home? But you could be accused of misusing funds. You’re putting yourself in an awful position!” I whined, by now becoming seriously apoplectic.

Gillian didn’t worry about such things. She was a very confident person, too confident in many ways, and she really believed that she could simply talk her way out of any problems that arose. I, on the other hand, did worry about such things. And now I was worrying about all the other possible things that might be going on without my knowledge. I knew that when the next inspection team landed, they would root out these scams and start asking questions that I could not answer.

It was too late to do anything about today’s raffle now. The audience was arriving and the raffle was clearly advertised. Two classroom assistants had taken up posts at the entrance to collect money with menaces from everyone who entered the building, shaking their raffle tins provocatively in their faces.

“A pound a strip!” Audrey, a rather ebullient classroom assistant said to a tattooed father.

“Here’s a quid then. Get your kit off!” he laughed.

“I’m talking about raffle tickets!” she barked.

The man looked her up and down and said, “Aye, come to think of it, that’s a better option!”

The hall filled up quickly. The chairs were all taken and so the next group of people began to pull PE equipment from the storage bay and sat on trestles, gym tables and anything else they could find. Later arrivals stood wherever space permitted, and sometimes where it didn’t. I was sure we had too many people and would be closed down by the Fire Officer if he visited. But I had never asked what our maximum capacity was on the grounds that, once I knew, I would have to abide by it.

“Can I have a word!” someone said from behind me.

I turned round and facing me was the Mad Woman. We had indulged in conversations every day or two since the beginning of term. Each time, ‘our Michael’ had been bullied by an infant, told off for doing nothing wrong or been the victim of a cruel murder that had gone unnoticed by all the staff. I wondered what today's problem would be and was rather annoyed that she had chosen this particular time to speak to me.

"It's happened again!" she moaned. "My husband's in a wheelchair and there's no space for him. Look, every seat's taken. You never put a sign up or reserve a space for him at this school."

"I didn't know you wanted a space. If you'd have mentioned it we could have sorted it out, but I didn't know he was coming. I'm sure somebody will understand if we ask them to move."

"There's no point, he's not here!"

"He's not here? So what's the problem?"

"The problem is that if he was here, there'd be no space for him!"

"But if you told me he was coming, there would be a space!"

"But he won't come because he knows there won't be a space!"

"But... Look, at the Christmas concert, we'll reserve him a space."

"Oh yes, that's it! You've always got a clever answer, you people!"

"No, it's a genuine offer."

"Forget it, he won't be coming and I don't care how much you beg me!" And with that she marched off and stood at the back. I noted that as she walked, the other parents parted so that she didn't speak

to them. She walked in her own fluid space that travelled with her wherever she went.
In the middle of all this, I was becoming very aware that Reverend Bob had not yet arrived. Assuming that he would be here, I had not prepared or even thought about a story or speech for the end part of the celebration. Consequently, in the midst of welcoming parents, grandparents and confused people who had wandered in off the street, I was desperately attempting to make up a coherent story. I was informed on more than one occasion that the school had always put on delightful Harvest Festivals in the past and this added spectacularly to the pressure.
And then the children began to enter the hall. The plan was that each class would walk into the hall with their offerings and take them to the display tables at the front of the hall where a member of staff would help to arrange them neatly. The children would then sit down to make way for the next class. It all sounded so simple. The older children came in first and the system worked well. It was smooth and organised and I proudly watched the display build into a sizeable montage of fruit and tins, along with the odd giant marrow from some cocky little sod who wanted to be different.

But then the infants arrived.

The uninitiated should know at this point that the relationship between parents and older children is very different to that between parents and younger children. The older kids pointedly do not acknowledge the fact that they have parents. Parents, to these children, are an embarrassment, an encumbrance. They do not like to be seen walking with, or talking with parents. Indeed, if at all possible, they prefer to convince the casual onlooker that they have never been inflicted with the disgrace of having a parent. The little ones, on the other hand, worship their mums and dads. They will happily kiss them goodbye at the school gate and they will run to them at the end of the school day. And therein lies a huge organisational problem.

Whilst the older children walk into the hall with no intention of catching the eye of the mum or dad they begged not to come, the little ones actively search them out from an audience of hundreds. And the parents of little ones call out to their child and wave frantically.

This is not problematic under most circumstances. However, when the small children are standing in a line, carrying fruit and tins the potential for disaster increases. When the front of the line is positioned precariously close to a finely balanced display of all things edible then a state of high alert must be adopted. And it clearly wasn't on this occasion.

Charlie Bates' mum burst forth with a shout of 'Charlie duck' and this prompted Charlie Duck to turn his head. The mother's wave was a signal that Charlie Duck should reciprocate and so he did. So engrossed did Charlie become in seeing his mother only twenty minutes after leaving her on the school yard that he failed to notice the line had come to a halt. He continued walking and bumped forcefully into the girl in front of him, thus becoming embedded in this unfortunate child. The domino effect was promptly put into action. Each child lurched forward one after the other, until the child at the front became part of the fray. This child fell headlong into an impressive aubergine display which added momentum to the fall. Within seconds of Charlie turning to wave at his long lost matriarch, the tins, bottles, fruits and even the giant marrow were in a wrecked heap on the floor.

Each child blamed the one behind for the accident. The more physical infants began to lash out with fists and feet. And then somebody noticed that a large grapefruit made an excellent weapon. This sparked off a fruit offensive, as cucumbers, pears and kiwis became artillery. I feared that in years to come one of these children would be showing their grandchildren scars and gashes, saying 'This is an old Harvest Festival injury.'

That was the point when the decorating table under the display of cans gave up the fight and collapsed, unable to cope with both the weight of its load and the constant pounding by young children who were staggering back and forth in their quest for supremacy of the harvest. A hundred tins crashed to the floor and rolled in every direction and in so doing, brought many children to grief as they stepped on a rolling tin. Terrified that a child would begin throwing tinned peas at an opponent, I yelled over the chaos and eventually the children stopped and stood still.

After frantic efforts from all staff, the order was once again restored and the display was rebuilt, although it appeared less attractive than previously. I began the proceedings by welcoming everyone to the school and quickly moved to the first item, a poem by the oldest children about the life of a seed. I was a little puzzled when, two minutes into the poem the entire school was captivated. The poem, in my opinion was uninteresting and yet every child was transfixed. And then the reason became clear. Above the readers was a row of high level windows. These were now in the process of being cleaned and window cleaner's sponge and squeegee had captured the imagination of every child in the hall. Their heads moved in unison as the sponge worked back and forth across the window. They nodded together as the squeegee moved up and down and then the whole process was repeated a few degrees to the right when the next window was cleaned.

By the time the window cleaner had completed his entertainment, the youngest children in the school were at the front, telling a story they had learned. This was the very first time these children had stood in front of an audience and they were clearly nervous. Some burst into tears and were ushered away but the remaining twenty stood proudly in position. Within a moment of beginning their story, there was a howl of laughter from the adults and older children. Their amusement centred on the now notorious 'Charlie Duck'. In an effort to overcome his nerves he had pulled down the top of his elasticated trousers and was playing somewhat vigorously with himself. He was oblivious to the fact that the entire audience could see his actions and did not even realise they were laughing at him. The situation was compounded when Charlie's line, 'I've grown a big cucumber' was enunciated loud and proud whilst still indulging in his personal pleasures. I knew from that this moment forward, young Charlie Bates would always be referred to as Master Bates. There was no escape for him.

This was the point when Reverend Bob arrived. He was breathless, having cycled to the school following the breakdown of his usual form of transport, a Harley Davidson motorbike.

"Sorry I'm late." He whispered.

"Don't worry." I replied.

"Have I got time for a drink?"

"No, you're on. I was just about to make something up."

"Well, at least you'll have had time this morning whilst you were sitting and watching this."

"You don't know the half!" I grunted.

I introduced Reverend Bob and he stood up to speak. Clearly he had listened to all my advice, and then he had ignored it. Amidst the cacophony of crying babies and warbling telephones he looked at the children and began to speak, quietly.

"I've got something small and furry in my pocket, children." He said.

This, after Charlie's recent exhibition was just too much for anyone aged nine or over, including the entire staff. Oblivious to their raucous laughter he continued.

"Would you like me to get it out?"

To screams of laughter and undeterred by the tears rolling down the faces of staff and parents alike he pulled out a fluffy puppet.

"It's Sam the Squirrel." He announced. "Who thought I was going to pull out a squirrel?"

No-one responded.

"Who thought I wouldn't pull out a squirrel?"

All the children put their hands up and Bob pointed to a cropped-haired boy aged about seven and said, "What did you think I was going to pull out?"

"I thought you were going to get your dick out like Charlie did!" the boy announced.

"No, it's Sam." Bob said, seemingly unaware of the vernacular.

Everyone tried hard to compose themselves. There was a collective deep breath and a tangible concentration of minds.

To the new found silence, Bob announced, "Sam's worried about his nuts." An explosion of laughter issued forth from almost everyone in the hall. The younger children who didn't understand joined in the laughter anyway because they didn't want to be left out.

"He knows that his nuts could be in danger from Sidney Squirrel because Sidney hasn't got any nuts. Who can guess why Sidney hasn't got any nuts?"

He pointed to a ten-year-old boy whose eyes were red from tears of laughter. "Because Sidney's a girl!" the boy called out.

Still oblivious to the laughter, Bob said, "No. Someone else have a go, how about you."

He pointed this time to a five-year-old girl who told him, "My dad lost his tie this morning and I'm going to a party after school. It's at my friend's house and you can come if you want to."

Bob laughed nervously and explained that Sidney Squirrel hadn't collected any nuts before hibernating and consequently wouldn't have enough food to last the winter. In some contrived way he likened this to a farmer working all year in the field so that he had a good crop in autumn. Just as I began to relax in the knowledge that Bob might have stopped asking unanswerable questions, he began talking about sowing seeds. He reached into a bag and pulled out a handful of small sweets. He explained that he was now a farmer and that the children were to take on the role of birds. With that, he threw out the sweets, showering the children with sugar-based precipitation.

There was a riot. The sweets had become bullion and every child wanted a share at any cost. They leapt up to intercept passing candy, they snatched, scratched, spat and bit. The religious festival had become an unholy war. Small children, parted from a newly captured sweet, sat crying. Older children tried to see how many they could stuff in their mouths at one time and Charlie took his trousers down once more and amused himself.

The celebration finished with a prayer asking for peace in troubled parts of the world and I wondered if the school qualified for inclusion. The prayer asked for those without food to be helped by those with plenty. Considering the recent scrum, the lead for such an act was hardly likely to start here, I considered. And then it was time for the children to return to their classes and for Charlie to return his trousers to their rightful position.

Tea and coffee were being served by a group of helpful parents whom Gillian had organised a week ago. Parents were invited to stay and to ensure they did so, Gillian would only call the raffle when plenty of drinks had been sold. Bob agreed to stay and informed me that he thought his story had gone down well and this had given him confidence to become more involved in the future. Curiously, all of this was precisely the opposite of what I was hoping he might say.

The raffle was drawn and it was a matter of great consternation that Mrs. Phelpington's strip of tickets attracted not one, but two prizes. The crowd looked jealously on as she walked away with both a bottle of apple juice and a box of embroidered handkerchiefs. There were comments that the draw had been fixed from certain contingents but such comments were balanced out by a scar-faced father's interjection of 'What does it bloody matter – all t'prizes are crap anyway'. Nods of approval followed this assertion and all claims of raffle rigging were promptly dropped.

Apart from one! The Mad Woman appeared from behind the large water boiler and demanded my attention.

"It's the same every time. I've never won a raffle at this place. I think my tickets get chucked out before the draw. I've lost count of how many raffle tickets I've bought. Probably thirty or forty over the years. I've kept this school open. And how many times have I won? I'll tell you, I've never won. It's a closed shop, jobs for the boys."

"Well, it's just a matter of luck. I never win raffles, I'm hopeless. But my daughter wins every time she enters. Some people are just lucky like that." I replied.

"I really fancied that apple juice." She said.

"Never mind. You didn't buy too many tickets, did you?"

"I didn't buy any! What's the point when you know it's fixed? I'm never going to win so I'll be damned if I'm wasting my money on tickets."

"But why are you complaining? You didn't buy a ticket so there's no surprise that you didn't win."

"Ah, you can't get me with that one. Trying to make me feel guilty so that I'll spend a fortune next time. Well, it won't work. I know what this place is like, you can't fool me!"

My mouth opened but no words came out.

There was no answer.

There would never be an answer.

Mrs. Phelpington left with her quarry of prizes and tried to ignore the whispers surrounding her obvious good fortune. In time a new scandal would break out and the Phelpington Files would be consigned to history but until then, she faced the sneering hatred of those who coveted the apple juice and hankies. I would do my best to protect her children from untoward attention whilst in school during these difficult times.

Reverend Bob also left but returned almost instantly. His earlier transportation problems were not yet over. The bicycle on which he had arrived had been chained to a drainpipe and secured with a padlock. In his frenzied generosity, he had – he assumed – thrown out not only handfuls of sweets, but also his keys to the padlock. As no child had complained of a broken tooth we guessed that the keys had either been dropped on the floor or alternatively, swallowed whole. The floor had been swept by a willing volunteer and all rubbish had been deposited in a bin bag. Bob and I searched through the bag but found no evidence of his keys.

As he was needed at lunchtime for a newly booked funeral, he decided to remove the wheel from his bicycle. And so with the offending wheel firmly chained to the drainpipe, Bob carried the remainder of his bike over his shoulder and trudged back to the church. The downpour, as expected, began as soon as he left. His boss was clearly unhappy with Bob's performance this morning.

It had been agreed that the produce collected at the Harvest Festival would be taken to the Riverview Nursing Home. I rang to speak to the manager to arrange delivery as soon as possible.

"Ah!" said the manager. "There's been a bit of a mix up, actually. My assistant had a phone call from another school and agreed to take their stuff and we got that yesterday. We can't manage any more, I'm ever so sorry."

"But I've got hundreds of tins and whole baskets of fruit. Are you sure you can't take some more?"

"We'll struggle to use what we've got. To tell the truth, we end up wasting half the fruit every year."

"Well, do you know of any other places that might be interested?"

"Can't say as I do. I'm sorry."

I put the phone down and sighed. I couldn't tell the children that their food was surplus to requirements. I was going to have to find somewhere for that food to go. But I was going to have to be quick.

Ringing round the list of local nursing homes produced no joy. The hospital would have liked to help but had regulations to abide by. I really needed a good old Victorian workhouse or orphanage, but they're just so hard to find. Progress, they call it!

I was just about to give up when I had a call from a man whom I had rung earlier. He had been thinking about our plight and remembered a group based in a church in a nearby town that accepted donations on condition that the food would be delivered to them. It sounded perfect and they were open for another hour. I commissioned a group of children to help me load everything into the car and then set off to the church. The traffic was moving at a snail's pace and road works abounded round every corner but I had plenty of time and there was no need to panic. The church was where the man said it would be, which is often the case as churches are not easy to move, and I parked outside and walked up to the huge wooden door.

It was locked. I tried round the back and the side and there was no way in. A man was tending the weeds in the church grounds and I went to ask if he knew anything about the food collections. He knew everything about the food collections, including the correct time of closing, which was one hour ago. I walked back to the car to find a traffic warden inspecting it.

“Is this your car, Sir?”

“Yes.” I answered suspiciously, whilst searching for yellow lines.

“I’ve been fancying one of these. Are you happy with it?”

“Yes I am.” I answered, relieved to not be on the verge of receiving a ticket.

“I’m going to have to give you a ticket.” He said. “This is a ‘residents parking only’ road and you haven’t got a resident’s sticker.”

I explained the situation to him and he agreed that the circumstances were indeed unusual. He also agreed that the story was likely to true considering the mass of produce filling my car. He knew of a nearby club that was on the point of having a ‘do’ for local old folks. There was a chance that they might take the food off my hands. I thanked him profusely and set off to find the place. The landlord, an ex-miner who made coal fall from the seam simply by looking at it, was puzzled by my arrival.

“So you’re an headmaster of a school, you say.”

“That’s right.”

"So do you sell food in your spare time then?"

"No, it's been collected by the kids."

"And then you go round trying to flog it? By heck, what has education come to?"

I explained more carefully and he began to see my predicament.

"So I'm not selling it." I said. "I'm giving it away for free. If the old folks are having a party you could use some of it to feed them or have a stall, or anything."

"If it's free, what's up with it? I don't want some old biddy croaking in here. It's bad for business is that."

"There's nothing wrong with it. I just can't get rid of it!"

"Should have thought of that before you bloody collected it."

He agreed to take a proportion of the tins. The rest would have to stay in the car and go back to school because I had no idea where else I could get rid of it. I was unhappy about going back with so much food and knew the children would be disappointed but I really could see no way round it. On my way back to the main road I drove past a school. On its fence was a banner which contained the words 'Harvest Festival Tomorrow'.

“Poor buggers!” I said to myself. “I hope they don’t have all this trouble getting rid of their stuff.”

And then I swung into a side road, turned the car round and drove straight into the school’s driveway.

“I heard you were having a Harvest Festival.” I said. “I’ve got a shop in town and I thought I’d give you a good start to your collection. I’ve got a car full of tins and fruit if you want it.”

My offer was gratefully accepted and a group of children were commissioned to help me unload the food from my car. Once it was safely stored in the school, I turned to the Head and said,

“Have you got somewhere to rid of everything when you’ve collected it?”

“Kind of.” She said. “An old folks home will take a bit. But there’s a club up the road that’s doing a big party for the old ‘uns this weekend. I’m going to ring them this afternoon and see if they want the rest.”

I left.

At the end of this week it would be the half term holiday.

Autumn Term: Week 8

I'm sorry, you seem to have mistaken me for someone who's interested...

The half term holiday was over. Not that it had been a holiday, more of a chance to catch up on what couldn't be done during last term because of all those interruptions. But now, after a 'week off', my 'things to do' list was shorter and could probably be completed in less than a hundred and seventy years.

So it was with this sense of achievement that I drove back to the school on Monday morning, ready to begin a new half term. This was the half term that ended with Christmas. It was the one where children would start to get excited about Christmas around the beginning of November. By December they would be so hyper that they would become anxious and agitated. They would fall out first with each other and then with their own reflections in the mirror. And to make matters worse, this was an eight-week half term.

Now that might not sound like a long time, but children tend to follow a particular pattern during the course of a school term. For the first five weeks everything goes smoothly, but then they become tired. Week six usually involves major fall-outs which impinge on their work. Week seven is where they begin to hit each other. Week eight, consequently, is a free-for-all. And when Christmas is part of the equation the outcome can be truly spectacular. I had experienced it many times, hence my rather impressive impersonation of Ebeneezer Scrooge when anyone mentioned Christmas, relaxation and fun in the same sentence.

Forcing myself to keep driving I turned into School Lane. Next to the school drive was a field, possibly owned by the council, and often used by the local children for football games or for attempting to kill each other. But today none of that would be possible. Today the field was occupied by caravans and other vehicles belonging to a group of travellers who had decided to stop travelling and settle there for a while. Some, already up and about, watched with interest as I swung off the road and into the drive.

As I opened the car door the sound of the word 'pancake' reverberated through the air. Walt was marching towards me and clearly my first problem of the day would begin *before* setting foot in the building. It was difficult to determine whether this could be classified as an interruption considering I hadn't started doing anything yet.

"Good morning, Walt. How are you?" I said cheerily.

"Bloody pancakes." Was Walt's unorthodox greeting. "Sodding bloody pancakes. I knew this would happen one day. And it has. Bugger!"

"Walt, I'm confused. Tell me what's happened and how it relates to your ancient prophecies and let's see what needs to be done."

"Well you know me, I'm not one to moan. I rarely complain about anybody. But I'll tell you this and I'll tell you now, them bloody pancakes take the biscuit."

Still feeling no further ahead I asked, "Which bloody pancakes, Walt? Who are you talking about and what have they done with your biscuits?"

"Them bloody travellers in them there caravans. And they've not got no biscuits, it's just a saying. It's one of them adverbs like 'a bird in the hand makes your lights work' or something."

"Too many pancakes bugger up your day! That'd be a good one." I joked. "Anyway, what have they been up to."

“They’ve been up to the pond, that’s what they’ve been up to. That wildlife area round our pond, I’ll tell you this and I’ll tell you now, it’s not seen life as wild as that since Moses were a nipper. They’ve been at it in that long grass. You should see what I’ve picked up!”

“Well perhaps you can introduce me to her later. But first, we’d better find out if there’s any evidence lying around the building. I don’t want the kids to find anything on the yard or the paths.”

“Aye, I’ve had a look and most stuff’s up in that long grass. I don’t reckon there’s any dodgy stuff round this part. I’ll tell you this though, they must have been at it like rabbits, judging by all t’condoms I’ve found.”

“Really? Incredible isn’t it, I never knew rabbits used condoms.”

“No they don’t, I’m just saying that they’ve been a bit wild up there. I reckon they’ve been having one of them there orgies. Well, we’re going to have to stop ‘em. Just imagine if a teacher took a class of kids up to do some work round t’pond and they came across a couple of prize pancakes having it away up there. There’d be some bloody interesting pictures in their sketch pads and make no mistake. And I’m not sure as mi pond liner’s up to it. If they get carried away and start thrashing about in t’water I could end up wi’ an ‘ole in mi’ pond liner. And that's a bugger of a job, replacing one of them. I reckon you'll have to go across and talk to 'em this morning."

"But how do we know it's really them, Walt? I know it's likely because the problem's suddenly started up since they arrived, but we can't prove it. If I accuse them it could be slanderous. I wonder where we stand legally."

"I wouldn't have though it were legal at all, whether you stand or not. But I reckon they were lying down. That's why they chose t'long grass.

"You could be right, Walt. Leave it with me, I'll see what we can do."

I quietly hoped that whoever was using the wildlife area would stop now that the school was open again. That way, the problem might just solve itself. That would make a very welcome change.

But I should have known better. As the children started arriving I was inundated with visits from parents. The first to arrive was Mrs. Precious who had brought her child early so that she could give the teacher a thorough interview before the term started.

"I need a word!" she barked as she flung open my office door.

There was a word in my head that she was very nearly treated to but I bit my tongue and smiled instead.

"When I agreed to allow this establishment to be responsible for my daughter's education, no-one informed me that those 'caravan people' lived here."

"No, because they didn't live here. They're travellers." I replied calmly. "And they've travelled here!"

"I want them removed." She snapped.

"Well it's not as simp…."

"I hope you don't intend telling me there's nothing you can do! I have been subjected to a tirade of abusive comments as I walked down the path and goodness knows what my little Precious thought of the language she heard."

"You didn't shout back at them, did you?" I joked, trying to lighten the situation.

"I think you are purposely misunderstanding me. Those, those, 'caravan people' and their children were shouting and swearing at each other and then to cap it all, they yelled abuse at myself and a number of other parents. Their language was foul and I will not have my little Precious put in a position of listening to such Anglo Saxon comments."

Anglo Saxon comments! That gave me an idea. If ever the law changed and primary schools had to offer foreign languages, that would be the one I'd choose. We could teach all the kids to swear. Our test results would be the best in the country. And half the parents would help their children with their homework without even realising it. This lovely thought had permeated my brain and suddenly I became aware that Mrs. Precious was still ranting and I hadn't listened to a word.

"Well?" she asked.

"Sorry, just go over the last bit again." I said.

"What are you going to do about it? It's a perfectly simple question."

"All I can do is register a complaint with the council. But as a local resident I think you should also contact the council."

"I would assume, my man, that it's your job."

"Not really. You see, however close they are, they're not actually on school property so I have no more jurisdiction over them than Mr. Smith down the road."

"Then get him to do it!"

“No, he’s fictitious, I’m speaking hypothetically. What I mean is that it’s a community thing. I can give the school’s point of view but to really swing it the council need to be bombarded with calls. That’s why I think you should get in touch as well.”

“Well I’m sorry but I have no desire to speak to ‘council people’. They tend to think everyone is claiming a benefit of some description. Someone else will have to do it. I expect to find them gone when I collect Precious this evening.”

“Then I think you’ll be disappointed.”

“How dare you speak to me like that! My previous headmasters have never spoken to me like that and I shall not accept glib comments from you!”

“Madam, your previous heads ran fee-paying schools and needed your business. I can take it or leave it! Now the rules are simple; if you make reasonable requests we do everything to accommodate you, if you make unreasonable demands it’s a different story. Now I do have other people waiting to see me and I have a very busy day ahead. I will do what I can about the problem but I can’t make any promises about the outcome.”

I watched that woman alter her demeanour at the point. She had clearly never been spoken to like that before, despite the fact that she *always* spoke to others in that way. I had a vague hope that it had done some good. Time would tell.

Next in line was the Mad Woman. She needed to tell me about the travellers also. Her argument was based on the premise that the travellers would quickly discover that 'our Michael' attended the school. Having made this discovery they would personally bully and abuse him to the exclusion of all other children. The school, of course, would turn a blind eye to this and 'our Michael' would end up in trouble for coming to school with his uniform in such a mess and sporting so many black eyes. It was then her concern that 'our Michael' would be seen as a victim by everybody and children from around the globe would come to the school on special day trips in order to punch him senseless. Even at this point, she predicted, the teachers in the school would see no evidence of bullying and would lay the blame firmly at the feet of 'our Michael'. The only way I could disprove her theory, it seemed, would be to march across the field and evict each traveller individually. It appeared that I could do this because I was a headmaster and was thus responsible for, well, everything. I suggested that I might put it on my list immediately after advising the president of the United States on his internal economic affairs. She neither laughed nor understood. She did, however, leave having convinced herself that I would be attending personally to the matter and that the travellers would soon be gone. It must have been the phrase, 'There's very little I can do' that assured her of this.

And so the morning went on. In the space of forty minutes I met nine parents and learned that the travellers and their children had shouted abuse, thrown mud at people, thrown stones at people and their cars, leapt out from behind fences and scared small children and made rather suggestive comments to three somewhat unattractive mothers and one father.

And then at twenty past nine there was a commotion in the corridor that sounded like a riot was taking place. Ann came into my room in a sweat and announced that the travellers were here and wanted to enrol their children.

"Tell them I'll see them in two minutes. I'm going to phone the Local Authority to find out if we have to take them."

We had to take them. Like anyone else, if they lived in the school's area and wanted to attend, we had to take them unless we were full. I wished I'd kept those wasps.

"Good morning!" I said to one of them.

"Are you the Boss?" he replied.

"Yes."

"We want our kids in school. We've got seven and we need them to start today."

I managed to convince him that we needed time to prepare books and equipment and that tomorrow would be the earliest they could start. He reluctantly agreed and gave me the names and ages of his children. The oldest child looked about fourteen but the man assured me he was eleven. A birth certificate would be very hard to come by and I had to rely on his word. This child was taller than me and built like an outdoor toilet. He hadn't yet learned to smile but could perform a number of gestures with his fingers. The younger children were systematically destroying my office as we spoke. I suggested they take the forms home to fill them in rather than sitting in my office doing so. There was no ulterior motive!

I quietly wondered if it would be possible to apply for, be interviewed for and be offered another job by tomorrow. Not only would I prepared to pull out all my stops if this were possible, I would be prepared to pull out all my teeth.

I spoke to all the children in the assembly later that morning and explained that the children from the caravans would be joining us for a short while. I made it clear that I needed to rely on everyone to keep things running smoothly as some of these children had a different approach to life than the one we were used to. Several children cried. Several others looked forward to the fights. They were both right.

Ann came to see me a little while before lunch. She had been getting on the wrong side of the cook because the numbers of children taking dinners had been wrong every day for two weeks before the holiday.

"One child every day!" Ann told me. "I don't understand how I can get it wrong so consistently. But there's always one more child having a dinner than I say there is."

"It's possible that one of the teachers is filling in the list wrongly." I said. "If a child starts having a school meal instead of bringing their own lunch, it's not impossible for the teacher to fill the register in wrong. I've done it myself, you just replicate what was in the week before if you're not careful."

"That could be it. I'll have to ask everybody to double check." She said.

"No, I'll tell you what. Let me take the lists into the dining room. I'll stand at the front of the queue and tick off all the kids who have a school meal. That should show us where it's going wrong nice and quickly."

So at lunchtime, armed with my trusty lists, I stood next to the serving hatch and ticked off each child who was served with a meal. Diane, the cook was overjoyed that the matter was being given high profile attention. The children, however, were a little uneasy to find me ticking off their names and at least twenty of them wanted to know if somebody was going to be in big trouble. Seven classes came through and there were no mistakes. The registers were filled in with total accuracy.

But when the eighth class arrived, one child near the back of the queue was marked on the list for bringing his own sandwiches. He was six years old and his name was Regan. His family was incredibly strict about what they ate and he was known amongst the staff as Regan the vegan. For a moment or two I failed to connect this fact with the inconsistent dinner numbers, assuming that Regan had simply started taking school meals and his teacher had not altered the register. But then it dawned on me that Regan brought a packed lunch every day because his diet was so carefully controlled. Regan's packed lunch consisted of a substance that looked like bark chippings and birdseed. It was free from artificial or actual flavouring and had a nourishment value of a small log. And yet here he was, in the dinner queue.

I watched him choose his lunch. He required chips, chicken curry and peas. His dessert was a choc-ice. I followed him to a seat and sat down next to him.

"Regan, do you normally have a school dinner?" I asked.

"I do sometimes." He told me, quite honestly.

"Don't your parents give you a packed lunch any more?"

"Yes, but I throw it away 'cos it's horrible. And then I have a school dinner instead."

"You throw your packed lunch away?"

"Yes. The school dinners smell really nice and I can have things that we don't have at home."

"You know they often contain meat and eggs and things, don't you?"

"Yes, they're lovely."

"Now there's a problem, Regan. You see, you're having a lunch every day but your mum and dad aren't paying for it because they think you're eating your packed lunch."

"I didn't know I had to pay for it."

"I realise that. But all the children in that queue have sent money at the beginning of the week to pay for their dinners. Then the cook buys the amount of food she thinks she needs. The trouble is, for the last few weeks she's needed a bit more than she's bought. Now if everybody had a lunch when they liked the smell of it, she'd be in a real mess wouldn't she. It'd be like you taking home fifteen friends for tea without asking your mum first."

"Nobody comes for tea at my house. They don't like it!"

I couldn't help feeling sorry for this boy. His parents were forcing him to do things their way and all he wanted was to eat dead animals like everybody else. And when he saw them being served in school he just joined the queue. And he got away with it for two weeks! I knew his parents would be furious with him if they found out what he'd been doing so I agreed with the cook that we would write it off as an accounting error and keep Regan's parents in the dark. Regan would have to make up his own mind when he was older. Hopefully he would be allowed to.

My moment of quiet reflection was dramatically broken by Maureen, the Senior Dinner Lady.

"I need you outside on the playground right now!" she announced.

"This is all a bit sudden, Maureen." I laughed. "It isn't very private out there at the moment. According to Walt, the wildlife area's a better option! That's where the travellers have been learning about nature."

"That's just the problem, the travellers!" said Maureen. "They've invaded the playground. There's about six of them and they're causing havoc!"

I rushed outside with Maureen who had now overcome her passion but had, in its place, acquired a tempting piece of flapjack. The playground was unusually quiet. The children were watching bemused as the travellers' children stuck a worryingly sharp kitchen knife into the football that until a few moments ago was being kicked by some ten-year-olds. I ran to intervene.

"What's going on?" I asked. This was a particularly silly question to ask as it was abundantly clear what was going on, but I needed an opener.

"I'm bustin' his ball!" explained George the eight-year-old knife wielder.

"I can see that. Why are you doing it?" I asked. At least we had a dialogue so the obvious questions may as well continue.

"Cos he's a dick head!" George responded.

"Why?"

"He wouldn't let me play. That's why. So I've bust his ball."

"But you shouldn't even be here. You're not allowed on the school premises yet – you don't start till tomorrow. And at this rate you'll be the first child to be expelled before even starting a school. Now I want you off the premises and I don't want to see that knife – or any knife – again. Understand?"

"I'll have him tomorrow!"

"No you won't. You'll behave yourself properly and if you try to attack anybody I'll bring a criminal assault charge against you."

"And I'll bring my dad against you. He's got an eight inch carving knife!"

The pleasantries were interrupted by screams from a group of children at the other end of the yard. Two of the other children had climbed onto the roof and were showering those below with small pebbles. The pebbles were meant to be part of the flat roof. Now they were part of people's hairstyles. Walt, who had been working in the boiler room had heard the patter of tiny feet on his roof and had rapidly climbed up to find out what was happening. Discovering the reality of the situation, he was now a very unhappy man.

He walked up behind them as they bombarded those below with stones. Upon reaching them, he grabbed each child by its ear and turned their heads to face him.

"Put them there stones down now, you pancakes!" he suggested.

"Bollocks!" was their witty return.

"Listen pal, I'll tell you this and I'll tell you now and I'll tell you reight and straight and when it's said it's said, nah then, you either put them stones down or I'll drop you off this 'ere roof like a couple of bricks. I'll leave it with you!"

"You'd never dare, you fat wassock!" one of the boys replied.

"Listen, plant-life, I've had pancakes like you for breakfast. This is my roof and no bugger goes on it without my permission. It's an elf and safety thing. And in t'name of elf and safety, if I find some twonk mucking about on my roof, I'll shove 'em off."

"We'd sue you!" they said, beginning to look a little convinced by his manner.

"I couldn't give a shite."

To add meat to Walt's claim, I shouted to the boys, "If you fell off that roof it'd be your own fault. There's three hundred witnesses down here who never saw anybody else up there with you. Your choice!"

The boys dropped their stones quietly. All the children cheered and Walt stood up proudly.

"You wouldn't have shoved us off really mister, would you?" one of them asked.

"I'll tell you this and I'll tell you now, yes!" Walt replied.

"But you could break our necks doing that. Aren't you bothered?"

"Listen pal, if you were on fire I wouldn't even piss on yer to put it out. Shoving you off a roof would be a pleasure!"

Walt made the two boys climb down and then followed them.

"And now you can pick all them there stones up off that yard. It's got to be done and I'll be buggered if I'm doing it. I've got a dodgy trip switch to fix!"

I suddenly felt a little more comfortable about them joining us tomorrow. They'd been put in their place and might realise that we meant business. To make things even better, all the children had been there when it happened and this was a serious blow to the credibility of any child who wanted to take the place by storm. Tomorrow would be interesting to say the least, but we were moving in the right direction.

At the end of the day the children met up with their parents and recounted the tale of the lunchtime knife attack and the rooftop shrapnel ambush. This, combined with the fact that the new children had been admitted to school and would be starting tomorrow prompted more than a few parents to call in for a visit. Of course, the first to arrive was Mrs Precious. She had arrived before collecting her daughter and did not know any of the day's developments.

"So, have you managed to do what I asked? I notice the caravans are still there. When will they be leaving?"

"I've no idea. I phoned the council but there's not a lot they can offer."

"So what will be happening?"

"Well, they'll be starting school tomorrow and we'll take it from there."

A ghastly look came across her face and was accompanied by a long, uncomfortable silence.

"But my baby! I will not have my little girl subjected to the disgrace of listening to their foul language and being witness to their animal behaviour. She is a delicate little flower. I expect you to protect her from these monsters at all costs."

"I'm tied up in red tape!" I said. "I have to follow the rules and the rules are that I admit them to school."

"If anything happens to my Precious, I shall hold you personally responsible!" she snapped. And then she left before I had the opportunity to tell her what a prat she was.

Many more parents visited and most were reassured to know that I would be doing everything possible to keep disruption to a minimum. I would spend every break on the playground along with supervising staff and I would be moving into exclusion measures if there were any hints of a threat to anyone's safety. I would also personally check that they did not carry any form of knife, machete, pistol, sidewinder missile, anti-aircraft gun or nuclear device. At one point, whilst assuring the Mad Woman of this, I did wonder whether I might be able to enter into an agreement with the travellers. It would involve them bringing a weapon just once and I would pay them handsomely. But on second thoughts, an anonymous contract killer still seemed a better option.

I had made a lot of promises and now I had to live up to them. And it was going to take up a lot of extra time and energy. But the parents were happy and hopefully would spread the good news to others. I foolishly allowed myself to feel a little satisfied. And then the phone rang.

It was the ever-pompous Chair of Governors. He had learned of the impending arrival of the new pupils and wished to pontificate.

"Not very happy!" he announced. "Seems you've imported some undesirables."

"They're starting tomorrow. But don't worry, we've got contingency plans and I'm sure we'll handle anything that arises."

“Problem as I see it is this. I don’t want one of these louts in the same class as my daughter. There’ll be trouble if I learn she’s got one in her class. Don’t like special favours and all that but this is one time where I expect a bit of preferential. Get my drift?”

“Oh, I get your drift. But unfortunately all the classes are arranged by age. One of those kids is in your daughter’s year group and so he’s going to be in her class.”

“Well move the little bugger. Put him in another class!”

“I’m sorry, but the teachers are going to have a hard enough time, aren’t they. If a teacher has a child in the wrong age group this will add to their problems of planning appropriate lessons. And I am not putting myself in the position of explaining to a teacher why I’ve taken one child out of its correct year group and put it in their class.”

“So you’re refusing to do as I ask?”

“Yes, I am!”

“And if I pull rank?”

“You don’t have any rank to pull.”

He went quiet for a moment and then came back with a different argument.

“Why didn’t you ask me before accepting these children?” he said.

"Because I chose to ask someone who knew the answer. I asked the Local Authority for the official position."

"Then I'll write to them and tell them to change their rules."

"They have to follow national rules. It isn't their decision. We're all doing as we're told."

"Well it's a bad show. It comes back to that discipline thing. If you'd have beefed up the discipline when I told you to, these people wouldn't have come!"

"It's nothing to do with that. They lived sixty miles away before they landed on the field next to us. It's just one of those things and we'll have to ride it out."

"That's all very well for you to say but you won't be dealing with an upset child every day, will you!"

"No, I'll potentially be dealing with three hundred of them!"

"Ah, bad example."

Eventually, after going round in circles he put the phone down, only for it to ring again immediately. Fearing another similar discussion, I answered and was greeted by a rep who wanted to engage me in conversation before telling me what he was selling.

"Hi, and how are you?" he said.

"Fine, what are you selling?"

"Did you have a good break at half term?"

"Forgotten it now. What are you selling?"

"Can I ask, what's your position in the school?"

"Sitting at my desk. Can we get on to what you're trying to sell please?"

"I had a week in Majorca myself, it was scorching."

"Look, you're mistaking me for someone who is interested. I'm not. I've had a crap day and I want to get on with some work before my brain caves in. Now, either tell me what you're selling or put the phone down."

He was selling advertising space in a diary. For the mere sum of two hundred pounds I could put the school's name in a quarter of a page of an obscure diary. The proceeds would help the plight of children who had been failed by the education system and removed from their school. I politely declined his offer to which he replied, "Shall I put you down as a maybe?"

"No."

"Well we do an eighth of a page for one hundred and twenty-five pounds. Would that be a better option?"

“The best option would be for you to get off the phone.”

“Look I’ll do you a special offer. One hundred for an eighth of a page. Now what do you say to that?”

“Bugger off!”

“Are you sure you’re the headmaster?”

“Only until my case comes up, now bugger off!”

And so ended the first day of a new half term. This, I reminded myself, was an eight-week half term, ending with Christmas. I wondered as I drove home how many of us would still be alive by Christmas.

Autumn Term: Week 9

It was not a fight between two children, it was a fight between two mothers. They were going at it like professionals and I didn't know whether to break it up or set out some seats for the audience.

I had been quietly working for about twenty minutes on Tuesday morning when at eight forty-five a child ran into the building from the playground and banged heavily on my door.

"There's a fight on the playground!" she shouted.

A fight on the playground first thing in the morning was unusual on a number of counts. Firstly, there were normally a considerable number of parents waiting with their children and this made it difficult for any child to become seriously engrossed in a good scrap. Secondly, fights tended to break out when children were getting tired, not first thing in a morning. Thirdly, the playground was often half empty until two minutes before the start of school and any really good arguments could legitimately take place off the premises where there were no adults to spoil the fun.

So with a certain level of confusion I left my desk and followed the child outside to see what the problem was. And what a wonderful sight met my eyes as I turned onto the playground. It was not a fight between two children, it was a fight between two mothers. They were going at it like professionals and I didn't know whether to break it up or set out some seats for the audience. They had, by now, accumulated a sizeable audience of both parents and children who were standing amazed at the curious sight. But sadly, the language the two mothers were using was not ideal for a school playground and so I decided it was time to bring the proceedings to a halt.

I waded across the yard and forced myself between the marauding mums. Lost in the adrenaline of the battle they had no idea I was there and continued lashing out. I narrowly missed the opportunity to have a week in hospital following a kick that skimmed past me only millimetres from a site of special scientific interest.

"Stop!" I yelled.

"Not till I've killed the little cow!" shouted one of the mums.

"Just try it, you fat slapper!" replied the other.

I pushed them apart and tried to hold them away from each other for at least a moment.

“You can’t do this on the school playground.” I said. “Come inside and calm down and let’s see if we can sort things out.”

“I can sort things out me bloody self. Just let me give her a good kicking! That’ll do it!”

“Sod off, you slag!”

“Shut up, you bitch!”

“No, you’re starting again.” I said. “I want you to leave the playground and either come inside the building or go home. Which is it to be?”

“Well I’m not going home till I’ve sorted her out!”

“Me neither!”

“You’ve got no chance!”

The mothers agreed to come inside, much to the disappointment of their respective children who had been cheering them on. This was ever so slightly surreal. As we walked from the yard to the office the mothers kept pushing each other and trying to deliberately trip the other one up. It was no different to bringing in a couple of ten-year-olds who had fallen out over a shiny pencil. I found myself saying ‘Walk properly!’ on at least three occasions. After being chastised they walked normally for a few seconds and then started pushing and shoving once again. And we wondered why their children were so out of control!

One of the mums was Kelly. Kelly was the lady I had met on my first day, requesting that I put her youngest child down. I wondered if a family discount might be in order on that point. The second mum was a lady called Lisa. She had so many studs in her ears, nose, eyebrows and lips that if she walked past an industrial magnet, there was a real chance she would never break free. Such a magnet would, I mused, be one of the few things on this planet that might be attracted to her.

They pushed, shoved and stumbled all the way to my office and on arriving they sat in chairs at opposite sides of the room and stared at each other. I never before realised that venom could be transmitted from the eyes. If I could avoid death by eye contact, it was time to find out what the problem was all about.

Kelly explained to me that Lisa had started the problem and that Lisa was a slapper and a bitch. Lisa's alternative explanation was that Kelly was the instigator of the current unrest and that far from being the respectable citizen I had assumed, Kelly was indeed a filthy slag who goes at it with anything that moves. Kelly took issue with the finer points of that statement and made it known with great certainty that Lisa was an old dog that got stoned every night and slept with anyone who offered. She then qualified her accusation with supplementary information relating to the dramatic reduction in the number of offers over recent months. Lisa's somewhat exuberant response to this was to stand up and offer to put Kelly's teeth through the window. Not to be outsmarted on such a technical point, Kelly clarified that her teeth were at least attached naturally to her gums. This, she proposed was unlike Lisa's as she had reason to believe that most parts of Lisa's body were either optional extras or still on approval from a mail order company.

But entertaining as this was, it was not helping me to understand the reason for the initial outburst on the yard this morning. As I prepared to ask for clarification of the situation, Ann came to the door and offered coffee and this was gratefully accepted.

"Right, start from the beginning." I said. "I don't want to know the background to why you hate each other and I don't need a list of your recent sexual conquests. I want to know, very simply, what happened on the yard this morning that sparked off a fight. Kelly, tell me your version."

"I'll bloody tell you…." said Lisa.

"You'll get your turn in a minute!" I snapped. "I want to hear both versions and I'm starting with Kelly."

"It's her kid!" Kelly explained. "Her kid, Tyler. He's that fat little bugger in Mr. Richards' class."

"Don't you call our Tyler a fat little bugger you nasty bitch!" interjected Lisa.

"Nasty bitch? Nasty bitch? You jumped up little…."

"Back to the story, Kelly!" I insisted.

"Sorry. Her Tyler, he's been bullying one of mine. He's been making fun of our Jonah for ages."

"For ages? How long exactly?" I asked.

"Since last Thursday." She replied. "And I'm sick of it. I'm at the end of my tether. He comes home telling me all these things that Tyler's said and done and I'm not having him bullied. He's a good lad, our Jonah and I'm not having her fat little bully upsetting him. And she can stop looking at me like that or I'll deck her, old slut!"

"OK, OK! Your turn Lisa."

"She talks out of her arse, she does. My Tyler's not fat and he's not a bully. It's her little brat of a son that's your problem. Mind you, she's got that many kids she probably doesn't even know who some of 'em are. Her Jonah comes up to my boy every day, well since they fell out last Thursday and he kicks him, punches him and spits at him. And I'm not having it. That might be how they do things in her house but I won't put up with it."

It seemed to me that these two boys had done what all children do from time to time. They had fallen out with each other. And in conversations with their parents they had each blamed the other child. And where most parents are adult enough to know that in a few days the children will be best of friends again, Lisa and Kelly did not. Instead, they got involved and perpetuated the problem. And as always, adult problems take longer to heal than children's problems.

I suggested this to Lisa and Kelly who clearly did not like to hear that they might be at fault in some way. Their response was to revert to their earlier conversation regarding each other's personal attributes. They seemed comfortable with this discussion.

Exhausting all relevant words after a particularly eloquent comment directed towards Kelly's early teenage escapades, the two decided it was time once again to put the argument on a physical footing.

Launching herself across the room Kelly scored a direct hit on her opponent by means of a kick to the shin. Lisa pushed Kelly away with a surprising amount of force and as she stumbled backwards the door opened and in walked Ann with her tray of coffee. Not expecting to have a parent landing on it, Ann was holding her tray too lightly to support the additional load now provided by Kelly. The leading edge of the tray plunged towards the floor and the cups were catapulted across the room, coming to rest on a pile of newly completed financial returns that were sitting on my desk.

Relatively unhappy about this turn of events I switched on the 'old headmaster' act and told the two ladies to sit down and shut up immediately. They responded instantly. They sat down, crossed their legs and looked at the floor.

"You cannot continue behaving like children all your life. I've tried to listen to your arguments but it's becoming clear that you have no interest in sorting out the problem. All you seem to want to do is carry on bickering and fighting. You're enjoying the attention!"

They sat motionless in their chairs with their heads still down. I suppressed a smile and continued.

“You’ve made fools of yourselves in front of the other parents and children and now you’ve ruined a pile of work on my desk, work that took around seven hours to complete.” I thought it best to not mention the fact that I had already made photocopies. “I am supposed to spend time working for the children in this school, not sorting out fights between adults and not repeating piles of work that have been wrecked by people who can’t keep control of themselves.”

“Sorry.” They both replied, still looking at the floor.

“You will be if it happens again. If I have to come and sort your fights out again, I will ban you from the premises.”

“Sorry.” They said again.

“School grounds are private property. Parents are allowed on them by invitation only. In most cases it’s assumed that the invitation is general and open to all parents but it doesn’t have to be. If I ban you, I can have it enforced by law.”

“We won’t do it again. We got carried away.” Said Kelly.

“Sorry we’ve messed up your work.” Said Lisa.

“I think you should go home and keep out of each other’s way.” I said. “Will you make it home without scrapping in the street?”

"Yes, we will." They replied.

I opened the door and they started to leave.

"Do you want any help cleaning up your desk?" Kelly asked.

"I'll manage!"

"I think it did us good, you telling us off." Kelly continued. "I think we need it sometimes. If you ever fancy a night out…"

"Goodbye Kelly!"

I didn't know if I had done the right thing. Maybe I should have called in Kelly and Lisa's parents. Maybe I should have made them stand outside my office at break time, or write a hundred lines, 'I must not smack the fat slapper'. But no, at least they were out of the building.

The rest of the day was less memorable. I was visited at break time by Lisa and Kelly's children. They wanted to know if their mums were in trouble and whether there would be a punishment involved. They seemed rather disappointed when I said no. I think the idea of their mothers being in trouble with the head for fighting on the yard had a certain appeal. It would certainly be a good story down the pub when they were older. Assuming, of course, that they didn't go down the pub already most nights.

By the early afternoon I had completed a surprising amount of work without interruption and this made me feel uneasy. Headship, I had decided was reminiscent of the eternal balance between pleasure and pain. There were syntactical differences in that the pleasure was in knowing that a task had been completed successfully and did not need to be done again. The pain was anything that stopped the aforementioned process. Consequently, the pain included children, parents, teachers, other staff, the local authority, the Government, inspectors, advisers, social workers, school health officials and governors. Of that list, the most significant were children. And parents. And teachers. And… well the picture is becoming clear, isn't it!

But at two forty-five I looked out of my window and caught sight of a large contingent of the traveller population from the field next door. They were storming up the path and I feared that my life was soon to be over. To be fair, their children had been relatively well behaved in the four days since they joined us. They had stopped bringing weapons to school after I confiscated three penknives and a paring knife on the first day. They had been more polite after I had punished them for telling the senior dinner lady to piss off on the second day. That act had annoyed me intensely as the pleasure of telling the senior dinner lady to piss off should be reserved for myself and senior management only. On the third day they had sat on an infant child in the playground and then threatened to cut off his feet so that they might procure his trainers. In fairness, the infant child in question had not long ago purposely trapped another child's fingers in the 'hinge side' of a door and so foot amputation whilst being sat on was something of a just dessert. As far as I was aware, they had committed no badness on the fourth day. Perhaps I was to learn differently right now.

Ann showed them into my office and I welcomed them. To further unnerve me, they smiled.

"We're leaving!" said one of the party. "We need our kids 'cos we're going now."

"What, immediately?" I asked.

"Immediately. We want to be gone by early this evening so we've come for our kids. Can we have 'em?"

"Well yes, wait here and I'll get them rounded up for you."

I went to the classroom that contained, or at least tried to contain, the oldest of the crew. I informed the boy of the situation and asked him to collect up the others and bring them to office. A few minutes later, my office was full to bursting point having, as it did, all the children and the large group of adults squeezed into it.

"Have they been good?" one of the female travellers asked.

"They've surprised me!" I replied. "It can't be easy trying to fit in at a new school. Especially when it's for such a short time."

"He's a good 'un!" the lady said, pointing to the eldest. "He's growing into a nice lad. And he's a good driver you know. We let him drive our van when we're moving on. It's handy having a kid that can drive, you can have a bit of fun in the back!"

"But he's only… how old is he?"

"Thirteen."

"So he shouldn't have been here. He should have been at the secondary school."

"Whatever!"

The adults, despite their unorthodox ways, were insistent upon politeness and the children were encouraged to shake hands with me and thank me for our hospitality. Jed, the nine-year-old reached out to shake my hand and as he did so, a calculator fell from his sleeve. I watched it fall to the floor and then looked at Jed.

"Shit!" he said.

"No, calculator!" I responded. "Got any more?"

Jed answered in the negative and then one of the adults clipped him round the ear, informing him that if they later found any school property on him they would inflict pain in a variety of curious ways. He consequently emptied his sleeves and pockets of three pairs of compasses, two further calculators, a CD-ROM and the school business stamp. He claimed in his defence that he had no idea how they had got there and that, despite their obvious bulk, he was not aware of their existence until now. As if to show he doubted his story, one of the men rammed the boy into a wall and informed him that his parentage was in question.

I thought it might be useful to know if any other school equipment was lurking in the pockets of any of the other children.

"Listen." I said. "I'm going to suggest we have an amnesty as you're leaving us. There's a table in the entrance hall. I want you to go out of the office and if you have any school property on you, put it on that table. No questions asked. But remember what your… your… the adults said. They don't want to find anything on you."

Without speaking, the children all left the room and walked into the entrance area. I gave them a moment or two and then suggested to the adults that we go and take a look.

I had anticipated the small table being large enough to hold any additional items that the children had taken a shine to. I was wrong. The loot filled the tabletop and then spread onto the floor below. The range of items astounded me. The other adults were also astounded, and just a little proud of the way their children could hide so many items in such a small space. On the top of the table was a pack of felt-tipped pens, a box of metal pencil sharpeners, a stapler, numerous pieces of Lego, an Internet connection lead, a blackboard rubber and seven paintbrushes.

The view under the table was truly amazing. To think that these children had stood in my office concealing the amount of loot that littered the floor was beyond comprehension. A hacksaw was the first object I noticed. This was accompanied by an array of batteries and small light bulbs used in science experiments. Behind those was a box of magnifying glasses and a small, but not *that* small, microscope. A couple of video tapes were under the microscope and a thermometer stolen from the weather station was also in the vicinity. From the music department were a wooden recorder and a pair of castanets. Finally a football pump and a skipping rope seemed to have drifted from the PE store and landed in one of the children's deceptively spacious pockets.

After standing with my mouth wide open for approximately five centuries, I turned to the children and said, "Thank you!"

"Mmm!" they mumbled, rather annoyed to have been 'cleaned out'.

"I'm just amazed you could conceal this lot." I said. "I'm tempted to ask you how you did it, but I'm not sure I want to know."

Ann, walking past at this point, stopped and looked at the display of treasure with incredulity. And then she looked at the shelves on the wall and her eyes opened just a little wider. She stared at me and subtly flicked her head backwards, signalling me to walk over to her, though I did not pick up on this immediately. I smiled at her and then ignored her.

She coughed loudly and repeated the gesture.

"Are you OK, Ann?" I asked, clearly missing the point.

"Yes!" she said. And then she coughed once more and signalled a little less subtly for me to go over to her. Once again, I spectacularly failed to connect.

Finally, she looked at me and said, "Come over here and look at this."

I walked to where she was standing and she leaned over to me and quietly whispered in my ear.

"The trophies! Two of the trophies are missing."

I honestly did not know what trophies there should be on the shelves. Having been immersed in people problems since my arrival at the school, I had not yet risen to the level of inspecting – or even being aware of – cups and trophies won by the school. But if Ann was convinced that two trophies were missing I had no reason to doubt her story.

The children were aware that she was telling me something and were beginning to look shifty. I turned to them and said, "I think you still have some more thi…"

"Run!" shouted the eldest. And with that, they burst through the front door and set off down the school path. I gave chase and as I ran through the door I caught sight of Ann following me.

"Don't worry, Ann. I'll catch them. Don't try to race them."

Ann had obviously taken notice of me because she was not there when I next looked round. I followed the children down the path as it wound round a ninety-degree bend, skirting Walt's storage room, a brick built garage with regular doors.

Suddenly to my astonishment, Ann appeared from the other side of Walt's room. She had used an overgrown pathway that I had never even noticed before. She burst out of the undergrowth with a vociferous war cry and a long broom handle and successfully tripped up the first of the escaping miscreants. In the collision that followed I was able to catch up with the children, just in time to observe Ann retrieving the stolen trophies. With the thieves in a squirming pile on the floor, Ann stood triumphantly holding two silver cups high in the air, victorious in her battle.

The travellers left us after that. By five o'clock the field was empty of caravans but rather full of litter and rubbish. And then at five-fifteen a group of pupils and parents knocked on my office window. In their collective hands were four black bin liners.

"We've found all this on the field." They shouted through the glass. "It's all stuff that belongs to the school. Do you want it back?"

At that point I decided that if any children were absent tomorrow I would ring their parents immediately. I needed to check they hadn't been stolen.

Autumn Term: Week 10

You can tell a lot about folk by their door furniture. You want to see my sister's knockers. Tarnished, they are. It's where people's hands have worn 'em down.

This was a big week in the history of the school. Work was scheduled to begin on the building of our new classroom. This was the first significant change to the building since it had been originally thrown together back in the sixties. There had been minor changes, of course. From time to time the place had needed new glue and sticky tape to hold its walls together and occasionally bits of damp card had been affixed to the roof to help the leaks become more dramatic. But no actual building had ever taken place.

When first built, the school was a technological marvel. It was built on reclaimed land, once littered with hundreds of bell pits. The land had been filled and now consisted of shale and other crumbly stuff. All of this meant that the foundations were something of a masterpiece. The new builders had been told all about this and I had reiterated it over and over again, but they seemed unconcerned. I assumed that building technology had moved on such that a dodgy bit ground was of little consequence nowadays.

Walt was as excited as a child with a new cuddly urinal. This week would signal the beginning of many months of maintenance talk with builders, plumbers and fitters of various devices. It would give Walt the opportunity to slope off and yet always appear to have a good reason for his vanishing. He would be ensuring that the builders had sufficient knowledge of drainage runs and the like. And they would, no doubt, be treated to a VIP tour of his urinals.

From everyone else's point of view, this was the start of the chaos season. Part of the playground would become a builders' compound, lorries would be reversing across the yard delivering girders and from time to time, certain entrance and exit doors would be blocked off. This would necessitate up to a hundred children being diverted through the school to a different exit, which they would share with another hundred children.

But it would all be worth it. No longer would the school be overcrowded. No longer would groups of children have to work in a draughty corridor. In just a few months we would have a shiny new classroom, fully equipped and ready to make the school a more comfortable place to work and learn.

Of great concern was that it started so well. First to arrive were two metal containers and these were unloaded from the lorry and placed on the playground. One was to be the builders' 'tea break room' and toilet, the other was to be a storage point for smaller items. A metal fence was erected around these containers so that the children could not go near them. Next came another metal fence, this time around the area where the new classroom was to be built. The site was currently grassed and was on a fairly steep slope. The foundations would have to go deep to cope with the slope, Walt had informed me and he wouldn't like to dig the buggers out. I had no reason to disagree.

The construction team arrived and Walt and I went out to greet them.

"Good morning!" I said.

"Good morning!" said Mick, the foreman.

"Nah then!" said Walt.

I introduced Walt, not as the caretaker but as the site manager, just like he had requested. He grinned as I stated this title and the construction team looked on in awe. Either that, or they could smell something.

"So you're the man to ask if we need to know anything, are you?" Mick responded, clearly buttering Walt up.

"That's me!" Walt replied. "I'll tell you this and I'll tell you now and I'll tell you reight and straight and when it's said it's said and I'll say no more. There's nothing I don't know about this place. I've combed every inch down to the last milligram and I know this place inside out. Anything you need to know, just ask me. Go on, ask me. I can tell you anything."

"Brilliant! Where does your waste water pipe leave the perimeter? We need to link up our caravan."

"I'm not sure." Walt replied, losing all credibility at this point. "But we can trace it if you want. We'll start off in some toilets – while we're there I'll show you my urinals, spotless they are – and we can perhaps work it out."

"Wouldn't it be easier to look for the inspection covers and see which way the drains run?"

"Aye, well that's another option. I were going to suggest that first but I thought you might want to see my urinals."

Mick sent one of the builders with Walt. Despite everything, they were heading inside the building. Walt clearly had a urinal tour on offer and the man was not escaping. Still worried about the grotty ground under the school I talked to Mick to ensure that things would be OK. He looked a little surprised when I informed him of the problem and told me his boss had never mentioned anything about it. But he was quite sure that a little shoring up would keep things in order.

Having prepared the site the builders went for a tea break and this coincided with the morning break for the children. As the day was warm, the builders had begun to drink their tea outside their caravan, but being aware that children were about to appear, they had stayed behind their metal fence. The children, being both inquisitive and tactless in equal measure were interested to find their playground somewhat modified when they stepped outside. I had expected a few problems based around so many children running about in a smaller space than usual, but they did not run about. Instead, they stood almost silently and watched the builders drink their tea. The builders behind their metal fence took on the appearance of caged animals in a zoo and drank nervously as their every move was scrutinised.

"What are you doing?" a small child asked after some time.

"Drinking my tea." Said Mick.

"Why?" the child asked.

"Because I'm thirsty."

"Who's put you in that cage?" a five-year-old girl shouted.

"Nobody!"

"Have you been bad? Have you killed somebody?"

"No, we're builders. We're building your new classroom."

"What, in there? How will you get it out?"

"No, this is where we…"

"What's your name?"

"Mick." Said Mick, quite accurately.

"What's their names?"

"Dave and Bob." Mick replied innocently.

A builder called Bob was too much for the older children to handle. Choruses of 'Bob the Builder' resounded through the yard and the poor man finished his cup of tea inside the caravan, looking longingly out of the window as if in captivity. In an attempt to ease the plight of the builders, the teacher who was supervising moved the children away and insisted that they act like they normally would at a break time. This meant thumping each other, poking smaller children with twigs and kicking balls at unsuspecting infants. Once this was under way it made the builders much happier and they were able to finish their tea break in comparative peace, bearing in mind they were still on a school playground.

Walt returned with the remaining builder, Jack, from their voyage of discovery.

"Have you found where the drains go?" I asked.

"Aye we have. I'll show you if you want, it's only across this field."

"It's OK, Walt. As long as one of us knows where they are, I'm sure everything will be fine."

Walt took me to one side and suggested that we go back into the building.

"I can't take to him!" he told me. "Do you know, nah then, I took him round every one of my toilets, showed him every bowl and every urinal and do you know what he said? Well I'll tell you. I will, I'll tell you. He said that when you've seen one toilet you've seen' em all. 'Not till you've seen my bloody toilets' I told him. I said as there's none to compare with mine. Bloody Queen could come and crap in my toilets and I'd be proud to see it happen. But is he interested? No he's not. He's a bloody pancake and I'll tell you that. Nah then, I'll leave it with you."

"So you're not keen on him!" I suggested.

"Not keen? Not keen? He'd better not want access to my ball cocks and waste traps 'cos it won't happen – and that's swearing!"

These were strong words from Walt. I only hoped that the rest of the construction team would fare better. If not, a troubled time lay ahead. But Walt informed me that he liked Mick and as he was in charge, that was all that mattered. It transpired that making friends with Mick could be beneficial to Walt as, in months to come, Mick might put timber offcuts and boxes of fixings Walt's way. It was, I mused, a little like winning the lottery, only different in every way! At eleven fifteen, I had cause to call to see Amanda Chaplin to discuss a child's poor attendance. Her room was directly next to the newly created building site and the new classroom would ultimately be next door to Amanda's room. On entering the room, I found the children working quietly and calmly with a lovely buzz of activity. I asked her to spare me a minute to give me her view on the aforementioned child and as she began to reply, the most deafening racket started up outside the room. It was the sound of a huge pneumatic drill ramming its way into the shale outside. The walls and windows shook and the ceiling tiles rattled in their frames. Pencils rolled off desks and three seven-year-olds started to cry.

"It's OK!" Amanda shouted over the din. "It's only the drills outside. It's not an earthquake!"

Unfortunately, although I could hear her, and possibly the four children closest to her could also tune in, the rest of the class could not make out what she was saying. To make matters worse, the drilling momentarily stopped when Amanda was yelling the word 'earthquake'. Consequently, twenty-six children, on hearing their teacher shout 'Earthquake' at the top of her voice, screamed and ran amuck.

In the midst of their screaming, the drilling commenced once again. A competition then ensued between the children's screams and the noise of the drill. The vibration in the walls was only equalled by that in my ear drums. As the drilling stopped once more, Amanda and I shouted over the children's voices and insisted that they stand perfectly still and remain silent. When we had their attention I said,

"Miss Chaplin was actually saying that it's *not* an earthquake! It's the builders outside. They're drilling into the ground. There's no need to panic."

"Will the school fall down?" asked a girl in the middle of the room.

"I promise you that nothing will fall down. Well, maybe a couple of posters might drop off the wall in all the vibration, but that's all. The walls will stay up, just like they have done since the school was built. There's nothing to worry about."

I invited the children to go back to their seats and to get on with what they were doing. The drilling wouldn't last too long.

"Why are they drilling?" a little boy shouted to me.

"They have to dig a very big hole and the ground is made of crumbly rock. They're trying to break through to find the some solid rock." I replied.

"Why don't they just build it on the grass?" the boy asked.

"Well, the ground under the grass might not be strong enough to hold a building, and it isn't flat. So they dig down and…"

"I know!" said another child. "They dig a hole and plant the new classroom in it so that it grows in the right place."

"That would only work if we were having a tree house!" I replied.

A cheer went up across the room.

"Our new classroom's in a tree!" a group shouted.

I suggested that the children try to ignore the drilling. If it got on their nerves they could count how many seconds the drilling lasted before it stopped. As if on cue, the noise started up again and this time the children remained calm and many simply listened and counted. The drilling continued for about forty seconds and then a rather loud clang was heard. At this point the drill stopped and through the silence was heard the drill's operator.

"Bastard!" he shouted, having obviously hit something erroneous in the ground.

It was at this point that we realised how well we could hear the conversations taking place outside the room.

"Sup?" shouted one of the men. I believe this was a verbal abbreviation of 'what's up', and was to be one of many abbreviated phrases for the class to learn.

"I've 'it dis bastard metal job!" the drillmaster informed his colleague.

"Daft git!" the colleague surmised.

"It were 'id under t'shale. Bloody hurt me that did."

"Jolt thi' did it?"

"Like 'avin' a pole shoved up mi arse!"

With the children enthralled by the builders' conversation, I decided it was necessary to go outside and inform the men that they could be heard very clearly inside the room. Mick, the foreman was very decent about it.

"Oh bugger! I'm sorry, pal." He said. "I'll tell 'em to keep it down a bit."

With that, he yelled at the top of his voice, "Stop bloody swearing, you twats, all t'kids can hear you inside t'building!"

"Oh shit, can they?" they replied.

"Don't know they're bleeding doing it, some of 'em!" Mick informed me. "I'll keep reminding 'em if I hear 'em. Foul mouthed bastards!"

I had a sneaking suspicion that Mick may not be quite as attendant as he hoped to be over the matter. It would probably be a good idea if Amanda allowed her class to be a little noisier that usual and perhaps play some Iron Maiden at full blast to help the children concentrate.

By lunch time a sizeable hole had been dug not far from the edge of the school wall. The ground underneath looked every bit as crumbly as I had expected and it was clear that the builders were going to have fun with the foundations. But never mind. I had been assured that they knew exactly what they were doing and that the job would be tackled with aplomb.

In the early afternoon the drilling was less of a problem. The men had resorted to digging away huge swathes of shale with their spades. That the shale was crumbling in on them seemed to be helpful to their cause and the whole picture reminded me of watching a child digging on a beach and making a futile attempt to achieve a vertical edge to their hole. Indeed, quite a considerable amount of shale fell in to the hole with every swipe of the spade, but whilst this made it difficult to empty the hole, it saved having to drill down from the surface.

I went back inside to check that everything was fine in Amanda's classroom and she confirmed that very little drilling had taken place since the earthquake had subsided. She also confirmed that the children's vocabulary was being considerably extended by the builders outside and was about to reach depths far in excess of the new foundations.

So it was with some surprise when, out of the calm, a frantic shout was heard outside the room. It was a technical comment made by one of the builders and it consisted of the words, “Shit! It’s sliding in!” Assuming that what was sliding in was not the substance he had suggested I rushed outside to ascertain the cause of the gentleman’s anxiety.

The ‘it’ that was sliding in was the ground. Above the part of the sliding ground was a wall belonging to Amanda’s classroom. Despite being a layman in building matters, I assumed that this was not an ideal situation, an assumption confirmed by the headless chicken impersonations now being acted out by the construction team. Upon seeing me Mick looked up and shouted frantically.

“Get them bleeding kids out of that room before it collapses!”

Convinced that I had enough information I raced back inside and told the children that we were going to have a walk to the main hall. I whispered the reasons for this to Amanda and she agreed that a break from their task would indeed be quite beneficial to the children. On arriving in the hall, Gillian’s class was in the middle of a PE lesson. Amanda’s class could sit and watch for a little while, I decided.

On hearing the reason for the arrival of her uninvited audience, Gillian offered to vacate the hall immediately, appearing as it did that Amanda's needs were just a little greater. It was now time to find Walt and tell him the news. This would increase his maintenance conversation repertoire and simultaneously give him something to moan about when I asked him to bring the children's desks and chairs to the hall.

"Walt!" I called out when I spotted him at the far end of a corridor. "We need your help!"

"Hang on, I'm just tightening up this door handle!" he replied.

"It won't stop them getting out, Walt. They're tougher than you think, some of these kids."

"No, it's not that. It's got a loose doorplate. If there's one thing I can't stand it's untidy door furniture. You can tell a lot about folk by their door furniture. You want to see my sister's knockers. Tarnished, they are. It's where people's hands have worn 'em down, nah then. They need a good rubbing down and a decent polish. I could do with a screw. It's lost one has this doorplate. That's why it's hanging bad."

"Walt, I need you to leave that job till later. We've got an emergency."

"Is it plumbing?"

"No, it's the new classroom. The foundations are caving in and…."

"Bloody pancakes! I told 'em they'd need shoring up. Elf and Safety, I said. I'll tell you this and I'll tell you now…"

"Walt, listen! They're getting their boss to bring in a structural engineer. In the meantime, Amanda's room is unsafe. The wall's about to fall in…"

"Well it's no good talking to me, you want to get them kids out. It's a basic bit of your Elf and Safety, that, you don't keep kids in a room what's collapsing."

"We've got the kids out. The problem is that they'll have to work in the hall. I need you to help us get desks, chairs and stuff out of that room and into the hall, preferably before it all gets damaged."

"Oh don't worry. They can't damage the hall."

Walt began moving furniture and I explained to Amanda's class that they would be working in the hall for a few days. I told them it was because of the noise outside. I told them this for two reasons. Firstly,

I didn't want anyone to panic and secondly, I'd already promised them that nothing was going to collapse.

By the end of the afternoon the hall had been turned into a huge classroom. Walt had done a sterling job of moving furniture and was now sweating profusely. Consequently his exclusion zone had expanded to around five miles. In the middle of joking with Amanda that she would now be the only teacher to receive any new pupils to the school, since she had the space for a class of three hundred, I was aware that Walt required my attention.

"It's going to bugger up my cleaning schedule, this is!" he exclaimed. "And Joan, my new cleaner, she's still finding her feet. When she gets wind of this she'll be well confused, I'll tell you that and I'll tell you now and I'll leave it with you."

Joan, the belching cleaner, getting wind of a problem was a curious thought.

"Can't do much about it, Walt." I replied. "We can't have the kids in the classroom and there's nowhere else for them to go. Everybody else will be messed around too. We'll have to cancel all the PE lessons, make special arrangements for dinners and assemblies and we'll probably have a whole pile of other problems cropping up that we haven't thought of yet. But there's not a lot of choice. We either evacuate the class or the thing falls in on them."

The arrival of Joan the cleaner was announced by a gust of wind as she opened the door and then confirmed by a further gust of wind as she opened her mouth. Walt dashed over to inform her of the day's events and to discuss an alternative cleaning strategy.

"Nah then, Joan!" Walt said cheerily.

"Nah then, Walt!" she replied. "I see your building's started."

"Don't talk to me about that bloody building. I'll tell you this and I'll tell you now and I'll tell you reight and straight and when it's said it's said and I'll say no more, nah then. They've been here one bloody day and they've wazzed it up already."

"How do you mean, Walt?"

"It's bloody collapsing, that's what I'm saying!"

"How can it be collapsing? They've not built any of it yet!"

"Bloody foundations are falling in. We've got a wall coming down in t'room next door."

"Eee! Has it come down on t'kids? That's a bugger."

"No it's not come down yet. They're trying to stop it. But I'll tell you this and I'll tell you now, it's buggering up everything. They've had to evaporate a class."

"How do you mean?"

"You know, evaporate 'em. They've got 'em out of their room and put 'em in the hall. So we'll have to change how we do things, I'll have to come up with a plan."

"Ooh, I bet them there kids are excited though, being evaporated. How long will it last?"

"Well I reckon it could be a couple of months but I'm talking off t'top of my head and I might be talking out of my arse 'cos I don't really know."

A teenage girl with radioactive acne appeared at that moment. She opened the door and looked at Joan. It appeared she was Joan's daughter and she had come to help her mother. She was eighteen and was introduced to Walt as Gail. I found it wonderful that a lady who suffers from chronic wind should name her child Gail. But no one else knew why I was laughing.

"He were telling me as how they've had to evaporate a class full of kids today to stop 'em getting crushed." Joan explained to Gail.

“You wouldn’t get me going in a room that were about to come down on me, I’ll tell you that. It’d put t’wind right up me, going in there.”

I walked away, leaving them to discuss the merits of evaporating seven-year-old children. They appeared to find it a most agreeable option.

Outside, the builders had finished for the day. Their hole was deep and impressive. Bits of shale were still falling into the crevasse but so far the classroom wall had remained standing. Walt had joined me outside to offer his opinion of the situation.

“Well they should have known as this were going to happen, bloody pancakes!” he opined.

“It sounds like their boss didn’t take the problem too seriously, Walt.”

“You can’t mess with construction and maintenance. I’ll tell you this and I’ll tell you now, you need to take care with construction and maintenance. You can dig yourself into a bloody hole if you’re not careful.”

He edged towards the hole to peer into it.

“It’s still crumbling, nah then. There’s bits dropping in. I’ll be surprised if there’s any bloody school standing tomorrow. Bloody pancakes, they come to build one new room and they demolish all t’rest!”

He leaned over, looked deeper into the hole and shook his head.

“I’ll tell you this, they haven’t got a clue. You have to know what you’re doing with ‘oles and they don’t!”

As if to demonstrate how weak the ground was, Walt stepped a little closer to the edge. The ground beneath him creaked and crumbled and then, within the space of a second it gave way. Walt took what looked like a short toboggan ride from the surface, down into the depths of the hole. He landed with a heavy crunch which dislodged further pieces of shale, causing what could only be described as a personal avalanche. Dazed and rather puzzled, Walt sat in the shale attempting to dodge falling debris.

“Bugger!” he shouted, thus confirming that he had not intended to visit the bottom of the hole. “Bugger and crap!”

When he had completed his soliloquy, he decided to remove himself from his predicament. Unfortunately, each time he attempted to climb out of the hole, he only succeeded in dislodging yet more shale. This brought small pieces of rock raining down on him and offered him no possibility of escape.

“Wait there, Walt. I’ll go and get a ladder.” I called.

“I don’t need no bloody ladder. I can get out on my own, nah then!” he stubbornly replied.

I watched as he grasped at the side of the hole, pulling endless pieces of shale out of the ground. My gut feeling was that Walt really could make use of a ladder and that attempting to get out without one would only benefit the builders, who would have far less digging to do tomorrow than they expected. With that thought in mind I set off to retrieve Walt’s ladder.

The ladders were locked in the store room and Walt had his keys with him in the hole. So to avoid damaging his pride I went to find a cleaner so that I might borrow a set of keys. Joan, the belching cleaner, was busy in a junior classroom. She could be detected, sonar-like, by standing at a junction of two corridors and simply listening for the wind. The belches came with such regularity that even if one had just passed, another would be along within a minute or two.

“Can I borrow your keys to the store room, Joan?” I asked.

She smiled, belched and offered me her keys.

"Have you seen Walt?" she asked. "I need to ask him something."

"He's a bit busy right now. I'll tell him to come and find you when he's done if you like."

I left Joan and went to pick up the ladder. As I came back out of the store, Joan was standing at the door.

"What's that for?" she asked.

"Walt needs it. I'm going to give him a hand with something." I told her.

She followed me, offering to help carry the ladder. I told her many times that this was not necessary, but she was insistent and would not go away. As we rounded the corner of the building, Walt could be heard like a grumbling sea-monster, ranting below the ground.

"Bollocks! Bugger!" he moaned.

I leaned over to speak to him and as I did so he caught sight of Joan.

"Oh that's all I need! Now everybody's going to know!"

"Eee! What a sight. I thought I were supposed to look *up* to my boss! Who's put you down there Walt, have you been a bad boy? Wait there, I'm going to get everybody to come and see!"

Walt began to say 'Don't you bloody dare, you pancake!' but Joan had gone. She had not expected live entertainment when she accepted this job.

Walt had actually been quite busy since I left. The hole was much bigger now than it had been earlier and whilst there was a lot of debris on the floor, the sides were coming down very quickly. I lowered the ladder into his little pit and offered him the chance to escape. Even the ladder knocked away some of the shale and I had a slight worry that things still might go wrong, but Walt managed to steady the ladder and begin to climb up.

As his head appeared above the surface once more, there was a cheer. Joan had, with immense speed, rounded up every member of staff still in the building. His audience watched as Walt climbed out of the hole and stepped on the ground once more. His first sentence was shorter than I expected. It consisted of the words, 'Bugger off you bloody…' and then a momentary silence. The cause of this silence was related to the fact that the ground was once again slipping beneath Walt's feet. With the ancient war cry of 'Shit!' Walt threw himself clear of the hole, landing face down at Joan's feet. Joan gave a loud belch of appreciation as she watched her line manager lie in grovelling position for a few seconds.

It was never clear whether it was the weight of Walt's landing on the ground or the rumble of Joan's belch, but the hole collapsed with great gusto at this point. Fortunately, the caving in was moving away from the building itself.

"Anyway, Walt," I said, "what were you saying about taking care with construction and maintenance and not digging yourself into a hole?"

"Bollocks!" he replied.

That was an angle I hadn't considered.

Autumn Term: Week 11

Mr. Miller arrived. He was a smartly dressed man, well-spoken and appeared to be a caring father. Consequently, I was not at all sure he would fit in.

A week into the building project and the classroom was still standing. Amanda's class continued to work in the hall and we were learning to cope with the disruption. A structural engineer had visited, shaken his head and left some time last week. This action was to lead to the delivery of some underpinning equipment which would ensure the relative safety of the school building. Once it had been given the 'all-clear' it would be safe for Amanda to work in her classroom once again, but sadly she would have to take her class with her. I had pinned the construction people down to a tight timescale for the remedial work to be done and was very happy with my guarantee of 'some time fairly soon'.

Tuesday morning dawned wild, wet and windy. It was going to be one of those awful days where the children would have to be kept inside all the time. This would mean that they would become irritable by the middle of lunchtime and positively hostile towards each other by mid-afternoon. It would also mean that the teachers would not get a proper coffee break in the morning and afternoon, as they would have to supervise children having a 'playtime' in their classroom. The staff, consequently would also be at the end of their tether by the close of school.

In the middle of remembering my own days as a teacher during 'wet break times' I became aware of a man approaching the entrance door.

"Art materials." He announced.

Unsure whether 'Art Materials' was his name or his consignment I replied, "Eh?"

"I'm delivering art materials. This is Hilltop Primary, isn't it?"

"Yes it is. And we did order some art materials. I remember now. Have you got much to bring in?"

"Middlin'."

"Hold on then, I'll get the caretaker to give you a hand. He's got a trolley thing that you can use."

Walt duly arrived with his trolley thing and he and 'Art' set off to the van. Walt enjoyed unpacking vans and complaining that there was nowhere to store anything that was delivered, so this would be a real boon to him.

Before I could return to my original thoughts I was approached by a delegation of parents, mostly mothers, who all wanted to tell me something I should know.

"He's back!" I was informed.

"Who's back?" I asked.

"That weirdo!" they all said in unison.

I was unaware that an additional weirdo existed, being deluded that I had now met them all since my arrival in September. However, this particular weirdo was not a mother, father, granny or other relative. This particular weirdo was a man sitting in his car watching the children.

I had never been keen to embark upon tales of evil strangers. I worried that children might be unnecessarily scared and grow up to be over-suspicious of everyone. Instead, I preferred to tell them that whilst you can trust most people, it can be wise to back off if their conversation or action is not going in a way you feel happy with. I remembered reading that more children die through drowning in a holiday swimming pool whilst their parents are unpacking the cases than through being abducted. And yet we don't tell them that in schools! I also remembered reading that 'Strangers' are not usually the problem. It's more likely to be a perverted uncle or mum's jealous new boyfriend that causes the problems – assuming that it *has* to be man, which it doesn't. So now I was puzzled. What did a man need to sit in his car and watch children for?

"When you say he's back, does that mean he's been here before?" I asked, rather unnecessarily.

"He were here on Sunday. He were walking round and looking through your windows. He's a shifty git, that's what I think." Said the spokesperson, elected for her oral skills.

"Was he still there when you came inside this morning?" I asked.

"He were!" she confirmed.

I suggested we walk up the school drive and find out what the man was doing. I promised that I would speak to him if the mothers would point him out. They duly agreed and we set off to find him. His car was still parked there as we walked up the driveway and the mothers began flexing their muscles and their tongues. They began winding each other up such that by halfway up the drive, he had been promoted from small time pervert to doctor of mass abduction. I became a little concerned that I might not be able to speak to this man as first, I would be unable to get a word in edgeways and second, he might lose interest in my questions once his limbs had been ripped from his torso.

As we neared the end of the drive, he switched on his engine and drove away. The sound of his car was drowned by the screaming and shouting of the gang of mothers who, having now decided he was guilty of planning to abduct a child, were disappointed to have their chance for a good slanging match so cruelly torn away. I made a mental note of his car number and turned back to return to school. The mothers, still in need of donating a tongue-lashing to someone, chose to have a go at me.

Apparently, I should have set off up the drive sooner. I should have walked more quickly. I should have run after his car. I should have worn a blue flashing light on my head and skateboarded after him. And now because of my lack of interest their children were in mortal danger. Maybe some of them were already dead. And all I could do was turn round and go back inside.

I pointed out that if he left *because* he saw us, it would have made no difference what time we set off or how fast we walked. They reluctantly agreed with that statement but still believed I should have chased the car. So then I pointed out that instead of shouting at the man, I took note of his number plate and was now going to check it with the police. That, they conceded, was probably better in the circumstances than standing at the gate and shouting at a car half a mile down the road. I was both reprieved and relieved.

Back inside the building the mail had arrived and there was a rather urgent looking letter that I particularly wanted to read.

Consequently, I gave the car details to Ann and asked her to contact the police. The man's car was a rather old Nissan and was painted in an unusual shade of insipid yellow. I had considered that if he wanted to be anonymous, this was not the car to be seen in. It also had a private number plate, 818 BUU, probably of considerably greater value than the car itself. This would again make the car stand out from the crowd. Ann picked up the phone and began to speak to the police officer on the other end of the line.

"Hello dear!" she said. "It's Hilltop Primary School here, well you know, *I'm* not Hilltop Primary, I'm Ann, the secretary. Now I've been asked to ring you by the Head because he's found a man. No dear, nothing like that! He's a bit worried that we've got a pervert hanging around. It happened once at my daughter's school but he turned out to be a solicitor trying to get parents to put in claims for accidents and things. It's very wrong isn't it! We had an election candidate giving out balloons at the gate last year. They shouldn't…sorry? Oh right, the pervert. It's a funny shade of yellow, you see. His car dear, his car is yellow. A nice one, I think. What make? I don't know, he just said it's a nice one. Oh, a Nissan! I got mixed up with nice one and Nissan. It might still be nice but that's not the point is it! Oh the number, yes we've got that. Have you got a pen? Right, I'll say it slowly. It's eight. Got that? Eight. Got it? Teen. OK? No, eight, eighteen. Eight-one-eight, yes that's right. Yes, there are letters as well but I thought you just wanted the number. Oh, I see. Right, the letters are 'B' double 'U'. No, there aren't any more letters, just the three. No, I haven't only told you two letters, I've told you three, 'B' double 'U'. How do you mean 'W' what? Just double 'U'. No it's three letters. Let me do it again 'B'. That's a bit sarcastic, Bravo. There's nothing clever about saying a letter. Oh it's the thingy that you use. We use those in school when the little ones are learning to read. I'll do that if it makes it easier. OK, Bouncing Ball, Uppy Umbrella, Uppy Umbrella, 'B' double 'U', like I said. Yes, two U's. Oh you thought I said W. No dear, you'll have to listen more carefully. So have you got it now? Good! Can you find out about the car and ring Mr. Jeffcock to tell him whether he's found a pervert or not? You can? Oh I am pleased. Have a good day won't you!"

I hadn't read a word of my letter. Instead, I had stared incredulously at Ann throughout her conversation. She informed me that the officer she spoke to wasn't very bright and she didn't hold out much hope of getting any results. I quietly assumed that, once he had slept for a while and recovered from his conversation, he would be more than competent.

Having finally read my letter and started dealing with its contents, a child knocked on my door at ten past ten. The child had just arrived at school, having been for a hospital appointment. He informed me that as he walked up the drive he had passed a blue van. Somebody was inside the van banging on the door and shouting. The child had been concerned by this unusual event and had rushed inside to bring the matter to my attention. I thanked him and then went out to find out for myself.

The van in question was the Art Materials delivery van. I had suspected that this had long since left the premises and was surprised to find it still parked near the inner gate and even more surprised to note that was rocking vigorously from side to side. Approaching the van I could hear what the boy had described. Someone inside the van was banging on the side and shouting. And one of the voices I recognised as the dulcet tones of Walt.

I opened the side door and there stood Walt and the now legendary Art Materials.

"Did you want something?" I asked.

"Did we want something? Did we bloody want something? I'll tell you this and I'll tell you now and I'll say no more, we did want something. We wanted to get out. Nearly an hour we've been banging in that there van!" Walt exclaimed, unaware that his choice of words could be construed as less than fortunate. To further compound his double-entendre, he added, "I've never know such a pain in t'arse. We're just about out of breath, nah then and I've hit t'side of that van so many times that I've lost count."

Walt and his accomplice climbed out of the passion wagon and breathed a sigh of relief.

"What happened, Walt?" I asked. "How did you end up trapped in the van?"

“A bloody gust of wind blew t’door shut!” he announced. “And then this bloody pancake tells me that his inside handle dropped off last month and no bugger’s got round to fixing it back on. So we were stuck.”

The school was not called Hilltop Primary because it was in a sheltered valley! It was indeed on the top of a hill and could be quite exposed. A gentle breeze in the valley could equate to a gale on our playground and it was quite reasonable that the wind could have slammed the van door. My sympathies were with the delivery man who had spent over an hour trapped in a small space with Walt. He was probably glad of the strong breeze that was still blowing when he emerged from the van.

Walt, however, was not glad of anything. He was in a seriously black mood as would befit a man kept in captivity in a van containing no plumbing or maintenance offerings.

“Buggered up my day completely, this has!” he remarked. “I’ve got jobs to do that can’t wait. I’ve got a new socket to install in t’kitchen. I’ve got things that are coming loose that need tightening. And to cap it all I promised to put a new shelf in Paul’s classroom. Everything were ready and then I got locked in that there van. I’ll tell you this and I'll tell you now and when it's said it's said and I'll say no more, I weren't expecting to get locked in nowt, never mind a van. I shan't be after doing it again in a hurry, nah then, I'll leave it with you."

There was still the matter of bringing the art materials inside and it was amusing to watch Walt carrying out (or indeed, carrying *in*) this process. He and his little trolley approached the van with extreme caution every time a new load was being collected. It appeared that Walt had a fear that the van itself was responsible for his imprisonment and that it might once again wait until he climbed inside and then entrap him amongst the crayons.

"You can get in and pass it all out to me!" he barked at the poor driver. "I'll not be wanting to go in there again and I'll tell you that now, nah then. I've got things to do, I have. And I've not even *started* on my toilet routine!"

"I'm busy as well!" the driver complained. "I've lost nearly half a day's delivery time and you're not the only one who needs to go for a piss!"

"Bloody pancake!" Walt muttered.

"Don't start on me!" the driver advised.

"Well, you can't go about your business when your handle's dropped off! Basic rule of maintenance is that. If something drops off, you stick it back on. It's turned into an Elf and Safety for you, I reckon. I'll tell you this, if you check you'll find that being locked in a van with your egress knackered is an Elf and Safety."

I assumed that a lack of ventilation might also be an issue for the poor man and may well come back to haunt him in later life.

Ann came running out to me at that point with the cordless phone in her hand.

"It's the phone!" she said to me.

"Well done, Ann! You're getting very good at recognising things nowadays, aren't you! To think, only three weeks ago you'd have thought it was a kettle." I answered sarcastically.

"It's for you!" she snapped.

"For me? Oh I couldn't – I've already got one."

"It's the police."

I put her out of her misery and took the call. I was informed by the policeman that the owner of the car was a Matthew Miller who lived about six miles from the school. The police had contacted this man and he had been devastated to learn that his actions looked suspicious. Far from being a prowling pervert, he was a dad who was thinking about moving into the area. He had looked round the outside of the school on Sunday and now, having a day off work, he had wanted to get a look at the school's clientele. He had done this on his own so that he didn't risk wasting my time.

The constable told me that Mr. Miller was happy for the police to pass on his phone number so that I could contact him and so that was done. I called Mr. Miller immediately and we chatted. He apologised for doing his research in a way that aroused suspicion and I apologised for trying to get him arrested. He was reassured by the speed in which the school reported anything that might be a danger to the children and this made him keen to let us take responsibility for his son's education. We arranged an appointment for him to take a proper look round. As it was his day off, this afternoon seemed perfect and we planned a meeting for two-thirty.

It seemed like only a matter of moments before two-thirty arrived and when it did, Mr. Miller arrived with it. He was a smartly dressed man, well-spoken and appeared to be a caring father. Consequently, I was not at all sure he would fit in.

“Thank you for seeing me at such short notice.” He said. “I specifically didn’t want to waste your time looking round if I wasn’t sure about sending my son here. I didn’t realise the problems I was causing. I’ve probably taken up a lot more of your time as a result.”

“Don’t worry. It’s good to know that we’ve got parents who are on their guard.”

“I wouldn’t like to get on the wrong side of them. They shouted some foul things at the gate this morning. At the time I didn’t realise they were shouting at me.”

“They can be a little, shall we say, over-exuberant at times. I think some of them inherit it from their children. But they mean well.”

“Will you tell them who I am? I’d hate to get shouted at if I turn up as a parent one morning.”

“I’m hoping to catch one or two this evening when they collect their children. I’ll tell them that it’s OK and that you’re just a parent looking at the school. The message will get round quickly enough.”

“Thanks, I appreciate it.”

I felt quite sorry for this man. His wife had found herself a boyfriend and then, at the age of thirty-four, had developed a drug habit. As a result, Mr. Miller would not let his son stay with her and her new boyfriend. On the odd occasion when the boy had seen his mother he had been left alone whilst she went out with friends and left to fend for himself. When she came back, she came back to the same house but on a different planet.

He now had a court order to stop his wife from seeing the child and was trying to juggle his job around child care and school. He had decided to move to a house closer to his work and this happened to be in the area of my school. Always suspicious as we headteachers are, I had already found out the name of the child's current school when we spoke this morning. I had since rung the head of that school and checked that there were no hidden secrets that might complicate things. Indeed, the man I spoke to said the boy was delightful, dad was delightful and mum used to be delightful but was now a complete arsehole. My impressions so far gave me no reason to think otherwise.

We chatted for twenty minutes as we wandered around the school. Every classroom at this point in the day was musty and stuffy. The rain had never stopped and so the children had never been outside. The wind had been both wild and cold and our position on the hill meant most rooms had their windows shut. To open them produced the effect of welcoming in a blast of icy cold air which not only caused the inhabitants of the room to freeze, but also picked up papers and thin books, throwing them round the room with abandon. One or two teachers had tried to create the tiniest gap by sliding the windows a matter of millimetres from their frames. The result was a screaming and howling from the wind followed by a screaming and howling from the children who assumed that a ghost was attempting to infiltrate their literacy lessons. Consequently, the air inside each room was stale and smelly and made chloroform seem weak by comparison. Despite this, Mr. Miller found the school a very pleasant place. He liked the attitude of the children and thought they all seemed very happy. I would have to do something about that!

We then ventured very briefly outside. I intended to show him the school field and the playground but at this point our tour took a rather unexpected turn. Mr. Miller had parked his car on the school drive, close to the inner gates. When he had arrived, the drive had been empty but now, at ten past three, it was not. A number of parents persisted in arriving more than half an hour early to wait for their children and to find a good parking space. On wet days they sat in their cars but on fine days they were able to stand at the gate and slag off the school. I called them the Gate Gang.

I had never really taken much notice of which parents were members of the Gate Gang before now. But today I discovered that it consisted of three of my morning visitors. These three ladies had arrived early as usual and then one of them had noticed the distinctive yellow car that belonged to Mr. Miller. Assuming he was prowling around the premises, the ladies had procured lipstick and, incredibly, a can of red spray paint, presumably from the boot of one of their cars, and taken matters into their own hands.

The yellow vehicle was sprayed and daubed with the word ‘Pervert’ in huge letters along each side, and across the bonnet was written ‘Prevert’ which I assumed was an Olde English spelling of the word. Smaller messages written in lipstick abounded on the windows and around the back end of the car. These messages proclaimed ‘Leave our kids all one’, ‘Nobody liks a pervert’ and ‘The driver of this car is a child mole’. On a line below, and a little smaller were the letters ‘ster’ completing the word ‘molester’ from above.

Mr. Miller looked as one would expect him to look. His eyes were almost bulging and his mouth had opened wide, although no words came out. He turned to me whilst at the same time pointing to his car. I felt somewhat cheated that a large question mark had not descended from heaven and hung above his head at this moment. Although I desperately wanted to comment on the atrocious spelling, I refrained out of respect for this poor man who had not only had his vehicle vandalised, but also had to now drive through the streets in it and then convince his neighbours that this was all a mistake.

"I really don't know what to say." I finally said.

"It's not your fault. But I'd like to know who did it!"

"Perhaps I should have phoned some of these mums and told them the situation."

"You shouldn't have to do that. They knew you were tracing the car so they should have worked out that I wouldn't come back if the police had been in touch."

He was right of course. What these parents had done was inexcusable. The trouble is that, like most things connected to a school, people become very emotionally involved if they think their children are in danger or have been badly treated. If you buy a pair of shoes and they fall to bits, you take them back and get a refund and then it's over – it doesn't become personal. But where someone's children are concerned things are different. It can get very personal.

I, of course, should have not subjected Mr. Miller to the possibility of this happening. I was used to things being blown out of proportion when someone's child was unhappy. It went with the job and although it could be stressful, it had to be accepted. Mr. Miller on the other hand, had no hint that this might happen and I couldn't help thinking that I should have asked him to park elsewhere, or wait until I had set the record straight before he visited.

We walked over to his car and he stood looking at the red spray paint. The lipstick would wipe off easily but the paint would not. It was clear that his thoughts were already onto his journey home through town. And there was nothing he could do.

Suddenly, from behind us there was a shout.

"He's there, the bloody pervert!"

Three mums came rushing towards us wielding tongues sharper than swords. Other parents were pushed aside as the mothers made their bid to be first to castrate this poor man. I stood in the way and prepared to protect him. It seemed the least I could do. And I always thought it advisable to do the absolute least.

"Stop!" I shouted. "It's OK!"

"Don't side with him. Get him locked up!" shouted one of the mothers.

"He's looking round the school so that he send his son here." I explained.

"Never! We're not having no pervert's kid mixing with our kids!" the lady yelled.

"He's not a pervert. He was looking at the school and at the type of people who come here."

"What yer talking about? What type of people? What yer mean?"

"He wanted to see if the kids looked friendly. He was interested in whether they behaved well or not. He's found out that the kids behave but the parents don't, hasn't he!"

As she went a little quieter I became aware that Mr. Miller was looking at one of the other members of the gang. The mother in question was vehemently trying to avoid him. She clearly did not want to make eye contact. Eventually, Mr. Miller shouted across to her.

"Linda? Is that you?"

Linda pretended not to hear. She was a huge woman with a temper that could flatten a small nation. I had heard about her before but only in the context of a local public information poem which stated:

> Don't mess with Linda,
>
> Or she'll put you through a winda!

And I had every reason to believe this prophecy to be accurate.

"Linda! It is you, isn't it?" he called once again.

This time she had no alternative but to look round. "Yes." She warbled. "I'm sorry Mr. Miller. I didn't know it was you."

Mr. Miller explained to me that he was Linda's supervisor at work. She was currently on a final warning from those in charge. This was due to her appalling temper and bad language. She had been informed that any further outbursts that came to attention of her bosses would probably mean the end of her job. She came over and stood with him.

"I didn't know it was your car, honest I didn't." she grovelled.

"But I take it to work every day. You must have seen me in it."

"I go on the bus. I don't walk through the car park. I don't know what anybody drives. You've got to believe me. I didn't know it was yours."

"But it looks like you knew it belonged to a pervert. What am I going to do? How can I drive around in that?"

The other mums had stopped to listen. They were feeling very guilty and I sensed they were struggling with the sensation of having their mouths closed for a moment. They knew they had gone too far and they knew that Linda was on the verge of some serious trouble. They'd helped get her into this and now she had a lot to lose, they couldn't help get her back out. Finally Linda turned to Mr. Miller and said,

"Look, my husband's brother does car bodywork. How about I ring him and get him to respray your car. I'll get him to lend you one while it's being done. I'll pay."

"Nice idea, Linda!" I interrupted. "But how's he going to get the car down there? He doesn't want to drive around with 'pervert' painted on it, does he! Can you drive, Linda?"

Mr. Miller smiled.

Linda changed colour.

"OK, you win. I'll drive it down there. Oh God, this'll look great, won't it!"

"Treat it as a learning experience, Linda. After all, that's what people come to school for." I remarked.

I invited Mr. Miller in for a coffee whilst he waited for his replacement car to be delivered.

"As far worst days of my life go, this one's giving me a curious sense of satisfaction." He told me. "Can my little lad start next week?"

Autumn Term: Week 12

Why Chicken Drummers, I asked myself? Why never Chicken Bass Guitarists?

Wednesday was the first of two parents' evenings. Appointments had been made two weeks ago and the children were either excited or terrified about the prospect of their parents meeting their teachers. About half the parents had promised to attend and from experience, around a quarter of that number would forget and an additional twenty parents who had not made appointments would appear out of the blue.

But there was a whole ordinary day to get through before the joys of Parents' Evening began. And the ordinary day began, ordinarily enough, with an early visit from the Mick the Mower Man. Mick worked for the Local Authority Landscape Department and every few weeks he would appear with his tractor and mow the school field and surrounding grass. He had once appeared during a games lesson, sending a class of eight-year-olds fleeing for their lives as his blades careered across the field towards them. They dropped everything and ran and just moments later, a shower of shredded tennis balls rained down on the grass. Mick, with his radio blasting out at full volume in the cab of his tractor, remained blissfully unaware of the mayhem he had caused. As he signed in I was somewhat relieved that his eight-thirty start would avoid such carnage during today's visit. He would be long gone before any games lessons began this afternoon.

I heard his tractor start up and I watched from my office as he began to mow the grass that ran along the driveway into the car park. Remembering that one of the teachers had asked for a patch of grass to be left uncut – either for a scientific experiment or to assist with burying a child – I rushed out to inform Mick of this requirement. Walking towards him I spotted the arrival of Ann the secretary. She was driving into the car park in the new little yellow car she was so proud of, when there was a sudden rattling sound which would have reminded me of a machine gun if I had ever heard one in real life. Ann's car came to an immediate halt and she leapt out and performed a dance for Mick the Mower Man. Initially he continued mowing but then he spotted Ann and waved. Her dance became rather more agitated and Mick assumed that she was requesting his attention. He stopped and opened his door.

By this time I had reached the scene and was becoming aware of the reasons for Ann's gyrations. Mick's mower had picked up numerous pebbles and stones from the area where the grass met the drive. Having picked these items up, his mower had then proceeded to fling them violently at Ann's passing vehicle. Her pride and joy now looked as though it had been driven through a 1920s gang war. It was peppered with chips, all the more noticeable because of the bright yellow paint on the rest of her car.

"You've just sprayed my car!" she informed Mick. "He's just sprayed my car!" she then informed me.

"He has." I answered.

"I haven't!" Mick replied.

"You have." I reaffirmed. "I saw you do it."

"Well, bloody hell!" Mick asserted. "And I'm normally so careful. I don't think I've ever done any damage with this thing before."

The word 'balls' was on my mind but I chose to not mention it.

"Are you sure *I* did it?" Mick asked Ann.

"Yes dear, I'm very sure. I was coming up the driveway and you were in your mowing thingy…"

"Tractor." Mick offered.

"Tractor, yes. And then suddenly I heard a noise, crrrrrrrr. And I felt it hit my car door, ping, ping, ping. And then I got out and opened my door, no, I'll get it right, I opened my door and got out. That was when I saw the mess. Crrrrr, ping, ping. That's what it did."

Mick pulled a tissue out of his pocket and attempted to polish around one of the marks. He looked at Ann as he did so.

"It might polish out if I give it a good rub." He said.

"Looks like it's getting worse to me!" Ann suggested.

Mick turned to look and saw that he had collected in his tissue a tiny piece of grit from the stone chip. This was now producing circular scratches around the area Mick was polishing.

"Bugger me!" Mick announced. "I'm sorry love. I've gone and made a right mess of it now. Have you got a nice clean cloth in the school, I could…"

I interrupted him whilst taking away his tissue.

"Mick, don't try to fix it." I said. "Let's talk to your department's insurance people and they can deal with it."

"You'll need it spraying." Said Mick.

"I thought that's what you'd already done." Ann replied, utterly confused in these matters.

Walt appeared on the scene. He always claimed he could smell a problem from a mile away. Personally, I could never understand how the smell of anything other than his own armpits could get within sniffing distance of his nose.

"Eee, what's happened here. Looks like you've been blasted wi' stones, lass. That'll take some shifting. It's gone through your paintwork has that, I said it's gone through your paintwork. You'll not get that out for a fiver. That'll cost you a fortune will that. Did it happen on your way to work?"

"No, the mower man did it." Ann replied.

"Mick? He's done it? That'll be a black mark, Mick. They might take your tractor off you and send you out to cut all t'school fields wi' a Flymo. If they do, I'll lend you my long extension cable, nah then."

Ann took her car to the car park and Walt explained to Mick about what had happened. He told him how a mower could pick up stones and fling them haphazardly around. He pointed out that this could cause damage to a passing vehicle. Mick listened for a while and then when he could stand no more he made the comment, 'I know, I've just bloody done it!'

The insurers were more than happy to cover the damage to Ann's bodywork and the morning progressed smoothly from that point onwards until the heady hour of eleven thirty-five. At that precise time I was aware of Ann in the office next door shouting to me.
"I can see a big car coming through my window." She called.
"You'd never get a big car through your window!" I replied.
"Besides, it'd make a hell of a mess. Is the car park full?"
Ann explained in immense detail that she had meant to tell me that she could *see* it through her window, not that it was *coming* through her window. I replied that I could now see the car coming through *my* window! When Ann had described this vehicle as a 'big car', I had thought nothing of it, assuming it to be a large family saloon car. But when it came into view I discovered that it was actually a limousine. A black, chauffeur-driven limousine. This was most unusual as I was only expecting a boiler-servicing engineer and I was under the impression that those people still turned up in little vans.
The chauffeur got out of the car and opened the back door. The Lord Mayor and Lady Mayoress climbed out. The Mayor wore his Chain of Office and his wife was suitably attired to accompany him. No

sooner had the car door closed than another smart vehicle pulled up behind it. This one was not quite in the same league as the limousine but was nevertheless very formal and dignified. Its occupants emerged and they, along with the Mayoral party walked towards the school entrance.

I frantically searched through the diary to find out if I was expecting a formal visit from the local dignitaries, but there was nothing written down to suggest this. I racked my brain but could remember no mention of such an occasion being planned. Ann had absolutely no idea, nor did she know anything about the current visit! Was I about to be awarded the OBE? Or sacked? And should I greet these people with the phrase, 'Dur'?

They came into the entrance hall and before Ann or I had time to speak they apologised for being a little early and explained that the others would all be here by midday. It was now time to look a fool and admit that I had no idea whatsoever that these people were coming, or indeed who they were.

"Well, good morning." I said. "I wonder if I could ask you…"

"To sign in? Of course we will. Got to follow the security rules! Ah, look, here's a couple more of them."

Another car rolled into the car park and was discussed by three dinner ladies who were just arriving for work.

"I'm not really sure…" I began.

"Where to put us? Anywhere will do. We'll sit in the entrance if you like. I don't want you to feel we're in the way."

"No, no, it isn't that." I attempted to continue. "It's just that, well, I've been checking the diary and…"

"Another appointment before us? Don't worry, I told you we were early. Carry on with what you were doing. We're not supposed to be here till twelve. Just thought we'd rather be here early than late. It's disappointing for the children if we get stuck in traffic and don't turn up on time. Are they excited, the children?"

"Well actually, I haven't…"

"Haven't made a big deal of it? Best not to, I always think. Keep it till the last minute."

This infuriating man insisted on finishing every one of my sentences for me. And every time he was doing it wrong. As a result, I couldn't explain that we still had no idea what the hell these people were doing here. And then another car arrived and a lady emerged carrying something wrapped in a cloth. The entire party began to make noises which suggested that this was what they had come for and they waited with eager anticipation for the lady to come into the building.

On entering the building she made a number of sounds that resembled the phrase 'fwah, fwah, fwah' and then peeled back the cloth to reveal a plaque. The plaque, a very beautiful piece of brassware, was inscribed with the words,

'The Rotary Club, in association with the Mayor's Office presents this new picnic area, complete with seating for twenty-four children to Hillside Primary School.'

"Shall we pop it on a wall close to the picnic area?" asked the infuriating man.

"No, you'd better not. You see, this isn't…"

"Isn't the best place for it? Well, you suggest a suitable spot, old chap."

"I suggest the best spot would be at Hillside Primary School. This is Hill*top* Primary School."

"Beg pardon?"

"This is Hilltop Primary. Hillside Primary is across the other side of town. It's a little village-type school with seventy kids."

"But why didn't you tell me?"

"Never got the..."

"Never got the chance? I know, I must stop butting in. My wife says it drives her..."

"Mad?" I suggested.

"Indeed! How long will it take us to get across there do you think?"

"About half an hour."

"Well blast and buggery! So much for being early."

The motorcade attempted to leave but found it extremely difficult to turn round in the now crowded car park. All but the limousine left in a great hurry. The chauffeur of the limousine performed an eleven point turn in the record time of four minutes, but embedded the limousine's bumper into Ann's unfortunate stone-splattered vehicle on point nine. The Lady Mayoress ran into school to tell us to put it through the Council's insurance and then ran like the clappers, dived into the limo and sped off down the drive. So very dignified.

Ann, still dazed from seeing her pride and joy become today's pot-shot target, ran out to turn away four other cars over the following five minutes. All four left emitting a vapour trail. The fifth car she attempted to turn away was the man who had come to service the boilers. He was puzzled why a ceremony was being held as normally he just did his job and left. He was even more puzzled that the ceremony was across town but promised he would attend as soon as he had calibrated the pressure sensors.

Inside the school hall, the children knew nothing of the chaos that had just passed. They were innocently tucking into their 'Chicken Drummers'. Why Chicken Drummers, I asked myself? Why never Chicken Bass Guitarists, Chicken Keyboard Players or Chicken Trumpeters? And what was the musical connection anyway?

At the end of the school day the children went home and the teachers either went for a snack in the staff room or drove down to the local sandwich shop to buy something to eat. They had a long evening ahead of them. Intending to join the staff for a drink in the staff room, I set off out of my office but heard the distant belch of Joan the cleaner resonating down the corridor. I then realised she had attempted to shout my name but had belched instead and she was now running to catch up with me.

"Are you OK, Joan?" I asked, assuming that she wasn't.

"No! I've got a serious complaint!" she said.

"Can it be cured?"

"It can if you have a word with that Jenny woman what teaches Year Four!"

"Jenny? What's she done?"

"It's her bloody classroom! It's in a right tip. Normally she's tidy, she is. I'll give her that, I will. She's tidy. Tidy is Jenny."

"I think we're getting in a loop here, Joan. I understand that Jenny's normally tidy but what's the problem?"

"Well, she's normally tidy, but today she's, she's, well, what's the word? Untidy. She's left out all her kids' drawers full of work. She's not got no chairs up on t'desks and she's left books out all over her room. I've had a right job tidying it up. I've got it all put away now but it's taken me ages. I'll not be able to get round my other rooms if she does that sort of thing."

She concluded her complaint by putting her hands on her hips and emitting a belch to rattle the windows.

"Joan, it's parents' evening. Do you remember Walt telling you? The teachers leave out examples of work for the parents to look at. They leave the chairs on the floor for the parents to sit on. It was intentional. They get the children to put everything out before they go home. Now Jenny's gone for a sandwich. Get the chairs back down and when she comes back, she'll have to find the drawers and books and put them out again. And this time she'll have to do it on her own, without the kids' help."

Walt, passing down the corridor at this point, asked the vexed question, 'What's to do?'. On discovering the Joan had cocked up, he comforted her with the words,

"You daft wassock! You bloody pancake! I telled yer it were parents' evening. You don't have to go in a bloody classroom tonight you soft arse! It's worktops and bogs tonight, then we're done. I telled yer it were worktops and bogs. Worktops and bogs I said. I said it on Monday."

Joan promised to see Jenny when she returned and help her find all the books. Jenny was an unpredictable character and I was unsure how she would react to the problem. But the first parents were already arriving so I returned to my office so that people knew where to find me if they wanted me. Most people, of course, simply needed to see their child's teacher and not me so this evening afforded me some time to catch up on jobs that I needed to do.

Watching parents arrive made me smile. Sometimes, the parents were identical to their children in all but size. They had the same hairstyles, the same facial expressions and often the same intonation to their voices. Others who arrived were huge ex-miners, tattooed on every visible part of their body (and their husbands were almost as big!) who transformed from confident, beer-swilling lads into jittering nervous wrecks as they approached the school.

A knock on my door was effected by a Mr. Barnes. He came in and wished to tell me that he disagreed with his son's teacher's comments.

"Have yer gorraminit, headmasster?" he enquired.

"Yes, come in."

"I'm a bit bothered about our Ian's teacher. She says he never listens."

"What, to instructions?"

"Aye. She says that when she's trying to explain things to him, he starts talking to her about summat else. I'm surprised, cos he's a good lad, is our Ian."

"Well it's probably that something sparks off a train of…"

"Have you been to Paris?" he asked, doing precisely what he claimed his son never did!

"Yes, but…"

"Have you been on t'Metro?"

"Yes, but…"

"Well you'll have noticed them there drainage ducts that run alongside t'rails."

"I can't really say I've…"

"I used to make them. I worked in t'factory what made them." He said, proudly. "Well, it's nice to meet you. I'll have to go on account of I've left my dog in t'car and he's incontinent."

I watched him leave and retraced the conversation. I guessed that my mention of a train of thought made him think of trains and this brought us to the Parisian Metro. I decided to not worry about his complaint too seriously.

What I would take seriously, however, was the appearance of the Chair of Governors as he marched towards the door. Without knocking, he flung open my door and barked at me.

"Thought I'd put in an appearance!"

He explained that he intended to set out a chair and table in the hall and sit on ceremony. He would introduce himself as Chair of Governors and let the parents meet him and discuss any concerns with him. He proudly showed me a sign that he had made to inform people of the reason for his solitary chair in the hall. I was not impressed by him doing this but had no authority to stop him.

As the minutes passed, so did the people. No-one stopped to talk to him and most studiously ignored him as they walked through the hall. The exception to this rule was one middle-aged father who had quite clearly had a little too much to drink before embarking on his visit to the school.

"Warra you doin' sittin' here?" he slurred.

"I'm the Chair." Came the reply.

"You're a chair? You're bloody dafter than I am!"

"No, no, I'm the Chairman of the Governors."

"My mate's a chairman at the club. He stacks 'em away every night and gets 'em out next day. Is that what you do?"

"No, I don't deal with chairs, I…"

“Well then, you’re not a bloody chair man, are you! I’ve come to see Mrs, Mrs, one of the teachers. I’ve come to find out how our Kyle’s getting on. Who’s class is he in?”

“I really have no idea!”

“You’re no bloody use at all you aren’t. You’re sitting here telling everybody you’re a chair and you know nowt. I’m not standing here talking to a bloke that thinks he’s a piece of furniture and then doesn’t even know our Kyle’s teacher. I think I’ll find t’headmasster and ask him who she is.”

He walked away and as he passed a couple heading the opposite way through the hall he stated,

“Watch him! He’s a bloody nutter. He thinks he’s a chair. I reckon if he is, he’s one of them there commodes ‘cos he’s full o’ crap.”

I pointed the gentleman in the right direction for Kyle’s teacher and decided to stay close by to ensure he didn’t outstay either his welcome or his bladder. That was when I heard a scream from the Year One classroom. Fearing that an aggressive parent had become violent, because a parents’ evening rarely goes by without such an incident, I rushed into the room. I discovered Mrs Johnson, a heavy, heavily pregnant lady reposing in the most curious of positions. She had attempted to sit on a small plastic chair to look at her daughter's books. Her weight, coupled with the age of the chair had broken the welds that held the plastic seat on to the metal legs. As a result, the seat had slid backwards off the legs, taking Mrs, and Embryo Johnson with it. At first glance I assumed she was partaking in a rehearsal for the birth-giving process until the true extent of the situation dawned on me. Fortunately, she found the episode highly amusing and apologised for trying to sit on a chair that was made only for small children. I offered to make her a cup of tea, as this appeared to be the only compensation she might require.

As I returned with the promised cup of tea I wheeled in an adult sized swivel chair in a gesture to show that subjecting heavily pregnant women to experiences reminiscent of an earth tremor was not a regular occurrence. She accepted the tea and the chair as gracefully as might be expected from someone in her condition and then continued her discussion with the teacher. I, however, did not stay in the room because my next disaster was commencing down the corridor. So much for catching up with the jobs!

The newest disaster to hit the building was a rather aggressive slanging match. Many parents had stopped to listen, thinking that we had been innovative and provided entertainment whilst people waited for their appointments. Central to this aggression were three parents, a man and two women. The man was a rather scrawny looking character wearing an old leather jacket and shabby jeans. He was thin and had receding greasy hair and a moustache that was decidedly not receding. The women were both fearsomely overweight and were seemingly equipped with built in radio microphones. It appeared that this weedy gentleman was an object of desire for both of these women. As I approached I became aware that one woman, the fat one, was his wife. The other woman, the fat one, was his lover for whom he had left his wife. Both women had children in the same class at school and both had been given consecutive appointments. This had not been a wise move.

I asked if they could lower their voices so as not to create so much of a disturbance.

“Piss off! It’s our bloody argument!” one of the large ladies suggested.

I invited them to continue their discussion outside but they, in turn, invited me to carry out an anatomically impossible experiment upon myself.

They began to get physical. Whilst getting physical had probably been the cause of their troubles originally, it was now taking a different turn. The physical session this time involved pushing and shoving. The little man was sent reeling into a mother and father who were trying hard to ignore the fracas. He apologised, stood up and was then clouted over the head by his wife's handbag which sounded like it contained a few cans of lager. The wife made a comment to him about his seemingly constant search for a bit on the side and I quietly mused that he actually appeared to have rather a lot on the side. The 'bit on the side' took exception to the wife's comments and the ladies then began pushing each other forcefully. This ultimately resulted in a display cabinet being wrenched of a wall by a passing bosom. I decided to call the police as there seemed to be no stopping this rather exuberant discussion and innocent people were on the verge of being hurt. I refrained from reporting the incident as an out of control bosom and instead described it as more of a rapid-fire sumo contest.

In a matter of minutes the police arrived. Two squad cars had been deployed, leaving me to assume that they would come back later for the little man. As the officers entered the building seven parents ceased waiting for their appointments and departed rapidly. Simultaneously, quickly moving footsteps could be heard on the roof as a gang of spaced-out teenagers left a makeshift campsite. I had no idea they were there. Maybe they lived there permanently or perhaps this was just a temporary stop in their search for the perfect snorting spot.

The two love rivals gave each other a last punch before their imminent arrest. The wife was thrown backwards into a desk, crushing both the desk and a chair as she fell. She let out a scream and remained motionless on the floor. The closest officer assessed the situation and decided she had broken her leg. He called for an ambulance and led the other two miscreants away and out of the building. One officer remained with the broken leg and its owner until the ambulance arrived.

Two paramedics entered the building with a stretcher. They looked at the huge lady lying on the floor. They then looked at each other and finally at the stretcher. The stretcher was laid on the floor and carefully they attempted to put the woman onto it. Suggesting that the position of the lady was difficult for them, they enlisted help from three dads nearby. The efforts of all five resulted in the lady being deposited on the stretcher

With a paramedic at each end of the stretcher, it was now time to take the lady to the ambulance. But as they grunted and struggled, they found that lifting the lady from her position on the floor was not going to be easy. As they raised the handles of the stretcher, they were aware that it was bending in the centre. As her head and feet left the floor, her well-endowed middle regions remained firmly planted on the ground. She was slowly raised higher as perspiration poured from the foreheads of the paramedics. The stretcher wobbled precariously from side to side as the party began to inch forward. The woman, screaming in pain was now ignored by the two stretcher-bearers who appeared by this time to be in considerably more pain than their patient.

I walked with them to the ambulance, convinced that she would drop to the floor before the end of her journey. As we passed the hall I caught sight of the Chair of Governors still sitting there, alone. Not once had he tried to find out why parents had been fighting, why the police arrived or why an ambulance was called. And as I passed by he shouted to me, "I'm going to call it a night. It's been pretty

uneventful really but I felt I had to give it a shot. What time will you be finishing?"
"Whenever the last teacher finishes." I replied.
"Have you managed to read that new LEA policy on Governor Training this evening?"
"Funnily enough, I haven't!"
"You'll really have to prioritise a little more."
I was about to make an angry remark when it happened. There was a shout of 'Shit' and a thump. I rushed out of the hall to find the paramedics had dropped their huge patient in the main entrance. She was howling with pain but nothing was broken – the chairs and tables were all intact. I called to the Chair of Governors to help and between us we placed the woman back on the stretcher and helped get her to the ambulance. The Chair of Governors asked me if I knew what had been going on but I pretended to not hear him. I simply couldn't be bothered to listen to his pontificating about how a parents' evening should *really* be organised.
Jenny was the last teacher to finish for the evening. Her last appointment ended at nine forty-five. As I prepared to lock the school up she said, "Thanks for waiting. It's strange isn't it, how

these evenings are so hectic for the class teachers and yet for you they must be incredibly boring. I bet it feels like you've been here for days, doesn't it?"

"Oh, I keep myself busy!" I replied. "There's usually something to do."

Autumn Term: Week 13

"We've had a break in."

"Did the alarms go off?" I asked.

"No, they've bloody nicked 'em!" Walt replied.

It was December. We could no longer put off the onset of Christmas. Once the decorations were up there would be no chance of the children concentrating on anything that seemed remotely reminiscent of school work. We had studiously ignored the switching on of the town's Christmas lights and we had paid no attention to the local shops' decorations which went up in late October, but now it was December and we had to concede that Christmas was close. We had to accept that the children would surpass being as high as kites, many would be so high that they would look down on orbiting satellites. And this excitement, coupled with increasing tiredness as the eight-week term dragged on, would result in arguments and fights. And parents, already tired of their hyped-up children and dreading the prospect of a school holiday would come in their droves to complain about the behaviour of other children. And I would, tired as I now felt, be accommodating and polite and listen to their every word, knowing that they simply needed a place to vent their frustration. And then I would walk away and kick something. Yes, the Season of Goodwill was upon us.

On Monday afternoon our own Christmas presents arrived. Eight new computers were delivered at one-thirty. I had ordered these a few weeks ago, to replace some clapped-out models that were gathering dust in certain classrooms. The order had cost far more than I could afford from the school budget, but legislation dictated that I must have a set number of Internet-accessible computers according to the number of children in the school. Interestingly, no legislation dictated a set number of teachers for that same number of children, so if all else failed, I could sack some teachers in order to buy additional computers. Perfect educational sense!

I had decided to set the computers up myself as this was cheaper than having it done professionally. Besides, by the fifth one, I would be able to do it with my eyes closed and then I would be able to go back to the first two and set them up properly. I had managed to install three by the end of Monday and the children were very excited to see the boxes being unpacked and shiny new computers being set up on their desks. The old wrecks were left on the floor for

Walt to dispose of when he had the time, which wouldn't be till Thursday because he had a serious sanitary situation that required his urgent attention.

So a busy week was in store. Tuesday would see the rest of the computers installed and this would coincide with the delivery of the Christmas tree, which would be placed in the hall and decorated profusely. I planned to do no real work on Tuesday. This was no different to any other day except for the fact that doing no work had this time been *planned.*

Arriving at school on Tuesday I was greeted by Walt.

"You'll not be happy!" he cheerily commented.

"Good morning, Walt. Why not?" I replied.

"We've had a break in. They've smashed a window in Year Three and the buggers have infiltrated us."

"Did the alarms go off?" I asked.

"No, they've bloody nicked 'em!" Walt replied.

"They've stolen the burglar alarms?" I asked incredulously.

"Smart buggers. They know more about these things than we think. They disconnected all your outside units before they got in. I don't know how they did it but they didn't trigger a bloody one. They must be experts."

"So what have they taken, apart from the alarm system?"

"I don't know properly. I've only just discovered it a few minutes ago."

I had a horrible feeling inside. I pretty much knew that a child would have gone home and told someone about the new computers and some weasel in their family would have decided to break in and take them away. And some were still in their boxes.

There appeared to be no evidence of theft as I walked along the corridor. I peered into a few classrooms along the way and everything seemed to be in order. The rooms where the new computers had been installed were fine and I was becoming a little puzzled about the whole situation.

On reaching the Year Three room I went inside and found, as Walt had described, a broken window and a badly damaged lock on the fire escape door where someone had tried to force it. I rushed to the corner where I had yesterday installed the new computer. Yes, the thieves had been inside. They had taken a portable CD player, the video machine from the TV trolley and the computer was gone.

But not the *new* computer! The knackered old wreck that had been left on the floor was the prize that our bungling burglars had chosen. Walt would not have to find room in the bin for this particular pile of rubbish as our visitors had kindly removed it for us.

Walt decided to carry out an inspection of the school whilst I contacted the police and reported the robbery. No sooner had I put the phone down than Walt appeared at my office door once more.

"I've had a quick climb up on me roof. They've smashed a skylight window. Might have been when they ran across."

"Which room does it belong to? There'll probably be some clearing up to do."

"I reckon it's that Visible Room. It'll be alright cos nobody uses it much."

The 'Visible', or Audio-Visual Room as it was correctly called, was a curious little place. It had been included in the original design of the school back in the days when just one television would have sufficed for everyone, and when programmes were watched 'live'. The room had a strong door with a lock and it had no windows, thus permitting intense darkness for watching TV. It was currently hardly used because pairs of classes now had a TV and video to share. The room thus remained empty, save for an occasional wet painting left to dry there.

"Well, we'd better go and see if there's any mess to clear up." I said. "I don't want somebody walking in there and getting sliced by a sharp piece of perspex from that roof light."

"I'll get me brush. I'll need a long-handled, hard-bristled model and an eight-inch dustpan. That should make a clean job of it."

"Whatever!"

Walt selected the optimum brush for the job and I accompanied him to survey the damage. Walt had his huge bunch of carefully colour-coded keys and selected the one labelled 'Visible Room'. He unlocked the door.

On the floor was shattered perspex from the roof light. But in the corner were two men aged about twenty-five. They had jumped in through the roof light and once on the ground they had discovered that they were in a locked room with no windows. The room was devoid of desks and chairs to climb on and the roof was too high to help each other up to their only means of escape. They had broken in and caged themselves. They tried to make a run for the door so Walt and I slammed it shut and locked it once more. Amidst the frantic banging from behind the door I assured Walt that the police would be here very shortly.

Upon their arrest they explained that having removed the computer and hidden it under a hedge, they remembered that the school had a room full of TV and video equipment, which it had when they attended as children fourteen years ago. They could remember the layout of the building and so they carefully chose the right room but assumed that it would contain furniture like it did in the past.

As it had rained the previous night, the stolen heap of computer junk was now even further from salvation and all in all their mission had been less than successful. But I was puzzled how a couple of electrical wizards, with the ability to disable a sophisticated alarm system, could cock up quite so spectacularly.

“Disable it?” one of them answered, “I just ripped the bugger of the wall. I thought it’d go off but it didn’t, so I ripped all t’rest off just to be sure. They’re under that hedge wi t’computer. Do you want ‘em back?”

I didn’t answer. I simply smiled as the arresting officer led the two gentlemen away. And then I spent the morning installing the remaining computers and scrawling security markings on them in permanent ink.

"You want one of them there invisible pens for that job!" Walt announced as he wandered past on his way to a cistern.

"I know, but I couldn't see any!" I joked.

"I've got one I can lend you." Walt replied, missing the joke altogether.

"No, I don't really want one. Can't see the point!" I said. "By the time they realise it's been marked, they've already nicked it. I prefer permanent markers because you can see it's been marked before you try to take it. Theoretically, that should mean you *don't* take it."

"Well bugger me backwards with a broomstick handle! I never thought o' that." Walt thoughtfully responded.

The end of lunchtime brought the arrival of a huge Christmas tree. With it came a whole new learning experience for me as I had to become acquainted with the Christmas customs in the school. Traditionally, the arrival of the tree prompted a decorating session which included the involvement of the oldest class of children in the school. By the end of the afternoon the tree would be completed and then the entire staff would congregate in the hall to decorate the walls and ceiling in an ingenious manner which would be explained to me later. I had also learned that mince pies would be heated up in the staff room during these festivities. All told, it should be an enjoyable – and relatively trouble-free – afternoon.

After clearing away the lunch tables, Walt procured a large bucket in which to sit the tree. Ann and three dinner ladies joined us in our quest to stand the enormous tree vertically in a corner of the hall. This went surprisingly well and once the tree was upright, Walt secured it to the walls using rope. It was now time to enlist the help of the children.

The oldest children in the school were in Alan Barnett's class. Alan was a very serious sort of man possessing the kind of personality that took many months to understand. Many of his pupils still were not sure how to react to him even though they had known him for almost a term. He was a keen teacher and always inspired his pupils but he found life in general very difficult to cope with once outside the security of his curriculum plans. Consequently, this afternoon was one which he had approached with a sense of foreboding. An afternoon of allowing his class, unplanned, to decorate a tree did not fit comfortably into his schemes and plans and for his own part, he had absolutely no wish to be associated with such frippery.

Alan glumly led his excited pupils into the hall. There was a buzz of anticipation amongst the children. Not only was this an afternoon without work, it was also a privilege for which the children had waited since they first joined the school.

"I don't see why the children have to do this." Alan groaned to me. "They only get the chance to hang a couple of baubles and they spend all afternoon wondering where to put them. I could be getting through the Science work this afternoon. It'd be a lot more profitable."

"It's one of those special things, Alan." I replied. "They look forward to it. They tell their parents that they decorated the tree and pretend they did it single-handedly. Besides, one afternoon out of a whole year won't destroy their education. And if we're honest, it'll only take half an hour."

"It's still disruptive. I can't see the value in it. I'm sorry, but I'm not a lover of frivolity. There's too many people going around trying to enjoy themselves at every end and turn. They've got no structure, no direction. Headlong into trouble, that's where it takes them."

“You’re not a party animal, are you Alan!”

“I wouldn’t like you to think I’m miserable because I’m not. It’s just that fun doesn’t appeal. I’m not a lover of fun. I prefer order.”

“Well, just remember, it’s only one afternoon.”

“The thin end, that’s what it is. And once you get a thin end in, it gets bigger. And it’s harder to get it back out than to get it in in the first place. I’m not a lover of getting thin ends in.”

I asked the children to wait for a few moments whilst Walt climbed his step ladder to the secret cupboard. The hall was panelled with wood and one section of the wood was a cleverly concealed door to a high level storage space, about ten feet above the floor at its lowest point. Walt climbed his ladder and swung the door open and the children gasped in amazement, having never noticed the cupboard before.

Sadly, this meant they watched Walt’s every move from this point on. With the cupboard door open, Walt’s very next move was to enter the storage space. Whilst not small, the space was not huge and Walt entered head first, leaving his not inconsiderable backside protruding through the doorway and eclipsing the light from the windows as it wriggled its way inside. The children giggled and Alan looked on disdainfully.

"I take it you're not a lover of fat backsides squeezing through small gaps!" I whispered to him.

"It's not what I went into teaching for and that's for sure." He replied.

"Still, it's a different slant on your thin end, isn't it!" I joked.

I climbed part-way up the ladder and offered to take the boxes of decorations from Walt as he passed them down. I asked Alan to stand at the bottom of the ladder and take the boxes from me and place them on the floor. Whilst he had no written action plans for this event, Alan performed his task very well, creating a very ordered pile of boxes on the floor, very much unlike the pile I would have created. Walt, by now enjoying himself immensely in the cupboard, had reached the pile of tinsel and as he passed out his next box, a piece of shiny red tinsel had attached itself to the box. As Walt let go of the box, the tinsel dropped and draped itself beautifully around Alan's head and shoulders. A roar of laughter from the children only served to embarrass Alan even further.

"You look gorgeous, Mr. Barnett!" I called out.

“It isn’t funny. I do not enjoy being draped in décor!” and he tugged it forcefully off his body. The small amount of tinsel that had come loose and entangled in his beard was mentioned by no-one. An unspoken conspiracy had caused us all to leave Alan to wander around for the rest of the afternoon with metallic red highlights in his facial hair, reflecting his exuberant personality.

The boxes were now all on the floor and Alan had returned to a position close to his children, his beard shimmering in the moist winter sunshine. How I would have loved to have added a few fairy lights to that beard, but I guessed he would not have taken it well. Ann beckoned me to answer a phone call and as I left the hall I was unaware that Walt was reversing out of his cupboard. I was also unaware that his left leg was swinging back and forth in search of the ladder. And then I became aware that the children were all looking at something and as I turned round I watched Walt strike the ladder full on. It wobbled and then began to fall. This huge triangle of ladder, twelve feet at its highest, toppled and landed with an uncomfortable smash on three boxes of glass baubles. Bits of bauble flew in all directions and the children shielded their eyes. Walt was hanging from his cupboard with his left leg dangling, his backside poking out of the door and his right knee rested on the cupboard floor. The words 'shit' and 'bollocks' were being emitted from inside the cupboard at regular intervals, much to the children's amusement.

"Help me get that ladder back up!" I shouted at Alan. He trickled into action as we pushed the ladder back to where Walt was dangling.

"Chaos!" Alan commented. "No structure, you see. You can be sure of impending disaster when there's no structure to the activity. I'm a real lover of structure. I like everything in its place." He said, his beard still catching the light each time his head turned.

Safely on the ground, Walt regained both his breath and his odour and then set about sweeping up the broken glass. The children began placing the baubles from the surviving boxes on the tree and Alan looked on and checked his watch at regular intervals. With thirty-two eleven-year-olds working with great enthusiasm, it wasn't long before the lower part of the tree was fully, if not altogether tastefully, decorated. The upper parts of the tree had to be dealt with by adults because the use of a ladder was required and Walt was preparing the lights and tinsel.

"Got to PAT test me fairy lights." He announced, producing his little machine that he had been trained to use on a City and Guilds course two years ago. He was very proud of being able to do his own PAT testing and informed me many times just how much money his skill was saving the school. "A few quid an item!" he would often bark. "Think how many items we've got in here. It'd cost you hundreds, maybe more. Think on when it's pay rise time, I'm saving you a fortune! I'll leave it with you." He was right, of course, but I usually just smiled and nodded. I would make no commitments to future finances before I knew the exact figures.

Walt and I draped the lights over the tree and Alan stood thoughtfully, planning tomorrow afternoon's history lesson. We switched on the lights to test them and the children said, "Aah!".

Alan, clearly trying to be a part of the situation looked up and said, "Ah yes, the lights are on. Children, the lights are on. Very effective. Right, back to the classroom, we've got things to do."

Ann appeared with the mobile phone for me to take another call and whilst I spoke, I took note of Walt showing great interest in being in charge of the fairy that went on the top of the tree. By the end of my call, the step ladder was in position behind the tree and Walt, fairy in hand was making his ascent. I returned the phone to Ann and we stood and watched Walt emerge over the top of the tree. As his head appeared from behind the highest branches I called out, “God, that’s an ugly fairy!” and Walt responded using the well-known fairy retort, “Bollocks!”

After the children had left school for the day it was time to involve the whole staff in decorating the top half of the tree and putting streamers and decorations around the hall. Gillian had switched on the oven in the staff room and was taking charge of the mince pie situation. Everyone else was doing decorative things, except Alan, who was moaning.

“It’s really not an efficient use of my time. I’m not a lover of wasted time. Minutes are valuable commodities, you know. There are so many things I could be doing and instead I find myself here being involved in frippery. I’m not a lover of frippery.”

“So shut up and get on with it so you can go home!” Jenny snapped. “And get that daft bit of tinsel out of your beard!”

“What bit of tinsel? Nobody told me I had tinsel in my beard. How long has it been there? Have I been walking round with tinsel in my beard all afternoon? I don't like to look foolish. I'm not a lover of looking foolish."

"Alan, you've got a big bushy beard!" said Jenny. "You can't claim to be concerned about your appearance with that thing attached to your face!"

Alan went to look in a mirror to find out how foolish he looked with his metallic adornment and I listened to Paul's instructions regarding the streamers. Paul was the Art Co-ordinator and always came up with novel ways of making things look impressive. His plan was to attach thin streamers to a hoop which would be hoisted up, on a pulley, in the centre of the hall. The other end of the streamers would be stapled to the wall of the hall and when the central hoop was raised the effect would resemble the inside of a colourful tent. It was a superb idea, but rather time consuming. However, with as many step-ladders, chairs and tables as we could collect, we stapled the streamers to the walls.

Paul had climbed to ceiling height and fitted up a pulley system that could be tied off at the edge of the hall. He attached strong string to the hoop and the streamers were tied in place. We were just about to raise the hoop when the phone rang. The phone, however, was not where we expected it to be. As it persisted in ringing we homed in on the sound and discovered that it was coming from the Christmas tree. Indeed, the mobile handset was lodged four feet up, in a bushy branch, where Ann must have lodged it earlier in the afternoon. This time wasting caused Alan to pontificate once more.

He stood in the middle of the floor commenting that he was not a lover of lost phones and that he really did want to hurry up and finish because he had a lot of work to do when he got home. He was so carried away in his speech that he didn't notice Paul begin to raise the hoop. Nor did he notice the yellow streamer that was positioned between his legs. The hoop began to rise and the streamer pulled tight in the crotch of Alan's trousers. Alan stood bolt upright and let out a whoop.

"Stop! Stop!" he yelled. "Inconvenient moment. I have a streamer between my legs! Shouldn't be there."

A burst of laughter issued forth from the staff.

"This really is becoming tiresome. I can't afford to have Christmas decorations affixed to my nether regions, it plays havoc with the concentration. Get it away from me!"

Clearly Alan's detailed plans for the day had not involved Christmas decorations being put up his arse and this was causing him to have to reassess the progress of his day's work.

But in a handy twist of fate, his complaints were interrupted by Gillian who suddenly shouted, "Bugger, I've forgotten the mince pies!"

Indeed she had, and we ran to the staff room to try to rescue the situation. The room smelled of burning and as the oven door was opened, thick, black smoke filled the room. The pies were burnt to a cinder, blacker than soot and probably not terribly tasty. The smoke reached the ceiling at a remarkable rate and set off a piercing alarm. Within seconds Walt was on the scene armed with a fire extinguisher with which he provided an unappetising foam topping to the evening's delicacies.

"Have I put it out?" he yelled, above the noise of the alarm.

"Yes Walt. We're out of danger. You've saved us. You're a hero!" I remarked.

"What was it? An electrical fault?"

"No, a mince pie."

"A mince pie? I've extinguished a bloody mince pie?"

"With gusto."

"I'm not bothered what flavour it was! It were a waste of foam. I'll have to get that refilled now and that'll be a bugger. It always is. How did a bloody mince pie set t'smoke alarms off?"

"Gillian forgot to get them out of the oven"

"Bloody pancake!"

"No Walt, bloody mince pie!"

"Aye well, now you know what you get when you let a bloody pancake cook a mince pie. It's an elf and safety. I'll have to get me log and put it in. I don't know what I'll write. Fire extinguisher required for burning mince pie. That's what I'll put."

He rushed off on his new mission, racing past Jenny and Alan who were getting ready to go home.

"Where's he going in such a hurry?" Jenny asked.

"He's gone for his log!" I announced.

"Oh, it's very good of him but I'm not a lover of chocolate." Alan remarked. "It doesn't really matter that the mince pies were ruined. Well, not for me personally. I'm not a lover of mince pies."

"He's gone to get his Health and Safety Log, not a bloody yule log, Alan!" I moaned, getting very close to the end of my patience.

“Ah, goodnight then.” He said.

“Goodnight Alan.”

“Got to call to the supermarket before getting on with my work.”

He walked out of the building, excited at the prospect of planning tomorrow’s lessons, blissfully unaware that someone had pinned a green tinsel tail to the back of his jacket.

Autumn Term: Week 14

The collision between Jesus and the shepherd was considerable and the shepherd suffered a nose bleed, a rather less severe injury than that sustained by the Christ Child, whose head flew off and landed in the audience.

Christmas was edging closer and with it came the traditional events in the school calendar. Next week, the final week of term would see the delights of the party season and the compulsory visit from Santa, but this week, the penultimate week of term, was performance week. Rehearsals for the Christmas concerts had been taking place for approximately the last four decades, at least that was how it felt to me. I knew every line of the scripts and every song, having heard them incessantly for the last three weeks. I even woke up in the night playing the part of the donkey, but that could be badly construed so nobody was told about it. The teachers had decided upon the themes for the concerts back in early October and by the end of the half term holiday the scripts were ready. Surreptitious rehearsals then took place from early November. Whilst the normal curriculum should have been continuing, teachers cajoled their pupils into sneaky, under the counter preparation for the approaching festivities. If I took to wandering around school and happened to enter a classroom, the rehearsal would miraculously turn into a Literacy lesson, a Music lesson, or even a Technology activity. The entire school, it seemed, was conspiring against me in pretending to be working as normal but in reality, indulging in major theatrical rehearsal.

There were to be two main concerts. The infants would perform on Tuesday afternoon and the junior children would execute, in every sense of the word, their performance on Tuesday evening. Official rehearsals had taken place for the last three weeks, when the hall was commandeered for musical variety purposes by each department. Curiously, the weather had taken a turn for the worse during this period also.

And now it was Tuesday morning. The big day had finally arrived, the children were suitably excited and the staff were suitably panic-stricken. The junior department had planned to have a final rehearsal in the morning, the infants had completed their last practice yesterday and their failure or success was now in the lap of the gods.

In the midst of all this it had fallen to Walt to put out the huge, wooden stage blocks each morning, clear them away and put out the dining tables each lunch time and then replace the dining tables with the huge stage blocks each afternoon. This process clearly had a detrimental effect on the amount of love he could lavish on his urinals and, consequently his mood during the run up to Christmas, was very black indeed. He had informed me on numerous occasions that things like bloody Christmas cock up your routines and cause a lot of extra work. He failed, therefore, to understand why schools had to waste their time bothering about Christmas when the telly did it for them perfectly well. He had also taken the opportunity to add that he held a similar level of enthusiasm for Easter, sports day and after-school football matches. Yes, the only Christmas spirit Walt had in mind was a stonking great bottle of whisky, nah then.

And so it was that the entire junior department assembled in the hall at nine-fifteen, shrouded in curious costumes made from old curtains or stolen from senile family elders. This was the dress rehearsal for their Victorian Music Hall Christmas Extravaganza, a snappy title if ever there was one. I had intended to sit in and watch this delight but my time was instead encroached upon by Gillian. Her infant concert was, she informed me, doomed. It appeared that the children playing three of the main parts in her Nativity play had fallen ill. She did not even smile at my comments regarding the curse of a certain Shakespearean play but instead quickly retrieved the phone numbers of these poor, sick mites, to enquire whether they might be planning to attend this afternoon.

They were all too ill to attend this afternoon. The young lady who was to play Mary had been vomiting since two in the morning. Morning sickness being out of the question, she was confined to a sofa and had to be given liberal doses of children's TV. She would remain thus for the next two days. The boy who was in line to play Joseph had found himself in casualty, having inhaled a small magnet that he had chosen to attach to the inside of his nostril. This, I concluded, would not have been a good example to set his rather important new-born son and so a short spell of recovery until the problem 'passed' may, in the long term, be the best option. Lastly, the innkeeper had developed a nasty case of food poisoning, bringing into question the standards of hygiene at his hostelry. Consequently, the forecast was for our alternative Mary and her new boyfriend to give birth to their child at the local Holiday Inn whilst taking advantage of special midweek rates for stays of two or more nights.

Gillian replaced the telephone handset and rushed back to the infant department to attempt to train three children to play these vital roles in her concert. I attempted to walk to the hall to watch the junior rehearsal but was once again sidetracked. This time, the reason for my change of plan centred around the arrival of Reverend Bob. He had come to offer his services for the last assembly of the term, next week.

"I hate Christmas!" he somewhat surreally informed me. "It's non-stop in my job. Services for this, services for that, Christingles, Carol Services, it never ends. And that's before you get stuck with Midnight Mass, Morning Service on Christmas Day, Boxing Day Services. Bloody ridiculous, you never get a break! I've got three on the big day, I have. Three! Some merry sodding Christmas that'll be!"

"I suppose it kind of goes with the job though, doesn't it?" I commented. "I mean, you tend to know that Christmas will be fairly hectic for a vicar."

“Hectic? I could cope with hectic. It’s Christmas I can’t handle. It’s a different speed altogether is Christmas. And everybody expects you to be full of the bloody joys. I’ll be glad when it’s over. Get back to normal and have a rest.”

“Bah, humbug, eh?”

“I’m with him on that one!” the vicar replied. “Anyway, I’m going off the subject. I’ve come to see if you want me to do a special assembly on your last day…”

My mind had drifted. I was imagining the assembly he might do. ‘Good morning children, it’s nearly bloody Christmas. Christmas is a time for giving and sharing and it’s also a time for never getting a bloody minute to yourself. You think you’ve got it bad because your granny’s visiting? Let me tell you what I’ll be doing. I’ll be preaching the same sodding service over and over again until I’m well and truly pissed off with it…’. I began trying to check that there was no way Walt could have disguised himself to play a huge trick on me, but Reverend Bob was considerably narrower and was not nasally detectable from across town.

And so it was agreed that Bob would visit us on the last day and would absolutely not throw out sweets or suggest that he had small furry things living in his trousers. He understood my concerns and gave me his assurance that my comments would be heeded. I explained that I really had promised to see the junior dress rehearsal and that I should have been in the hall fifty minutes ago. He offered to join me because he enjoyed watching children perform, he explained.

As we walked to the hall he attempted to show interest in the progress of our concerts. "How's it all going?" he asked.

"Very well, I think." I hesitantly replied.

We arrived at the hall as the children were about to stop for a break. Celia Short, our drama expert had decided to give them all an encouraging team-talk before they dispersed. Bob and I stood quietly in the doorway so as not to disturb her.

"Useless!" she bawled. "I have never seen you perform so pathetically since we first started rehearsals. I can't hear a word you're saying. You're all mumbling at the floor. You're bumping into each other, forgetting to bring your props on, forgetting your lines, it's rubbish. And if you've sung one song in tune this morning, I must have missed it, probably when I fell asleep through boredom!

When you come back in from your break it will be a hundred times better and if it's not you'll rehearse through your lunch break."

I looked at Bob and smiled. "As I said, it's coming on really well." I decided not to stay and watch the second half of the rehearsal.

As soon as lunch was over the hall was set out for the infant concert. Masses of parents arrived as early as possible in order to get a good seat from which to wave to their children and thus cause them to forget their lines. Gillian had set up her raffle once more, despite my serious misgivings about the legality of it. I was rather nervous about confronting her again over this issue in case it was revealed that this was only the tip of an iceberg. She could be a supplier of crack cocaine or other narcotics and indeed, they could be the raffle prizes, but I preferred to not know.

As the hall filled to bursting point I figured I just had time to make a quick visit to the Gents' before my introductory speech. It was peaceful in the Gents'. I had often given consideration to spending entire days in there with its prominent lack of telephones, computers and most of all, people. It would, I had mused, be perfect for me. It had somewhere to sit and I could install a kettle in an appropriate spot. I could even have my lunch there bearing in mind that Walt had so many times informed me how agreeable it would be to eat out of the urinals. My thoughts drifted to the peace and tranquillity of it all as I stood facing one of the aforementioned urinal-cum-tureen combinations. Outside this room was a hectic, heaving mass of proud parents and crying children and yet here, in the bog, life was as relaxed as it was ever likely to become. And then the automatic flush made a screeching sound and sprayed my trousers. A horribly embarrassing wet patch appeared on the light-coloured trousers and I knew that, contrary to the tasks carried out on a normal day, my next job was to stand up on the stage in front of two hundred and fifty parents and make a speech. Not one of them would listen to a single word, but instead they would snigger at the fact that the Headmaster looked like he had peed himself. I had never been closer to moving in permanently to the Gents'.

Two minutes of thrusting my crotch at a badly adjusted hand drier made absolutely no difference. The wet patch remained as prominent as ever. And the cursory glance at my watch told me that I should have begun the proceedings exactly three minutes ago. I crept out of the Gents' and walked, crab-like along the corridor, attempting to hide my embarrassment. This was futile, as in less than twenty seconds my trousers would be viewed by everyone and would be, no doubt, captured for eternity by the plethora of camcorders attached to the front of many of the fathers' faces.

I stood on the stage and announced, "Good afternoon, ladies and gentlemen!" with the result that the hall fell silent, save for six crying babies and four mobile phones. Not knowing whether to mention my misfortune, and thus draw it to the attention of everybody or to ignore it and let people make their own assumptions, I decided to make a brief comment. "If you wanted to go somewhere warm for Christmas, I promise you that this hall will be it by the end of the show. I've already prepared by damping myself down." I smiled at the audience and they sat, stony faced, waiting for the children to appear. "The children are going to perform a traditional nativity this afternoon and before we start, I should tell you that Mary, Joseph and the Innkeeper are all last-minute replacements. The originals were struck down. Well, not *the* originals, of course! They're long gone, er, in the past. Our originals, however, are… Let's get on with the concert!"

The children were led in, wearing an assortment of dressing gowns and with their heads draped in tea towels. To the casual onlooker, they resembled an entourage from a dishwashing-fetish party. True to the nativity scene, many sported trainers with flashing lights beneath their dressing gowns. They waved and smiled at their parents as they walked into the hall and once assembled, the music began for the first song. This was sung beautifully by the teachers. The children had frozen with fear at the sight of so many faces in the audience and had uttered not a single syllable. The phrase 'your mum will be coming to watch' clearly did not translate to the children as 'and so will everyone else's mum'.

The new Mary and Joseph, trying desperately to remember what they were supposed to do, clomped onto the stage, looked at the audience and seized up. Gillian, down at the front of the stage tried to attract their attention.

"Psst!" she hissed. They continued looking at the huge audience.

"Pssssst!" she hissed again, sounding like a rattlesnake on steroids. This time they looked at her.

"We've come on the donkey…" Gillian hinted. And suddenly, Mary's face lit up and she spoke.

"We've come to Beflem on a donkey because everybody else has gone in the taxis." The little girl announced proudly.

“Taken their taxes!” Gillian hissed.

“We’ve come to Beflem on a donkey but everybody else has taken a taxi.” The girl shouted in a piercing voice. “I think I’m pregnant and I need to stay somewhere for the night.”

“We need to stay somewhere for the night!” Joseph suddenly yelled, ever the agreeable husband. A song began and once again the teachers sang it, but this time a select group of children joined in. At the end of the song the scenery on stage had altered and there were four doors visible. Joseph banged on the first door and a child wearing a blue checked tea towel opened it. “What!” he barked.

“Have you got anywhere for us to stay?” Joseph yelled.

“Yes come in!” the boy replied.

Evidently he should have said no because at this point Gillian jumped up and down on her seat and performed a silent rant of anger. “No!” she said. “Say no!”

The boy, realising his mistake, attempted to correct himself whilst not upsetting a potential customer.

“Hang on.” He yelled. “I’ve changed my mind. I don’t like the look of your wife so you can’t stay here.”

Joseph knocked on the next door. “Have you got a room for the night?” he yelled.

“No, bugger off!” the young proprietor answered. Gillian, red-faced, could not make the boy hear her over the laughter from the audience. She scowled at him, staring until he caught sight of her and making him feel truly uncomfortable. Thinking he had made a mistake, the boy revised his offer.

“Hang on! I have got a room, come in.” he announced, thinking this was what his teacher wanted.

“No, no!” Gillian hissed at him. “No room! No room!” The boy’s head leaned to one side, clearly confused at his director’s constant changing of the story and he once again spoke to Joseph.

“No I haven’t got a room. So you can bugger off again and don’t come back. Dick heads!”

I was sure by this time that many of the audience would have wet themselves and so my own little problem would be forgotten about. This pleased me. Joseph, after successfully being turned away by innkeeper number three, finally knocked on the door of our new substitute landlord.

“Have you got any room for us?” he asked.

The innkeeper looked at Joseph and then at the audience and began to cry at an alarming volume, stating without reserve that he wanted his mother. He then ran off the stage. Joseph, by now a confident actor, turned to Mary and announced, "Come on love, we can have *his* room if he's not staying!"

Mary duly gave birth and, like any good mother, proceeded to carry her new-born child around by its foot, frequently hitting its head on the floor or the 'rustic stool' that Walt had found at the back of the boiler room. Clearly bored with her visitors bearing gifts she plonked the baby down on top of the log fire for the duration of the penultimate song, which was now sung by the teachers and twenty children. And at last, at long, long last, it was time for the finale. This involved a seemingly huge number of children climbing onto the stage to sing a final song and take a bow.

The first sign of impending disaster came when one of the shepherds stuck his crook up Mary's dress as he was climbing onto the stage. This resulted in Mary belting the aforementioned shepherd with the only weapon she had to hand – the baby Jesus. The collision between Jesus and the shepherd was considerable and the shepherd suffered a nose bleed, a rather less severe injury than that sustained by the Christ Child, whose head flew off and landed in the audience. Mary, left with only the torso of her baby was understandably distressed and chucked it at the offending shepherd who was now being led off the stage by a first aider. As a result of the shepherd leaving, the baby's torso hit one of the three kings who responded by smacking Mary over the head with his beautifully packaged gift of frankincense. I suggested that next year's nativity should be renamed Jesus' Birthday Bash in order to have a chance of compliance with the Trade Descriptions Act.

Gillian was less than happy about the way her concert had gone, commenting that three weeks' rehearsal had been a total waste of time. And this despite my assurance that the choreography for the final scene must have taken many hours to perfect. She was clearly going to hold many post-mortems over this performance in the next few days but I was already beginning to dread the evening's junior department concert.

In the event it was successful. To begin, I made my introductory speech without a wet patch on my trousers. Secondly, the children sang loud and clear. Out of tune, but loud and clear! The individual music hall acts were entertaining on the whole. There was a momentary concern about the comedian whose two minute act extended to twelve minutes of ad-lib, with the jokes taking on a distinct shade of blue as the boy enjoyed the limelight. During this time two teachers were dancing frantically in front of the stage trying to shut him up whilst he made a convincing attempt to not notice them. It was left to Alan Barnett to finally walk on stage, shut up the comedian and introduce the next act. He sidled to the centre of the stage and in his inimitably flat voice announced, “Yes. Well done to Christopher, our comedian, as it were. I’m sure we’d all like to applaud his talent. Yes. Well done. Yes. It’s time to bring on the next, as it were, people. I’m not much of a dancer myself, don’t go in for it, two left feet, no rhythm but the next act is a… it’s a…, ah got it wrong. The next act is a magician. Not a lover of magic personally but I’m sure this will be truly… adequate. OK.” The magician walked on stage as Alan exited. Alan tripped over his own shoe lace and knocked the magician’s table, which consisted of her carefully arranged tricks, onto the floor. The magician cried and Alan pacified her by stating, “Ah, sorry about that. Never mind, carry on!”

On the whole the performance was highly entertaining and as the concert ended around nine o’clock there was rapturous applause from the audience which helped to keep some of the younger juniors from falling asleep. The hall emptied and looked a mess with chairs scattered around and no longer in neat rows and concert programmes dropped on the floor. The last child left at nine-fifty and I walked round school to close all the windows and lock the doors. Walt would be unhappy in the morning but at the moment I didn't care. I was tired. It had been an eventful day.

Wednesday morning Walt was unhappy. He greeted me as soon as I stepped inside the building.

"I'm not one to moan," he announced, "but I'll tell you this and I'll tell you now and I'll tell you reight and straight and when it's said it's said and I'll say no more, nah then. They left a bloody tip them parents did last night. A right bloody tip it were and I'm not joking."

"I know Walt. I did think about shifting it all last night but it had been a bit of a hectic day and I quite fancied going home. Besides, it was one of my daughters' birthdays and I hadn't seen her before I set off in the morning. I wanted to catch her before she went to bed."

"Nowt but trouble them there daughters. How old's yours?" he asked.

"She was ten yesterday."

“Mine are older. Twenty-nine and thirty-three.”

Funny, I’d never thought of Walt as a family man. I just assumed he went home and polished his toilet.

“Gone on bloody holiday with her boyfriend she has, my youngest. Gone to one of them there tropical islands. It worries me to death.”

“Oh, she should have a great time. And it’ll be a lot warmer than it is here.”

“Aye well, I worry about these here foreign parts. I’ve never been to a foreign part myself, except for a coach trip to Wales. They have these freak tornadoes at this time of year, don’t they?”

“Not in Wales, Walt.”

“No, I mean these tropics.”

“Well, it depends where you go, Walt.”

“I don’t want her getting hit by a bloody tiramisu.” He announced.

“A what?”

“One of them tidal waves. I’ve seen programmes on telly about ‘em. They’re called tiramisus.”

“Tsunami.”

“Aye, well they probably have different names in different countries. It can still kill you whatever it’s called.”

"Not so likely if it's a tiramisu though." I answered. This seemed to put his mind at ease and he informed me that he had plumbing to contend with in the lower junior department and promptly left. I had escaped without a serious reprimand for the state of the hall. I had also not heard the word pancake in the entire conversation. However, the discussion of the tiramisu led me to wonder whether he had moved on to dessert.

My day was to be something of a paradox. This afternoon I was taking the school choir to sing at the local old folks' home but before that I had to endure my termly visit from my school's allocated Education Adviser. This was a man named Tim who had once been a headteacher but now worked for the local authority as an education expert, running training courses and keeping an eye on – or supporting – his group of schools. All schools are subjected to this form of monitoring.

He arrived at nine-fifteen and opened his briefcase. It contained masses of data about Hilltop Primary School. Some data was general background information but the majority was related to the results of last summer's SATs tests. He had analysed these figures in immense detail and I was expected to have done the same. I had. My analysis looked at every pattern and every trend. I had discussed the results with the teachers and I had put into place any measures that I had felt might help more children to achieve better scores next year. All internal tests had been analysed in this way for all year groups as well and I kept detailed tracking charts of each child's progress. I was happy that we were on track for a good set of results in the next tests.

"Girls a little behind the boys in Science at Key Stage One." He announced. "Serious lack of Level Five scores in Science across the board at Key Stage Two. It's brought your average points score down significantly. Any thoughts?"

"Plenty. We've worked on a more 'girl-friendly' science curriculum at Key Stage One." I began. "We decided to adapt topic content away from things that typically interest boys. The infant staff spent a lot of time revising the work but I think it should pay off." I produced a revised curriculum plan for his perusal. "Key Stage Two is a bit more tricky but I've suggested that all teachers build in a 'generalisations section' into their Science lessons so that the children get used to looking for general patterns. So far it's quite successful but it's going to take time to become fully established. Here's the junior planning evidence."

He seemed impressed and asked for a copy of each set of plans.

"Maths has slipped eight percentage points across Key Stage Two and improved by six points in Key Stage One. How do explain that startling difference?" Tim asked.

"I'm afraid it's down to the group of children!" I explained. "Last year's Year Six were a poor group, according to the teachers. All the back-up material suggests that to be the case. They weren't typical of the school. We had thirty-three percent on the special needs register and …"

"You're copping out, Peter. We can all say it's the kids' fault, can't we! When those kids were in Year Two their results were ten percentage points higher. Somebody hasn't been stretching them, let's be honest."

"When those kids were in Year Two, they weren't all the same kids!" I replied. "Look at the list of names. Fifteen children left that class between Year Two and Year Six. The ones who replaced them generally were of lower ability. You can't compare the two years' results."

“That’s what the Government does, so I have to go along with it.” he replied.

“You don’t have to go along with it. You should be helping to put honest discrepancies like that into context. Children change schools and this affects the school’s predictions, it’s obvious. If the smartest child in a class leaves and two weeks later somebody moves in who can’t read, it affects the results. And you can’t predict it eighteen months in advance like we’re expected to.”

“Well, I’m afraid I have to go by my figures. You’re well down in Maths and I need to see your action plan for sustained improvement.”

“There isn’t one. The class did better than we expected. Look at the predictions and the test results as they came up through school. They were poor all the time and those kids did wonders in their final tests. The teachers gave it a hundred and ten percent and the kids tried their absolute hardest. The results were miles ahead of what we predicted.”

“Then your predictions were unchallenging. I need to see an action plan.”

"There is no action plan. This year's class is a different level altogether. They're much brighter and the results will be vastly different this year. No action plan is needed."

"So, you haven't produced an action plan. I will have to report this back to the Senior Adviser. That means that a Numeracy Consultant will be allocated to the school to monitor planning and teaching. You'll have to do a full-blown remediation plan to ensure that results improve."

"But they will improve! All you're doing by sending in a consultant is making me look like I haven't got a clue about the way this school works. And then you're making this consultant look like a bloody genius when our results suddenly get better, when we've already got the problem sorted."

"I'm sorry, it's already on my report." He replied. "You should have sent more children to secondary school on higher levels last year. It's as simple as that."

"No, it's absolutely not as simple as that. We could, I suppose, have coached those children to get a better level. We could have done everything short of cheating to bring their levels up, but what for? If we send a child to secondary school with an artificially high score, they'll be expected to do things that are beyond them. When the secondary school finds that the child can't cope, they have to humiliate them by demoting them to a lower group. What does that do to a child's motivation, especially one who is already struggling?"

"You're missing the point!" Tim snapped. "It's about results, figures, Local Authority targets. If a school misses the target we expect it to achieve, our overall average slips back."

"But if the children are not able to…"

"It's not about children, it's about data!"

"Thank you! I've waited so long to hear an adviser actually say those words!"

"Well, what I mean is…"

"No, don't spoil it. Send your consultant, fill in your reports, but just let me get on with doing the best for the children in this school. Because to me, these kids aren't data, they aren't potential points on a chart. They're real people with real abilities and real difficulties. It's how the school responds to those abilities and difficulties that matters to me. Yes, I have to crunch numbers just like you do. But each number I crunch has a real child's name and history attached to it. And after I've crunched, I do the hard bit – I try to figure out what action to take to improve things next time round. I use it to help decide how to make things better in this school for these kids. Test results can be massaged, manipulated and misconstrued. My interest is in each child's improvement."

"But that's the same thing. We're aiming for the same thing."

"No. A child might come into school unable to even *talk* properly, never mind read or write. To get that child to the magic Level Four will be an impossible task. We're talking about a kid who at the age of four is already three years behind everyone else. But if I can get that child to Level Two or Three, that's a fantastic achievement. It means the kid has a basic grasp of reading and writing for life. To me – and to the child – it's a great result, but to you, the child hasn't made it to Level Four, so we've failed. So what should I do? Pile on so much pressure that the child starts failing and bunking off school? Or ignore that child and just concentrate on those who are guaranteed to hit the required level? It's the same result whichever way you look at it. Except my way gives the kid a chance to cope in the real world."

By the end of our meeting we had looked at every graph and chart that had – and could – ever be produced for the school. Tim thought we were basically a good school but was still not happy with our Maths results. I concluded by pointing out that the government data he was basing his assumptions on was, academically speaking, a pile of crap. Of the two graphs that really mattered, one compared the class results now to that same class' results four years ago, when they left the infants. I had already explained that as half of the children had been replaced by others, this comparison was pointless. The second graph compared our results to that of similar schools. The way that schools are construed to be 'similar' is decided by calculating the percentage of children entitled to free school meals. The more free meals that are taken, the lower the results are expected to be. The assumption is that those who take free meals are from poor families and are therefore thick! As some of the brightest children I had ever taught were from poor families where mum and dad had no job but devoted hours and hours to their children, I had reservations about these comparisons. But the Government knows best.

The afternoon brought my trip to the old folks' home. Riverside Nursing Home was an imposing building tucked behind a cramped housing estate. Once beyond the pitifully small car park the visitor was met with the disabled entrance. This consisted of a beautifully smooth ramp up to the front door, perfect for a wheelchair user to negotiate without help. On arrival at the front door, however, that same wheelchair user was greeted by a four-inch threshold built into the doorframe. Keeps out the riffraff, I expect.

I led the group of twenty-five children who formed the school choir down the driveway toward the door of Riverside. Half way down the driveway the sound of a vehicle could be heard and as I turned to ensure all the children were not in the middle of the drive, I observed that the vehicle was an ambulance. Quite a usual occurrence, I suspected, at a nursing home. The residents must be regularly taken to hospital for treatment and check-ups. So it was with some surprise that I saw the main entrance door at Riverside flung open with considerable urgency as the ambulance parked. With impeccable split-second timing, as we arrived at the door, the nursing staff brought out a stretcher on which lay a person, covered from head to toe in a blanket. It was a dead resident. The children had never been quite so silent as they watched the handing over of the dead person to the ambulance crew. The manager attempted to greet us but understandably had a little more on her mind at this point in time and consequently we stood outside, absorbing the event, prior to carrying out our role of singing joyful songs and wishing everyone a merry Christmas and We Hope You Make It to the New Year.

Inside the building it was unbearably hot and the curious smell of incontinence seemed to seep from every wall, every light switch and particularly, every inhabitant. The children took their place in the main lounge as I set up an electronic keyboard. The manager, returning hurriedly from the collection of her dead person, suggested that I make a brief announcement and get started.

"Don't worry if they don't respond." She said. "They'll be enjoying it but they might not clap or join in. Quite a few won't really know what's going on, but don't be put off."

"Sounds like one of my assemblies!" I laughed. "Nobody knows what they're about. Not even me."

I ensured the children had their song sheets and then turned to our audience. "Good afternoon ladies and gentlemen. We've come down from Hilltop Primary School…"

“Piss off!” shouted an old gentleman in the corner. “Piss off back there and let me get some kip!”

The children looked at me, unsure whether to laugh, and then laughed anyway.

“I’m sure you’ll recognise a lot of the songs we sing this afternoon. Please feel free to sing along if you want to.” I continued.

“Piss off, I said!” repeated the old man, clearly concerned that his point hadn’t been adequately made on the previous occasion. A nurse went over and spoke quietly to him as we began our performance. Her words must have had some impact because three bars into the song the old man took a swing at her and shouted, “Sod off you daft slapper. I don’t want to watch no bleeding kids!”

We completed our first song and a lady clapped. Three others snored loudly, one woman shouted, “Well done, now go home!” and the kind gentleman from before repeated his request for us to piss off.

Two songs later we had the audience in our pocket. Three of them were now clapping and one of the sleepers had woken up and was singing ‘Show Me The Way To Go Home’ in a loud voice, complementing our version of Little Donkey beautifully.

Midway through our next song a quiet old gentleman stood up and made his way to the door. The man who had earlier requested that we leave spotted this quiet chap and stuck out his walking stick to trip him up. He accomplished this with great aplomb, leaving the poor unassuming gentleman to fall face down on to the carpet.

"Arthur, why did you do that?" shouted the nurse in charge.

"He's a bastard!" Arthur replied. "He's been eyeing up Ethel this afternoon and he knows I've had my eye on her. Bastard!"

Ethel took exception to Arthur's comments. Within the space of just three and a half minutes she was on her feet and zimmering over to him. "Got your bloody eye on me? Aye, and your hands! You're a sex maniac. A bloody womanising gigolo, that's what you are Arthur Ramsbottom. I wouldn't touch you with a sterilised tramline. And you've got no right to trip Ernest up. If he were coming across to see me, that's his business and mine!"

Ernest, a little embarrassed, replied, "I were only going to the toilet. But I don't think I need to go now!" The identical stains on his trousers and the carpet served to confirm that Ernest had no more need for the toilet.

Twenty minutes later we had sung our entire repertoire and someone had clapped. A member of staff brought in a trolley with drinks and biscuits for the children. By now the children were bemused and bewildered. I had assumed that this might be a pleasant way to spend an afternoon but instead I had subjected the children to bad language, potential violence and dead bodies. In all honesty, they could have spent ten minutes on the school playground just for that! Arthur quietly wandered over to where we were standing. He prodded a girl in the back with his stick and when she looked round he nodded over to the luscious Ethel. "She's mine, you know!" he told the ten-year-old girl. "She wants me. Desperate for it! If he thinks he's getting in there, he's got no chance. He's a bastard!" The embarrassed girl tried to ignore him and choked on her chocolate biscuit. The nurse advised Arthur to go and sit down and his mood changed once more. He pointed his stick at us and yelled, "Oy! You lot, I told you to piss off. Stop eating my food and bugger off home. Go on, piss off!" The nurse summoned help and Arthur was manhandled out of the room shouting obscenities to the children and describing a few activities that he would be happy to pursue with Ethel.

The manager was going to wave us off but as we approached the door the cardiac arrest alarm sounded and she left in a hurry. I wondered if our being close to the door had a detrimental effect on the health of the residents, but didn't dare to suggest it.
I decided I should spend more time at Riverside because for the first time in many weeks, life inside school now seemed curiously normal.

Autumn Term: Week 15

A crying doll? What a pointless toy! I wonder what will be next sometimes. They cry, they wet themselves, they eat and drink. It'll be Baby Projectile Vomit next year, you wait and see.

It was the last week of term. With the concerts behind us, the only major event on the calendar was the round of parties. Groups of classes had their Christmas parties together and the activities chosen depended very much on the age of the children. The younger children in the school would receive a visit from Santa, the older ones would get a disco. All would have to endure party games and all would be provided with party food on an 'eat till you vomit' basis.

On the first day of the week, at ten fifty-five, I received a phone call from Mr. Cranshaw, an old man who lived down the road who had agreed to be Santa for the nursery party. The sound of his voice filled me with dread. I knew what he was going to say.

He had flu. He had a bad case of flu and being Santa was out of the question. He hoped I wasn't too disappointed and that I could find a replacement. I replaced the receiver and began to worry. Bearing in mind that the party was scheduled for this afternoon and would begin in just over two hours' time, how could I find someone to dress up in a Santa suit at such short notice?

There was clearly little point in seeking out other old men from the local area. That would entail many phone calls and promised a very low success rate. The two hours would be over before I would have a chance to make any headway in that direction. No, my choices had to lie with the adult male population already in the school. There were two advantages in this approach. Firstly, they were on hand and available. Secondly, I was their boss!

My list was limited. In terms of physical shape, Walt would make an ideal Santa. But that would be where the advantage would end. I couldn't risk the asphyxiation and subsequent lifetime respiratory problems of up to fifty young children. Knowingly putting their health at risk by expecting them to sit on his knee would be inexcusable.

Happily, I was unable to take on the task. All the children in the school knew me too well and would recognise my voice. Children have an eye for the oddest detail and it would be quite possible, even upon disguising my voice, for a child to identify my wedding ring, my watch or other seemingly insignificant attachment. All of this also applied to the two male teachers who taught in the lower junior department and occasionally came into contact with the infant and nursery classes. Both ran the risk of being identified and this could, of course, lead to a devastating turn of events if a young child discovered that they were being duped by their school.

So it was with these reasons that I went to see Alan Barnett at lunchtime. As the teacher of the oldest children in the school, there was less chance of any young child recognising him. This was compounded by the fact that he avoided at all costs any child younger than ten. His beard stood up with fright as he listened to my request.

"It's pretty simple." I lied. "All you do is put the suit on and sit in the nursery. The kids will queue up and you have a quick chat to them and give them a gift from your sack. Even the wrapping paper is colour-coded. Reddish paper has girly gifts inside and blueish paper has boy-type gifts. You can't go wrong. It'll all be over in half an hour."

“I’m not a lover of dressing up, I want to make that clear.” Alan moaned. “It’s a thing I don’t do well. And then there’s my class. What’s going to happen to them?”

“I’ve arranged for Celia to keep an eye on them. You start them off with their work and she’ll watch her class and yours. I’ll get a couple of assistants to go in there as well. It won’t be for long.”

“I’ve never considered impersonation before. I might not get the voice right.”

“The voice doesn’t matter. Just have a brief chat and dish out the presents.”

“I’m not a lover of idle chat. What should I say? What if they ask me about Lapland or the Aurora Borealis – I don’t have first hand experience.”

“They’re three and four years old Alan! They’re not going to ask you about the Aurora bloody Borealis. Besides, you were teaching your class about the Solar System earlier this term. Are you telling me you’ve been to Pluto just so you can get your facts straight?”

“They could ask how my reindeer fly. I’m not a lover of making things up on the spot. It’s a thing I don’t do well.”

“They’re special, they’re magic. That’s all you have to say. You don’t have to get into the aerodynamic qualities of a reindeer when you’re talking to an awestruck toddler.”

With masses of padding, Alan slowly turned into a rather professorial Santa Claus. He complained that the false beard itched and all those around him made comments about it being an improvement on his own, real beard. But eventually, replete with red suit, black boots and a sack full of presents, Alan Claus made his way to the nursery, rehearsing his cheery greeting as he went.

“It’s ho, ho, ho, isn’t it!” he confirmed as we walked to the nursery.

“Yes Alan. But it’s meant to sound confident and cheerful. Boom it out!”

“I’m not at all sure I can do this. I’m not a boomer. It’s not a thing I do well. It’s the same with sounding cheerful. I’m not a lover of cheerful in any of its manifestations. I prefer thoughtful. I’m just not a Santa at heart.”

“You’re hiding behind a costume. You’re disguised. Now be an actor, take on the role of the person you’re dressed as. The kids in there want to believe you’re Santa. They’ll only doubt it if you give them reason to.”

Alan's head nodded in agreement but his mind was still elsewhere. Inside his head he was planning next term's science curriculum for his class. We arrived at the nursery and I asked Alan to wait outside whilst I went in and told the children to get ready for their special visitor. And then, when the excitement had become almost explosive, I opened the door to reveal the man in the red suit.

"Ahem, er, ho, ho. Yes, ha, ha, ha." Alan began. Fortunately the cheering of the children drowned out this pathetic opening gambit and afforded him a moment to walk to the chair and sit down. Silence fell upon the room as the children looked on in awe at this hero of a man sitting in their nursery. They waited anxiously for him to speak. And so he did.

"Ah, yes. Right then. I'm, as you know, Santa. Santa Claus to be precise, and I hope you're going to have a pleasant experience this afternoon at your, er, party. Got a few little gifts in my bag here that I shall be distributing amongst you. Shortly I shall ask you to come forward and accept a gift and perhaps there may be time for a little chat. I'll make a start then and when you've all got a gift I'll wind it up and leave. Right! Oh, er, ho, ho, ho. Yes."

The children remained silent. It was entirely possible that these children, aged three and four, had not understood a single syllable of what Alan had just said. They remained with their mouths open for a moment and then looked at their teacher for assistance. She attempted to speak in words they might understand. “Now children, come and line up over here so that you can meet Santa.” She said.

“Yes, form an orderly queue. Not too close. I’m not a lover of crowds.” Alan added.

A small boy began to cry. “I don’t like him. I don’t want to see Santa. I want my mummy!”

Alan responded with sympathy. “Not an option, I’m afraid. Your mother won’t be along for an hour or so. So stop crying, I’m not a lover of crying children. It involves comforting and that’s not a thing I do well. Besides, it’s taking up valuable time and I’ve got things to do. Have you finished? No? Well go to the back of the line and see if you’ve stopped by the time everyone else is done.”

“Santa, he’s only three.” Said Elaine, the nursery teacher.

“Not good with young children. Never have been. Difficult to keep a sense of order with young children around. Wouldn’t do for me. I’m a lover of organisation and order. They're things I do very well, organisation and order. Right! Who's first?"

A small girl was pushed forward by the teacher. She sat on Alan's knee and his body posture changed instantly from uncomfortable to 'get me out of here'. She was wearing a headband embroidered with her name, Lise.

"Hello, er, er, Lice." Said Alan.

"It's *Leesa*." The girl replied.

"Well, it's spelt as Lice on your head thingy. Is that how you really spell it or did you get that thing cheap?" The teacher confirmed that the spelling was correct. "Are your parents illiterate?" Alan asked sharply.

"Er, er." Said the girl.

"Looks to me like they are. Not going to help you grasp spelling conventions is it! Ah well, any thoughts about Christmas this year? What have you got in mind?"

"Er, er." Said the girl.

"Well it's going to be a bit difficult for me if all you say is 'er', isn't it! Right, let's get you a present from the bag and get on with the next one. Here you are. Off you go."

Next in line was a small boy. He threw himself onto Alan's genitals as he sat on his knee.

"I'm Ryan!" he announced. "I want an TXB Mega Blaster for Christmas."

"You want a what?" Alan asked, his eyes watering.

"A TXB Mega Blaster."

"What in God's name is a TXE Master Blaster?"

"TXB Mega Blaster! It's an electronic weapon to kill people with."

"Oh I don't think I can sanction that. I'm not a lover of weapons, never have been. You'd be better with a microscope or a crystal garden. Much more educational."

"But I want a TXB Mega Blaster, Santa. I've wanted one for ages."

"Well I'm sorry but I'm not a lover of violence and toys like that make youngsters lose a sense of reality. Before you know it you'll be shooting air rifles at passing buses. No, sorry. Request refused, off you go. Oh, here's a gift from the bag. Ho, ho, ho."

Ryan climbed off Santa's knee and wept bitterly for the next fifteen minutes, unable to be consoled by his teacher or any other caring adult. When he finally spoke coherently, he made it clear that when he did finally become the proud owner of a fierce weapon, his first victim would be Santa.

Many of the other children were having serious misgivings about talking to Santa by this stage but they were cruelly pushed forward by Elaine. The next in line was Abbie, with her sister Amy. They were twins.

"Ah, one for each knee." Alan said, almost Santa-like.

"We're twins. I'm Abbie and this is Amy."

"Good, good. So, any preferences this year? Spotted anything in the shops that you'd like for Christmas?"

"I want a Baby Wee-Wee doll and Amy wants a Crying Baby doll." Said Abbie.

"Can't your sister talk? You'll have to let her talk sometimes or she'll end up with a complex. It can happen with twins, you know, mark my words. So, you want a what? A Baby Wee-Wee? I presume that this is some form of authentic urinating doll, is it?"

"It wets itself."

"That's what I said. Sorry, using big words. Simple speak is not a thing I do well. Not used to young children. And a crying baby? What a pointless toy! I wonder what will be next sometimes when I watch these ridiculous adverts. They cry, they wet themselves, they eat and drink. It'll be Baby Projectile Vomit next year, you wait and see. I'm not a lover of dolls. Right, here are your presents. Ho, ho, ho."

After forty minutes, Alan had given out twenty-nine gifts and caused eight children to become Santaphobic. He had also given out a gift wrapped in green paper to one young boy. This turned out to be Santa's thank-you present, a car care kit consisting of a bottle of wax and a sponge. The puzzled child had shown this to his teacher who then returned the gift to Santa for a replacement.

The visit ended ten minutes later.

"Right!" said Alan. "Well, it's been an experience. I hope the presents are acceptable and don't forget to put your wrappers in the bin. I'd like to take this opportunity to wish you a happy Christmas and I hope you get the gifts you're hoping for. Unless, of course, you've been hoping for one of those Blaster things, in which case I hope you get something more appropriate. Right, well, ho, ho, ho, as it were, and I'll go and check that my reindeer hasn't been clamped. Ha, ha. No, that was a joke. It's not a thing I do well, joking, clearly."

Alan picked up his empty sack, turned and tripped over a small chair as he left. The consequence of this action was that Santa's last words as he left the nursery were 'Sod it'.

Outside the nursery he turned to me and asked, "How did I do?"

"You were unique, Alan!" I replied.

"Good. Can't say I enjoyed it but it was marginally better than I anticipated." He began to pull off his beard.

"Alan, leave it on till you're in the staff room. If a little kid walks by, well, you know…"

"Ah. Not hot on discretion of that sort. It's not a thing I do well. Can I keep the car care kit?"

"Of course. You've earned it!"

"Quite useful. My old sponge is going a bit manky."

"It's probably the menopause."

"No, it's mould."

The next afternoon was the Infants' party. The Santa booked for this event was fit and well and turned up precisely on time. He was to appear in the hall at the end of the party and I was confident that he would be far more credible than yesterday's offering. The infant party had been organised by Gillian who, as Deputy Head, believed she was responsible for all forms of organisation within the school and for a thirty-mile radius around it. Many of the infants were a little nervous about attending the party in case they got it wrong, such was Gillian's influence over them. They were so used to being reprimanded for making small mistakes, or for breathing in the wrong place, that they genuinely feared punishment if they dropped the parcel in Pass The Parcel, or if they danced out of rhythm in the disco. I was sure, however, that today her personality would transform and she would become the life and soul of the event.

Her hidden sense of humour was instantly brought into the open when she appeared in her 'party outfit'. She had changed into a leopard skin dress which did not suit her immense bulk as well as it might.

Without being able to stop myself, I announced, "And the theme of today's party is, The Jungle!"

"No, there isn't a theme!" Gillian replied. "We never have themes. It's just a Christmas party." The other infant staff, knowing full well what was in my mind, simultaneously turned to look out of the window. The view appeared to make their shoulders bounce up and down and when they turned back, one had clearly been crying.

With all the children assembled, Gillian prepared to start the frivolity. “Right, children! Just a few things before we start. We want you to have a good time and enjoy yourselves. However, there is to be no running, no shouting, no pushing and no messing around when the games are being explained. Do not drop crumbs when you eat and under no circumstances allow your drinks to spill. When playing the games, stick to the rules and do not cheat. Have fun.” Gillian was in total control, not only of the children, but also of the rest of the infant staff. I had always presumed she was something of a control freak and today, in her ‘jungle dress’ the phrase took on an entirely new meaning. I watched dumbfounded as the festivities commenced. I had never before seen musical chairs played with military precision but the performance I was now watching could put the Royal Fusiliers to shame. As the game progressed, Gillian’s voice could be heard booming above the music. “Don’t run, boy!” she would yell at any child who mistook the game for a fun activity. “You! Stay in line!” was the response to any unfortunate being who took the corner a little wide at the end of the chairs.

As the chairs were being reduced in number, Gillian called upon the infant staff to assist. “Move it, move it!” she called to one of the teachers as she approached a chair. "Not that one! Leave that where it is! Move the one next to it! Now!" The poor, flustered teacher was behaving in an identical way to the terrified children, making nervous mistakes and developing a clumsiness that had never before affected her in more confident times.

The game ended, as musical chairs always does, with just one chair. The two remaining children had to walk round the 'track', which was now demarcated by teachers. One solitary chair remained in the middle. Exactly in the middle – Gillian had paced it out. When the music stopped the two children, a boy and a girl, made a dash for the chair and the little girl, whose name was Emily, reached it first. She had won the first game of the afternoon and she proudly looked up at Jungle Woman, hoping for recognition of her efforts. "Disqualified!" Gillian barked. "I said 'no running' and you ran. You both ran. Go and sit down!"

Two other punishments followed, namely Pass the Parcel and Musical Statues. Both games filled the children with terror as Gillian watched them with hawk-like vision, ready to reprimand any child who spoilt the flow of the activity. But then it was disco time. This was where the children could be free for a moment. Or so they thought!

With the music playing loudly on the CD player, Gillian patrolled, hands behind her back, in a manner reminiscent of an SS officer. Children who had chosen to sit at the side and not dance were informed that they had made the wrong decision. "Get up!" Gillian barked whilst simultaneously prodding them, "This is a disco! You dance at a disco, you don't sit there looking fed up. Now go over there and dance!" Eventually every child was on the dance floor and moving in some manner to the music. This still was not good enough. Gillian now proceeded to pick those displaying the least sense of rhythm and give them explicit instructions in how to dance. "Watch me and copy!" she snapped at a frightened little girl. Gillian moved her feet from side to side and insisted that the girl did likewise. Once happy that the girl had mastered this, Gillian swayed her torso and the girl copied. For a final flourish, Gillian began to swing her arms and in doing so, belted a small boy in the eye and almost knocked him off his feet. The girl, not daring to stop, swung her arms and danced in a paranoid fashion whilst Gillian turned to attend to the victim of her dance moves. She bent down to his level and lovingly said, “Look where you’re going next time, you could hurt somebody! There’s no room for people walking around half-asleep on a dance floor. Smarten your act up!” This must have made the boy feel better because he stopped rubbing his eye and moved away quickly at this point.

And then it was time for food. Gillian explained the process. The children would line up, class by class, in alphabetical order. They would be herded alongside a row of tables which contained food. They would collect a plate and place on it one sandwich, two biscuits, one bun and a packet of crisps. Should a child not wish to eat a sandwich, this could be exchanged for a further two biscuits or for one additional bun. No other permutations were permitted. Drinks would be available when the children had eaten their food and any spillages must be reported immediately to a member of staff. The member of staff would then mop up the spillage unless a child foolishly reported it to Gillian. She would probably insist that the child licked it up.

The first sign of commotion took place Amanda Chaplin’s children were collecting their food.

“You didn’t listen to me, did you!” Gillian growled at a young boy.

"Er, er…" he nervously attempted to reply.

"One sandwich, two biscuits, one bun, one bag of crisps. Is that, or is that not, what I said?"

"Er, yes."

"Yes what?"

"Yes please." The boy suggested.

"Yes Mrs. Crosby!" She snapped.

"Yes Mrs. Crosby." He replied.

"Well I can only see one biscuit on your plate. Where's the other one?"

"I only wanted one."

"I only wanted one, what?" she snapped again.

"One biscuit." He stammered.

"I only wanted one, Mrs. Crosby! Use my name when you answer!" she shouted. "Why did you only want one biscuit?"

"I don't like them, Mrs. Crosby."

"It's not about what we like and what we don't like, young man. You were told to take two biscuits. That's not hard is it? Go back and get another biscuit!"

The now distraught boy attempted to squeeze through the line to pick up another biscuit. His plate gently leaned to one side as he reached over. And then the food slid off it and landed on the floor. "You silly boy! Now look what you've done! This wouldn't have happened if you'd done it right in the first place."

As if God was looking down on the child, Ann came through the hall with a message for Gillian. Apparently the alarm on her house was ringing madly and she needed to go and reset it immediately. Flustered and clearly unhappy, she flounced out to her car and drove away, still wearing her ridiculous jungle dress, giving her assurance that she would be back as soon as possible. Amanda took over the running of the party and the children had a wonderful games session, followed by an exciting visit from Santa. They went home full of enthusiasm and some had even had two sandwiches, three biscuits or even, heaven preserve us, no bun.

Gillian arrived back in a black mood. Her alarm had stopped ringing by the time she got home and nothing seemed to be wrong with it. I kept very quiet about the call I made from my mobile phone to school, in which I pretended to work for the Alarm Company. Some things are best kept under wraps.

All the staff left early because tonight was the 'Staff Do'. A highly respected local restaurant had been booked many weeks ago and most of the staff had agreed to come. I arrived at eight-fifteen and once inside I was greeted by Jenny, Paul, Ann, Elaine, Amanda and Gillian. A few others were still to arrive but our seat near the window offered us a good view of the car park. Within minutes of my arrival, Walt's yellow Jeep flashed into the car park. Walt, not a regular visitor to restaurants of any description, had been invited out of kindness and then had accepted. I had been warned that he lacked understanding of the usual etiquette of eating out and that he might embarrass us. I was sure this would not be the case.

He looked surprisingly smart. I had worried that he might show up in his burgundy boiler suit, considering that I had never seen him in anything else, but I was wrong. He sported a cream jacket, light blue shirt and dark blue trousers. Everyone agreed that he would fit in adequately.

"Am I late? I'm not late am I?" he asked as he came into the bar.

"You set off on time but there's so many bloody pancakes on t'roads these days that you can't tell when you'll arrive. Am I late?"

"You're not late, Walt. A few others haven't arrived yet. Let me get you a drink."

I bought him a pint of beer whilst he made a quick call to the Gents'. On his return, he was firing on all cylinders. "You should see them toilets!" he announced to all. "I'll tell you this and I'll tell you now and I'll tell you reight and straight and when it's said it's said, they're like crap 'oles!" He looked at the female staff and asked, "Have you seen my urinals? Have you? You won't have, will you! Well, tomorrow, go and have a look at my urinals. You'll be impressed and no mistake. Nah then. Call themselves a restaurant? Not in there, they aren't. You could eat out of my urinals but I wouldn't want to eat out of theirs."

"Well, they prefer you to eat at the tables here, Walt." I reminded him.

"Aye and it's a good thing. I wish I'd brought a camera."

"What, you take photos of urinals?"

"No! I'd like to have a picture of us lot, you pancake!"

The little silver Mazda sports car that swung into the car park contained Alan. It was an unlikely choice for a man of his character but I assumed it was his one link to humanity. He rolled his long, lanky body out of the door and stood up, towering above the vehicle. He locked his door, checked it and set off towards the building. He then turned round and checked his door again and set off towards the building. He repeated this action twice more before finally entering and greeting us.

"Seventeen minutes!" was his opening remark.

"Likewise, Alan." I replied.

"It shouldn't take seventeen minutes to get from my house to here. I did a trial run at the weekend and it took twelve minutes. I had another check last night and it took thirteen and a half minutes. I was anticipating a journey time of twelve and three quarter minutes, basing it on an average of my previous trials, but it took seventeen minutes. It's spoilt my evening in many ways."

"Well, you're here now, Alan."

"Four and a quarter minutes later than anticipated."

"You should have flown here on your sleigh!" Walt suggested. "That'd solve your traffic problems. Mind you, I reckon you'd struggle to park it."

Alan ignored Walt's remarks. Being made fun of was not a thing he did well. That was surprising, considering all the practice he got.

We were shown to our table and we sat down. The table was decorated with candles and crackers. Helium-filled balloons were tied to the chairs and Christmas music was playing through the speakers.

"Would you like to pull a cracker, Alan?" asked Jenny, sitting opposite him.

"Not especially. I'm not a lover of crackers and festive décor." He replied.

"Oh come on. It won't kill you!" she insisted.

He pulled the cracker. Either it was incredibly tough, or he wasn't, and as he tugged, his face took on a crimson glow. With a last tug, the cracker snapped and Alan's chair tipped backwards, launching him onto the floor. Other diners looked round as Alan struggled to his feet. He gazed around the room at his audience and held up his half of the cracker. "Put up a bit of a fight, I'm afraid! Not good with crackers. Often have mishaps with crackers. They're not a thing I do well. Yes. Carry on." He took his place once again at the table and Gillian instructed him to put on the paper hat from inside his cracker. Not wishing to argue with her, he placed it on his head immediately.

"You look a prat in that!" Walt informed him.

“Unbecoming things, paper hats. Never been keen.”

Within five more minutes, we all looked like prats in our paper hats but no-one else had encountered a cracker-pulling accident on the scale of that suffered by Alan. The starter went well. Walt behaved impeccably, Gillian remained quiet because her mouth was busy doing other things and Alan got a small piece of lettuce from under his pate tangled in his beard. For someone who didn’t enjoy looking a fool, it seemed to me that the beard was actively working against him. The others, who all resembled normal people, had normal starters.

Walt was surprised that the waiter brought us all some soup. Having already eaten a prawn cocktail, he was under the impression that his starter was over. But to give him his due, he was very discreet when he asked whether this was correct or whether it would incur an extra charge. However, this occurrence had thrown him somewhat and he had to resort to discussing plasterboard in order to feel comfortable once more. Within a minute, he had moved from plasterboard to partition walls, then to cubicles and finally…

“Did I mention them urinals earlier?” he called out across the soup course. “Nobody’s been round them wi’ a clean sponge and that’s telling yer! Nah then. My urinals are in a different class. You could pour this here soup into my urinals and lick it out with your bare hands. I wouldn't be wanting to do that in this place. You'd never wipe your bread roll round these buggers."

Most people didn't finish their soup course. Those who did sat quietly, trying hard to think of other things. Suddenly Alan burst into conversation.

"Used the sponge!" he announced. "Gave the car a good clean and used the sponge. Works well. Always take pride in things like that. A good wash once a week and a buff twice a year and you can't go wrong. It's just a matter of routine. I like routine. It's a thing I do well."

"I can't see why you drive that little sports job!" Walt snapped, being rather disgruntled at having his urinal conversation stopped whilst in full flow. "You'd never get me in one o' them little things!"

"Well, perhaps you would need to diet a little." Alan said, utterly seriously.

The arrival of the main course brought a dilemma for Ann. Her meal did not turn up. Everyone else had their food but Ann's place mat remained empty. She signalled to a waiter and asked if something could be done.

"What did you order, madam?" he asked.

"I'm not sure. You see we filled in our orders over a month ago. Well, since then I've had to spend a bit of time with my sister and her leg. If she has it taken off she'll need all the support she can get. Anyway, after that I…"

"Shall I go and check the lists, madam?" the waiter asked.

"Yes please."

He returned with a copy of our order. "It seems to be the steak, madam."

"Ooh, that's right. I did. I ordered steak. I remember saying, ooh steak, I think I'll have that, so I will have done."

"I'll organise it now. It says here you wanted your steak medium."

"Well done, dear." She replied.

"Oh, well done. OK."

Ann's steak duly arrived as the rest of us were finishing our main course. She thought it was a little over cooked for her liking but she didn't want to make a fuss.

Everything continued smoothly until coffee. With our coffee cups, we each had a round, white mint placed on the saucer. The mints were quite large and had a rough texture. Most people took no notice of what Walt had begun to do at first but they all looked up when he called the waiter over.

"Oy, pal!" he shouted. "This sugar's crap! It won't bloody dissolve. It's made a right mess here, nah then." Walt had dropped his mint into his drink and proceeded to stir it with his spoon. The sticky mess that resulted was the cause of his loud complaint. Suddenly, Alan's paper hat did not look like the most foolish thing around the table.

The dinner was followed by a disco. I was a little concerned that if I appeared to lack rhythm at any point, Gillian might come over and give me a humiliating lesson, and so I attempted to dance enthusiastically whenever I 'graced' the floor. Ann was to be seen trying to tempt Alan into the groove, with little success at first.

"I'm not a lover of dancing. It's not a thing I do well. I'm more of a tapping my feet to the music sort of chap. Tapping my feet is one of my strengths, it's a thing I do well. But dancing is another matter, I'm not a dancer."

“Well I’m going to dance with somebody!” Ann exclaimed. “It’ll either be you or Walt. Tell you what, here’s a coin, let’s toss for it. Heads, I’ll make you get up, tails, it’s Walt. Here you are Alan, you toss the coin.”

“Oh it’ll end in disaster. I know I’m going to regret this. I wish I hadn’t come, particularly after the journey taking so much longer than I’d planned for.” Alan tossed the coin high into the air. It pinged off a ceiling fan and splashed down in a glass of beer owned by Wayne from Baldock Demolition on the next table but one. Wayne looked round in search of the person who appeared to require demolishing. “I knew I’d make a mess of that!” Alan moaned. “Tossing is not a thing I do well. I’m not much of a tosser when the chips are down. You’d have been better with Walt.”

“What’s that, pal?” Walt asked, seemingly awoken from a pleasant dream involving plumbing.

“I was just saying that you’re more of a tosser than I am.” Alan explained.

Walt took exception to this and began an eloquent soliloquy. “Nah then, I’ll tell you this and I’ll tell you now and when it’s said it’s said and I’ll say no more and I’ll leave it with you. When it comes to tossers you're in a class of your own. You're not just a tosser, you're a bloody pancake. And I know that's probably funny but I didn't mean it to be. I'm getting up!"

Ann followed him and within seconds she had steered him towards the dance floor and planted her handbag, like a victory flag between the two of them. Alan watched as Walt strutted his stuff. There was a considerable amount of it to strut and as Ann bounced off Walt's stomach from time to time as they miscalculated their moves, Alan began to realise that Ann was in need of rescue. He shyly got out of his chair and ambled onto the dance floor. Standing close to the various people from the school he rocked gently from side to side, clicking his fingers as he did so. This was too much for Gillian to ignore and she marched over to him, took him by both hands and treated him to the mother of all public dancing lessons. "Stop it!" Alan was heard to say, "I'm not a dancer. It's really not a thing I do well. I never have and I never will."

"Shut up and learn!" Gillian gently suggested. And Alan did as he was told. At least he was successful in the shutting up part.

Walt by now was playing air guitar and thoroughly enjoying being a rock star. Unfortunately, the excess activity had a detrimental effect on his odour, but on the bright side, the dance floor emptied significantly, leaving him much more room to display his terpsichorean prowess. This mass exodus of the dance floor left the DJ more than a little concerned regarding his choice of music and resulted in his trying every musical style known to mankind as the evening progressed.

Wayne from Baldock Demolition ventured onto the dance floor and was almost immediately smacked in the eye by Gillian's enthusiastic arm movements. He did attempt to take up the matter with her but within three sentences he had been reduced to a quivering wreck and wisely chose to let her off on this occasion.

The party ended at one-fifteen in the morning. Alan's journey home took only eleven minutes and this brightened up his evening somewhat and reduced his average journey time to fourteen minutes for each leg of the round trip.

In three days' time, we would take down the decorations in school and send the children home for their Christmas holiday. In our own homes, we would finally put up our decorations and begin to enjoy the season of goodwill with our own families instead of someone else’s. My first term was nearly over and I could no longer blame someone else if things were not quite right.

Final Words

And so the first book in the series comes to a close. The days have grown darker and we have reached midwinter, becoming fully aware that there is still so much to learn and so much that can still go wrong. But who could possibly have imagined that next term would bring a full blown school inspection, the most embarrassing fire drill in history and the world's biggest lake of vomit developing before my eyes in the middle of a school assembly! All this and much more appears in the second volume of my diaries, 'Get Me Out Of Here – I'm A Headteacher'.

Thanks for reading.

Books by Peter Jeffcock – all available right now on Kindle

For updates, quotes and other information, follow me on Twitter @peterAjeffcock and find me on Facebook at Peter Jeffcock Books.

A PIS OF CAK (Humour)

The original, best selling Pis of Cak is now available on Kindle. Bursting with unintentional humour, written by children when they are trying to be serious, this book has amused and delighted thousands of readers for over 10 years. Revel in the imagery of 'wild breasts roaming the jungle', update your knowledge of history by learning that there was a law 'demanding sexy quality for women', or simply smile at the idea that 'suspension bridges hang from a cloud'. Enter a world where haemorroids fly through space and where children in wartime had to be evaporated for their own safety and you may never view life in quite the same way again.

The A Pis of Cak series is now up to four books…

ANOTHER PIS OF CAK (Humour)

A THIRD PIS OF CAK (Humour)

A PIS OF CAK – THE FOURTH SLICE (Humour)

THE HEADTEACHER DIARIES: (Humour)

- **Headlong Into Chaos – The Diaries of a Primary School Headteacher**
- **Get Me Out Of Here – I'm A Headteacher**
- **More Repressed Memories of a Primary School Headteacher**

This series of three books document the author's first year as Head of a School in a North Midlands former mining town in the 1990s. It is hard to imagine what goes on behind the scenes of an apparently normal primary school and as the new Head starts out in his new post he meets his techno-phobic secretary, his terrifying deputy head and his incredibly foul-mouthed caretaker who has an obsession with polishing his urinals and categorising his nuts. With an array of parents that range from delightful to the insane (where insane makes up a huge majority) and a staff of rather eccentric teachers, life is never going to be easy. Every day brings about a new set of unexpected and bizarre problems that somehow interfere ever so slightly with the normal running of the school. From 50 children vomiting in unison during an assembly to getting the whole school locked outside during a fire drill, every day, indeed every minute, has the makings of a peculiar sitcom.

BEYOND THE FRAME (Sci-Fi Adventure)

Ross Carter has a unique ability. He can slip into old photographs and interact with the people in the pictures. After his boss asks for help in saving his wayward brother from an untimely death back in the 1960s, Carter accepts the mission. He travels back and prevents the young man from being killed, but when Carter returns to the present time he finds the brother's influence has changed everything for the worse. Carter has no job, no wife, no home and the man who was his boss is now dead – killed by the brother Carter had saved. His only chance of putting everything right is to go back and ensure that the brother dies, as he originally did. But once he returns to the past he meets up with an adversary who is hell bent on saving the brother's life – he meets himself...

MAD MAN – 100 Airport Codes to Brighten your Boarding Pass (Humour)

When the author noticed that a flight from Madrid to Manchester appeared on his ticket as MAD MAN, it prompted him to find out what other great journeys might be lurking out there. It turns out there are quite a few. If you want to know how to find HOT SEX, TOY BOY, FAT BUM or even DOC TOR WHO on your airline ticket, this is the book that tells you which flight to check on to.

PINK KNICKERS AND STUN GUNS (Comedy Adventure)

Even the kindest of people would describe Jemma Spicer as a complete flake! And when she inadvertently picks up the wrong bag from the airport carousel she sparks a series of events that place her in mortal danger. The bag's owner is desperate to get his luggage back before anyone discovers its extraordinary contents. But Jemma has already found them. And what she has discovered catapults her into the middle of an evil crime ring, threatening millions of lives – especially hers.

With only her delightfully scatty logic and the items in the bag to help her, she must stop one of the world's most powerful techno-criminals from destroying the future of her country. But first she has to work out what he is up to. How can an ordinary girl save an entire nation? How will she ever get over the trauma of a life and death pedalo chase! And should she really do that to the Queen?

If James Bond had been a fashion-obsessed girl who seemed to have absolutely no idea of what was going on around him, he would have been indistinguishable from Jemma herself.

THE ECONOMY DRIVE (Money Saving)

Use this book as if it is a distance learning project. Learn how to drive in a fantastically fuel-efficient way, whilst not sacrificing any of the fun of driving. You don't have to drive like a snail to be economical – and this book gives you all the methods. You will save serious money each year on fuel if you follow these simple methods.

JASON MASON'S SECOND WIND (Teenage Humour)

Sports day is approaching at Upper Gumtree School and Jason Mason is dreading it. He is the slowest runner in the class and, when under pressure, his legs seem to develop a mind of their own, causing him to stagger and wobble in a variety of directions as he attempts to keep up with his classmates. And if this were not bad enough, the class bully, Sam Lamb is, according to Jason, possibly the fastest runner in the entire world. But when Jason buys a particular brand of lemonade, he discovers it has an effect on him that is truly mind blowing – except the blowing doesn't come from his mind! And suddenly sports day feels far less scary.

Printed in Great Britain
by Amazon